Begin Again

About the Author

Kat Jackson is a thirty-something teacher/therapist living in Pennsylvania. She's been consumed with words and language for thirty-some years and continues to spend entirely too much time overthinking anything that's ever been said to her (this is a joke, kind of, but not completely). This is Kat's first book, hopefully the first of several if not many. When not teaching, therapizing, or writing, Kat is probably reading or running, as those are her gateways to maintaining her sanity in this challenging world. And yes, she lives comfortably with her clichéd three cats.

Begin
Again

Kat Jackson

BELLA
BOOKS
2020

Bella Books, Inc.
P.O. Box 10543
Tallahassee, FL 32302

Printed in the United States of America on acid-free paper.

First Bella Books Edition 2020

Editor: Katherine V. Forrest
Cover Designer: Kayla Mancuso

ISBN: 978-1-64247-129-8

Acknowledgments

This book could not have been written if not for the breaks my own heart has sustained (thanks, ladies!). Thank you to my parents, who have always believed in me…even when I've made some pretty stupid decisions. An extra big thank-you to my best friend, Kimho, who has been my quiet cheerleader for many years…even when I didn't follow the writing schedules she made for me. Katherine, thank you for your impeccable editing guidance and for teaching me that, much to my chagrin, I really do overuse commas.

There are three hundred eighty-seven reasons why this book came to life, and the moments behind the reasons mean more to me than anything. Thank you.

To all the hearts I have seen broken
Only to come alive and breathe again

CHAPTER ONE

The distinct patter of falling rain hitting the skylight pulls me from a semi-deep sleep punctuated with lively dreams. The latest, the one that dissolved as I opened my eyes, featured a walking, talking dolphin that sounded suspiciously like my mother—probably a subconscious reminder to call her or a sign that I need a vacation. Yes, a tropical vacation, away from my kind-hearted but prying mother, where I could swim with the actual dolphins and not be spoken to by them, or, well, anyone else. I roll over, rub my eyes and sigh contentedly at the alluring thought. A girl can dream, I think before sitting up in bed. And right now dreaming is all I've got.

"Wake up, wake up, wake up," I mutter, rubbing my eyes again and shaking the lingering sleep from my head. I'm alone in bed, which is not a sign. It's Saturday, and if Lauren is already up and moving, that means I should be too. An unspoken rule between us deems that Saturday is more a workday than a weekend, as chores and shopping tend to pile up unattended during our busy weeks. I've been unable to sleep past eight a.m.

since I turned twenty-five six years earlier, so I don't necessarily *mind* getting up early, but I also figure a little Saturday-morning cuddling wouldn't derail either of us.

As I flop back onto the pillows, savoring the final moments before I force myself out of bed, the rain picks up speed and sounds more like a near-downpour. A rainy Saturday has definite appeal. I could catch up on some reading after taking my time with my oh so important house-cleaning duties. Maybe Lauren could be persuaded to make dinner, which hasn't happened in months despite her being the absolute better cook, and we could lazily eat in front of the TV, watch something mindless and gratuitous, cuddle, kiss, have wild sex on the family room floor...

That too, I think with a tinge of bitterness, hasn't happened in months. Never mind the family room floor part: the sex part alone. And wild? I'm pretty certain Lauren and I haven't had anything close to "wild sex" in the last four years of our relationship, if ever before that.

"Em! You up?"

Lauren's voice trails into the bedroom from the bottom of the stairs. The sound of it tugs gently at my heart, spreading with it a mixture of warmth and sadness that keeps me wondering when, exactly, I last made love with my girlfriend of nearly five years.

"I'm awake," I call back, slowly moving myself out of bed.

"Your mom's called twice in the last hour. You might want to call her back."

"Seriously?" I mutter, recalling the annoying dolphin chasing after me. "I'll call her in a few minutes," I call down to Lauren.

"Mer is on the road and should be here around two. I'm going to run out to get coffee and make a Home Depot stop."

"Okay!" I yell back, rolling my eyes at Lauren's inability to climb a flight of stairs to a) say good morning to me, b) give me a good morning kiss, and c) speak to me like a normal person instead of yelling to me through the house.

With that, the sound of the front door closing signals Lauren's silent goodbye, one of her more annoying traits. I'm definitely the talker in our relationship and the more affectionate one. Our communication differences usually balance out, but Lauren has been relying too heavily on her avoidant nature lately. She knows I hate the silent/nonexistent goodbyes.

Not wanting to start the day off by belaboring the things that drive me nuts about my partner, whom I really do love and desire and all that, I give myself a mental shake as I pull on a sports bra and Nike shorts and T-shirt, grab an overflowing laundry basket, and head off to begin the day of chores. Maybe, just maybe, I'll still get a chance at that wild sex later in the day.

* * *

The first floor of our perfectly-sized house that's set close to the Sunnyside neighborhood of Portland is, surprisingly, very clean. I have no idea what time Lauren got up, nor when she came to bed last night, but it's nearing 9:30 a.m. by the time I emerge from the basement and step one of laundry duty, and I am definitely not expecting to see the house as orderly as it is, especially considering Lauren hasn't yet returned from her errands. For the past month, Lauren's been working on installing new hardwood laminate floors throughout our open concept living room and dining room, and while I knew she was finished, I also knew that as of last night there was a shit ton of random debris lying around the first floor. Now, nothing seems out of place. A tinge of guilt sweeps through me as I realize how much work Lauren has put into these new floors, as well as the cleanup process which, technically, I was supposed to take care of. I move toward the kitchen, half-hoping to find it a disaster…

…but, no. I don't think the kitchen has been this clean since we moved in roughly two years ago. All this unusual cleanliness is making me a little unnerved; Lauren is not known for being neat nor is she particularly orderly—that is definitely my role in the relationship—but she *is* known for caring deeply about people's opinions of her, and it suddenly seems as though she wants to be able to take the Housecleaning Credit when Meredith arrives.

I walk through the spotless kitchen and inhale deeply as I step outside onto the deck, phone in my hand. This deck was a *huge* selling point for both of us; it's nestled right into the lush greenery surrounding and encasing the backyard. It's big enough to hold a grill plus a table and chairs and still leaves room to spare in the yard for gardening (Lauren's thing, definitely not mine) and more entertainment space. I tuck my legs beneath me on the slightly damp built-in bench and look up through the wooden slats of the pergola, watching the clouds scatter quickly across the bluing sky, wondering where my rainy Saturday escaped to.

My mom instantly answers the phone. "Well, you *are* alive," she says, her tone light despite the salty words.

"I am indeed, Mom. Sorry I've been MIA this week; work has been crazy."

"So Lauren told me. You're getting ready to start a project with Whitmore Hill! How exciting!"

I shake my head, wondering why I need to speak with my mother when my loving, chatty-only-with-my-mother girlfriend obviously dished up all my dirt already. "Yep, we're kicking off on Wednesday. It sounds like a good project. I'll probably have to do some traveling." I'm a communications analyst for a consulting firm in Portland and while I love Portland, I *really* love being able to travel for work.

"Back east?"

"I'm not sure yet. Whitmore has outposts in New York, Florida, Texas, and Washington. I may end up closer to you on a trip."

"Oh, honey, that would be wonderful. Your dad and I would love to see you."

"I'd love to see you guys too." And I would. My parents are amazing: supportive, kind, and full of unconditional love. They're maybe a little weird, but after I got through my teen years, my mom truly became one of my closest friends—even if she is a bit of a nag at times.

"So, Lauren told me today's the big day?"

"Really? How do you know all of this? Do you talk to Lauren every day?"

Laughing, she assures me that, no, she only speaks with Lauren when she can't get a hold of me. "Besides," she adds, "Lauren always has more to say than you do."

I roll my eyes, thankful that my mom is two and a half hours north in coastal Washington, and not sitting directly across from me, because I'd be sure to get a love-slap on the arm for my roll of the eyes. Those little zingers are best ignored; I am in a constantly losing battle with my mother regarding how often we speak on the phone. "Yes, it's the big day. Meredith is moving in."

"And you're sure you're okay with this?"

"Of course I am. Why wouldn't I be?"

"Oh, I don't know…she and Lauren are so close, and you're accustomed to living with just Lauren. Do you worry that they'll spend more time together and you'll be left out?"

My mother, the worrier. And usually on someone else's behalf. "No, I'm not worried about that. Or anything else for that matter. I like Meredith. She's good for Lauren, and we've always gotten along. She needs a safety net right now and we're fortunate enough to be able to provide that for her."

"I'm glad to hear you say that. You're very kind, Emery."

"I learned from the best. Thank Dad for me."

"Oh, ha ha. Very funny."

I smile as she begins to blabber on about my older sister and her latest breakup. Helena isn't known for her ability to commit; my younger sister, Jaelle, prospers in that area and I hang out somewhere in the middle, typical for my middle-child status, I guess. Having grown up in a wealthy suburb of Philadelphia, we are all products of our parents' success, though in very different ways. Helena skipped the whole college thing, moved to New Hampshire when I was a freshman in high school, and is now a prospering sculptor and freelance writer. We all silently attribute her nomadic, free-spirited ways to having been born out of wedlock at our parents' tender ages of twenty. I came seven years later, a child of the literal honeymoon, and the youngest, Jaelle, arrived six years after my arrival. Jaelle and I have a stronger bond than either of us has with Helena. It seems weird to say, but I've never missed Helena; after I graduated high school and moved to the West Coast for college, my bond with her all but disappeared. I was happy when both my parents and Jaelle eventually moved to the west coast: Jaelle is currently living in northern California, a wicked drive for her to me or my parents up in Washington, so we all congregate at our family beach house in Rockaway at least three times over the summer. It's now April, and I haven't seen my family since Christmas, so I'm getting antsy for June to arrive.

"Your father wants to remodel the kitchen. Again."

My mom's voice interrupts my thoughts, which are again interrupted by the sound of a car in the driveway. "Oh, let him do it. He loves it. Listen, Mom, Lauren's back. I need to get going."

"Bye, sweetie. Don't forget to call your old mother next week and tell her all about your new project!"

"I will, I will. Bye, Mom."

* * *

"Em? The spare room is all cleaned out, right?"

I continue folding laundry and nod in Lauren's direction. "Yes. I moved all of my stuff up to the office and your stuff down to the basement."

"Thanks, babe." Lauren sidles up behind me and puts her arms around my waist. She kisses the nape of my neck, squeezes me, and leaves the bedroom.

I turn quickly, hoping to catch her for a more passionate interaction, but all I catch is the sight of her rather exquisite ass turning the corner.

"I got chicken for you to marinate for dinner. If you could do that when you're done with the laundry, that'd be great. I'm going to mow the lawn since everything dried out." Again with the long-distance talking. This is getting seriously old.

"Lauren, wait," I call after her, walking briskly to the bedroom door.

There she stands, already at the bottom of the stairs, looking up at me with a slight smile. God, she's pretty. Hot, really, and since she doesn't appreciate being called pretty, I tuck that word back into my mind to let it rest there while I verbally stick with *hot*. Lauren is tall, standing at nearly six feet, and decades of soccer have carved her body into a firm, muscular, taut specimen. She claims she was never curvy and has always had an androgynous build, which fits her personality perfectly. Her blue eyes are wide and touched with just a smear of gray, and her shoulder-length dark blond hair is pulled back, as always, into a loose ponytail. Years ago, I noticed Lauren because, yes, she was hot, but also because she looked really, really gay. I love that about her. She isn't masculine, she's just not feminine, and her androgyny is only slightly compromised by her lovely, small breasts. Yeah. Definitely hot. And pretty.

Now, she looks at me expectantly, wondering why I could possibly need to interrupt her schedule.

"I miss you," I say quietly, maybe even feebly, though I try to not have that tone.

"I'm right here, babe," she replies, her voice even and smile unwavering.

"Yeah, I know, but…I *miss* you."

Now the smile wavers. Lauren doesn't do heavy emotions, and she doesn't do whining. My plaintive declaration could easily fall into either category. I am running the risk of being dismissed for the lawnmower.

"In other words…" she prompts. Still with me. Okay. Go for it, Em.

"I'm thinking we should have sex soon," I blurt out.

Lauren laughs and takes the steps two at a time to meet me. She cups my face in her hands and looks at me, really looks at me, before kissing my lips softly and slowly. "Soon," she says, too quickly breaking the moment that I could have easily guided back between the sheets. Or against the hallway wall, whatever!

Words tangled in my wanting mouth, I stand silently as Lauren bounds back down the stairs and out of my sight. *Soon.* I've heard that one before. More times than I'd like to count.

* * *

Later that afternoon, I can finally see the end of the laundry. Yes, it gets that bad with two women who work *and* work out on a nearly daily basis, including one woman—not me—who is in denial about her clotheshorse status. The chicken is marinating, the lawn is mowed, and Lauren is working on making sure everything is in its place in the basement, which is finished and has a rec room and Lauren's "office," which is more of a catch-all room. Lauren doesn't do much in the way of needing an office, but we both need our own space. For the past seven years, Lauren has been working for a local engineering firm, struggling to move forward in her career. She seems to be stuck at a mid-level position, doing a lot of field analysis and assistance for the upper-level engineers in the firm. Because she's had very few projects that were hers alone, she virtually never has work to do outside of the office, hence the joking existence of her "office." On the other hand, my work in consulting demands a certain level of homework, mostly research, in order to effectively stay on top of things. So, my office is truly for work. Lauren's is more of a cave where she stuffs her sports trophies and blasts 90's music when she needs to decompress.

Right now, I'm realizing that it's a good thing our three-bedroom house includes a basement for Lauren so that we each still have our own space after prepping the third bedroom for its new inhabitant: Lauren's best friend from college, Meredith. Knowing my girlfriend as I do, I don't think she would have been so willing to let Mer crash for an undetermined amount of time if we were living in a two-bedroom house with no basement. Neither Lauren nor I are too keen on the idea of living on top of people, since we both lived that way during college. We definitely like having our own spaces. Mer, however, being quite the talker and attention-demander, will be an interesting addition to our low-key household.

I'm shoving the last of my clean underwear into its drawer when I hear the unmistakable sound of Meredith yelling Lauren's name. It isn't a normal yell; Mer's got this earth-shatteringly loud, deep, drawn-out bellow that ends in something like a cackle. It is unmistakable and one hundred percent Meredith.

Having Mer around is going to be somewhat of an adventure, I realize as I head downstairs. She and Lauren have been best friends for fifteen years, and, as Lauren sheepishly admits, Meredith is one of the few friends that Lauren never even attempted to sleep with—not that I know of anyone who ever turned Lauren down. Though resplendently open-minded, Mer is completely heterosexual, and about as experienced in that field as Lauren is in hers. They were quite the duo throughout college, and even after having been with Lauren for five years, I still blink twice when new stories detailing their sordid adventures come up.

"Emery, gorgeous girl! Hello, hello, hello!" Mer swoops into the living room and heads straight for my open arms. "I haven't seen you in ages!"

"It's been at least a year, huh?" I give her a good squeeze before releasing her to give her a long, thorough look up and down. "Too thin," I declare, poking at her suspiciously trim waist.

"Oh, shut up, I'm going through a stressful time. I'll pack it back on in time, especially with Lauren's cooking."

I snort. "Lauren's cooking? I think I've forgotten what that tastes like."

"Is my best friend not taking care of her woman?" Mer raises her eyebrows accusingly.

As if on cue, Lauren, weighed down by several of Mer's bags, walks through the front door. She grunts toward us and moves toward the first-floor bedroom, which will now be Mer's domain.

Mer turns back to me, a gentle look of surprise on her face. "Everything cool?"

Her intuition never fails, and apparently she still has us on her radar. "Yeah, of course. Everything's fine."

"Fine, huh. Fine. Fine's icky."

"Fine is…fine," I say unconvincingly, so I toss a grin in with it. "I'll go grab more of your things. Make yourself at home."

* * *

"This…this is delicious food." Mer leans back in her deck chair with a look of food ecstasy, eyes shut as she savors her final bite.

Lauren glances over at me and winks. "Em's becoming quite the cook."

I glare at her. True, I marinated the chicken, and it is pretty damn good. But Lauren did the actual execution at the grill, and she'd grilled some amazing corn on the cob as well. Is she seriously trying to make me the cook of the household?

"Oh, yes, on that note," Mer interjects. "What's this bullshit about you not cooking, Lauren Cabrian?"

"I cook!"

Mer shakes her head dramatically. "Nope. I don't buy it."

Lauren looks at me pleadingly, which is a very cute look on her. She could use those blue eyes to make me do just about anything.

"I can't defend you, Lauren," I say with a shrug, reaching for my glass of wine. "Things have changed around here."

"Who just stood at the grill for twenty minutes?"

"Who marinated the chicken and prepped the corn?" I shoot back.

"That's called *helping*, Em."

"No, that's called *cooking*, Lauren."

Mer sits back with an amused smile, watching our verbal ping-pong with a glint in her eye. "Oh, you two," she says finally, reaching both hands out to squeeze our arms. "You're just so adorable."

Lauren leans over and plops a loud kiss on my cheek. "So adorable," she repeats, getting up for another beer.

I focus my gaze on the nearly naked cob of corn on my plate. I know Mer is watching me, and I don't want her to see what I know my eyes are revealing.

"I hate cooking," I finally say.

"I know you do." Mer's voice is full of understanding and a touch of sympathy.

"And," I look up, having regained steady footing, "my work schedule is a little unpredictable. So, Lauren being the better cook with the more consistent, home-by-five-thirty-every-day schedule, it makes sense that she's the cook, right?"

Mer smiles at me and squeezes my arm a second time. "Absolutely right, Em. We'll get her back in the kitchen."

I nod in agreement, then turn my gaze out to the yard. The sun has set and the air is cooling by the minute. I tug the arms of my sweatshirt down and burrow into its warmth. I know Mer is still watching me in that slyly intuitive way of hers, and I know that if we keep talking, everything will tumble out of me, and her first night here is not the night for me to tell her how frustrated I'm becoming with Lauren and her seeming indifference toward our relationship.

Luckily for me, Lauren chooses that moment to return with a beer for herself and another for Mer, along with the bottle of wine I've been working on. I pour myself half of a glass, and sit back to listen to the two best friends banter and chatter, letting the night slowly drape itself over us.

CHAPTER TWO

The next day holds none of the rain vs. clear sky drama of Saturday. The air is crisp and clean, and the sun is pushing past fluffy strings of clouds as early as seven thirty a.m. I know this because I wake up alone, again, at seven and decide to show Lauren that I don't care about her absence from our bed. There's no sign of her ever having come to bed, again. I give myself a few minutes to stew amongst the sheets and pillows, then get up and dress to go for a run. I don't even bother looking for her as I quietly make my way downstairs and out the front door, phone secured to my arm. The house is silent behind me—and Lauren isn't on the living room sofa. I don't smell coffee, either, so I know Mer hasn't gotten up yet.

I push the mystery out of my head and stretch my legs at the bottom of our driveway. I honestly haven't given myself time to sit and dissect what's going on between me and Lauren. Given the amount of time we've been together, I assume we're having growing pains, or going through a bit of a slump. I'm not exactly well-versed in this area as Lauren is officially my longest relationship, but I figure I know enough from my own past relationships. We'd bounce back just as other couples did. In fact, two of our closest friends have tripped over bumps similar to what seems to be happening with me and Lauren. They're still together after eight years and still happy—so much so that they're trying to get pregnant. That definitely isn't in the cards for me and Lauren, but if it works for them, great. I'll be happy to be a lesbian fairy godmother.

As I jog through the quiet streets of our neighborhood, I think back to Meredith's concern about me and Lauren. I know that's not the end of it. She will gently push the subject with me before ever broaching it with Lauren. What is there to say when that happens? Do I love Lauren? Absolutely. Am I still in love with her? Yeah. Have things changed over time? Definitely. I know as well as anyone that the crazy, up-all-night passion that sparks the beginning of a relationship doesn't last in that form; it waxes and wanes over time and experience. I miss the closeness with Lauren. But I also know it's still there, somewhere. I just have to get her to remember it.

And the best place to start is figuring out where the hell she's sleeping, and why it isn't with me.

* * *

When I return home after my head-clearing jog, both Lauren and Meredith are working on breakfast in the kitchen. Lauren greets me with a soft kiss to my sweaty cheek, then sends me upstairs to shower. It's obvious that Lauren is happy about Mer staying with us; she seems more relaxed, and lighter somehow. Watching the two of them talk and laugh in the kitchen makes my heart swell. Sure, Lauren and I have friends in Portland, but Mer has always been her closest friend. Our other friends could never measure up to what Mer means to Lauren.

Later that afternoon, Mer and I find ourselves sitting on a blanket on the sidelines of the soccer field at Laurelhurst Park, which is a short walk from our house. Its proximity was another big selling point for us when we'd purchased the house, partly because of Lauren's need to be near a soccer field, and also because it's a great, open, green space, and we both love that.

Lauren has belonged to a soccer rec league since she graduated from college. The games take place on every seasonable Sunday of the year and I sometimes beg out in order to run errands or just have some time to myself. Mer insisted that I come along this time, if for nothing more than to enjoy the weather and the scenery.

It's an unseasonably warm and gorgeous day for spring in Portland, even warm enough for jeans and a long-sleeved T-shirt. A decent crowd heavily populated by lesbians has come out to watch their friends or partners. There are a few boyfriend-husband types lingering around, too, and a few have small children hanging on them.

I inhale deeply and lie back on the blanket, closing my eyes against the jarring rays of the sun. I love being outside—but only in temperate weather. I absolutely hate being cold.

"Lauren's looking pretty good out there," Mer remarks as she watches the team warm up.

"Yeah, she hasn't lost any of her skill. And she's in exactly the same shape she was when she graduated college."

"Incredible. That's a hell of a lot of devotion."

"Especially for rec league."

Mer snorts. "She could have gone somewhere with this, you know."

"I know. The national team. She knows too. But she won't discuss it."

"Family pressure, I bet. Her dad was hell-bent on her doing college the right way, all academics, no room for athletics."

"He's still like that. Every time she talks to him, all he asks about is her career."

"That's a shame," Mer says lightly, her voice trailing off as she looks around the field. "What is this, a lesbian flash mob?"

I laugh as I sit up to peruse the crowd. It does look as though even more lesbians have arrived. One particular crowd across the field is engaged in some rowdy laughter and playful shoving. "Soccer games are known for attracting lesbians, yes. If you were interested in coming to the dark side, you'd have your pick sitting right where you are."

"Maybe I should switch over. It's not like I'm having any luck on my side."

"Please. You're the least gay woman I've ever met."

Mer shoves me playfully. "I feel like that's an insult."

"It might be. What happened with McSteamy, anyway?" Mer had been engaged, which was a shock in and of itself, to a rather attractive plastic surgeon. It had seemed idyllic, but Mer wasn't known for her ability to commit, even when the man was absurdly attractive *and* obscenely wealthy.

"Oh, I tried to stick that out. I even went wedding dress shopping." She whispers those last three words, nearly shuddering as they slip from her lips. "But I couldn't do it. I went to see him in his office one day, and there was this guy in the waiting room. His mom was getting a consultation for a facelift, and he was gorgeous. Steamier than McSteamy, which I didn't think was possible." Mer laughs and shakes her head, her long black curls swinging across her back. "I slipped that rock off my hand and fucked that man three hours later."

"You cheated on Rob?"

"I did. I didn't mean to, exactly, but," she shrugs, a light blush staining her cheeks, "it happened. And I don't regret it because it was the best sex I've had in years."

"I thought Rob was good in bed."

"He was. It's just that Devon…Devon was even better. But you know me, Em. I'm not wife material. I'm every wife's nightmare."

I stare at her. I don't want to ask, but I have to. "And this Devon guy? Are you *his* wife's nightmare?"

"It would appear so, yes."

"Meredith! Jesus!"

"I know! I know. Seriously, Em, I know. I'm not proud." She finally meets my stare, her coffee-colored eyes showing some sense of shame. "I know you probably think I'm a whore."

I hold her gaze for a moment, knowing I have to choose my response carefully. "I don't think you're a whore, Mer. It's just…I don't understand your…lifestyle."

She winks at me. "Not many do."

"So is that why you're here? Running from both the broken engagement and the disgruntled wife?"

"Throw the obsessed man I cheated with in there, and yes, that's why I'm here. I hit the trifecta. I had to leave town."

I continue to openly stare at Meredith as she reaches back and sweeps her hair into a messy ponytail. Even messy, it can't hinder her beauty, which is one of the reasons she continually ends up in these situations. Mer's dad is from Spain, and her mom is Panamanian. Mer is a ridiculous, fiery mix of Spanish and Latin-American blood: her curves are killer, she's got this unruly mane of thick, curly black hair, and these eyes that tug you in, then drown you in their deep brown smokiness. Meredith had a very different upbringing than Lauren or I; she grew up in Los Angeles and her mom worked in the media, so she was constantly around older people. Mer's father died when she was in high school, but his work in the film industry further involved Mer in a world for which she was given no preparation. After a bottle of wine, Lauren once told me that Mer had first had sex at the age of twelve, and has not stopped since. I don't know, and probably never will, if that first experience was entirely mutual, but I do know that Meredith is over-the-top comfortable in her own skin. As she says: she doesn't regret anything she's done in her life. Meredith loves her life, including her promiscuity, which was at an all-time high during college. Never mind the fact that my girlfriend was right there with her enjoying her own promiscuous life, though hers was of course with women.

Mer's voice breaks into my thoughts. "Don't obsess over it, Em. I'm fine. They'll all be fine too."

"Of course," I manage, trying to not think about all the women Lauren has slept with over the years. She refuses to tell me how many. I figure she doesn't even know the total. That was something I had to get past very quickly in our relationship, as Lauren was fiercely protective of her rather experienced past. Our worlds pre-us were very different in that regard. I can count my total partners on one hand, Lauren being the last finger on that hand. I've never considered myself a "casual sex" kind of girl; I had three serious relationships prior to Lauren, and one longish affair during my first relationship. And no, I wasn't proud of that, nor do I talk about it, but, well, it happened.

I settle back onto my elbows and turn my attention to the game. Lauren is playing her usual position, center midfielder. It's a demanding position—she is constantly on the move and works her impressive foot skills to field passes and knock them out to her wings and forwards. She's played midfield positions since she started playing soccer when she was five years old. Throughout middle and high school, Lauren was always on the soccer field. Her dad had once joked to us that Lauren had permanent grass stains on her knees (and honestly, her knees still look off-color sometimes). Soccer is Lauren's life force. She has always known that she has the skills to take on whatever comes her way while on that field; in the other areas of life, she sometimes falters. It's not that Lauren isn't smart. She's just not *book* smart.

High school was difficult for her, and because she didn't graduate in the top fifty of her class, her dad informed her that she'd have to put soccer on the back burner if she expected him to pay for college. So she did—sort of. Lauren finished her freshman year at Portland State with a 3.7 GPA, and no soccer. No "real" soccer, anyway. She kept up a strict workout regimen and attended all of the women's soccer games. She'd become friends with a couple of the players, and occasionally kicked around with them to stay in shape. When the coach caught sight of Lauren on the field near the end of her freshman year, she'd approached Lauren immediately and asked her to try out for next year. The tryout was a formality; some of the team members had already mentioned Lauren's name and skills to their coach, and she'd been watching Lauren from a distance for some time.

Lauren kept her new soccer status from her dad during her sophomore year. She finally came clean with her step-mom over Christmas break. Beth was quietly supportive, understanding both her husband's and her step-daughter's fears. But Jake Cabrian remained clueless until Lauren's senior year when she invited him to her final game against Eastern Washington University. Both Jake and Beth, along with Lauren's younger brother and her twin step-sisters, were there to watch Lauren score two goals and help bring her team to victory. As Lauren tells the story, it wasn't so much that Jake was mad about Lauren's deception, nor was he surprised. He was proud of his oldest daughter, but also hurt that she hadn't felt she could be honest with him. That hurt spanned a few years of their relationship, and it was a big reason why Lauren didn't work toward post-college soccer. She knew her father wanted her to have a steady income through steady work, and she figured she owed him that much after having lied to him for several years. And true to form, Jake was over-the-top thrilled when Lauren landed a job with a local engineering firm, putting her civil engineering degree to work...even if it was just a mid-level job that didn't test her full potential.

Around me, people erupt with cheering—Lauren's team has scored. I cheer along with everyone else, frantically trying to determine who kicked the goal. Brenna, a woman Lauren has been playing soccer with for a couple years, jogs past Lauren and slaps her waiting hand. The smile on Brenna's face tells me what I need to know, and I relax. Not seeing your girlfriend score is not recommended, but missing your girlfriend's teammate score is not nearly as dangerous.

"Who's that cute girl?"

I follow Mer's gaze over to Brenna, who is bent over, tying her cleat, an act that slyly shows off her firm ass. "Brenna? You've met her, haven't you?"

"The one who just scored? Oh, yeah. Maybe I have. She's cute."

I cock my head toward Mer. "I thought you weren't coming to the dark side? Besides, Brenna's not on my team. She's on yours."

"Well, she's adorable. Is she single?"

"Habitually. She's an ophthalmologist, doesn't care much for dating. Why are you so curious?"

"Because I'm a curious person. But what I'm more curious about is why your girlfriend emerged from the basement this morning, and not your bedroom."

Oh. Well, that solved my mystery. I shrug, needing a moment to process this information and find a response. I know Mer is watching me closely.

"Maybe she was working on something late last night," I offer.

"Hon, I know she slept in the basement. And I know she isn't working on anything." Mer's tone is gentle, but not demeaning. She seems to understand that I'm at a loss.

"She hasn't really slept in our bed much lately." I exhale slowly. I feel a tiny bit better having shared this information with someone.

"Should I even ask when you last had sex?" Now her tone is low, still gentle, but almost teasing.

"Don't bother. I wouldn't be able to tell you."

Now it's Mer's turn to stare at me, mouth slightly agape. She shoves my shoulder. "Please tell me you're kidding, Em."

I slowly shake my head. "If I had to guess, I would say... around Christmas?" I rifle through the memories in my brain. Christmas *could* be right, but I might be thinking about the last time we *almost* had sex. "I know for certain that we had sex on our anniversary."

"Correct me if I'm wrong, but isn't your anniversary in August? And is it not currently *April*?"

I shush Mer, quickly looking around us to see if anyone is listening. Fortunately, most people seem focused on the game. My non-sex life is embarrassing enough in my own head, but to have the greater Portland lesbian athletic scene know how terrible it is? No thanks.

"Oh, Emery, what the hell is going on with you two? Are you sleeping with someone else? Is Lauren?"

"What? No! At least I'm not." My stomach clenches suddenly. How had I not considered Lauren having an affair? It makes perfect sense. Too perfect. And with Lauren's college track record...

"I'm sure Lauren's not either, hon. Really. She's never cheated on anyone."

And how could she? I'm Lauren's second serious relationship; after her promiscuous college years, she threw herself into a relationship that lasted for four years which, according to her, fizzled out on its own. I cringe inwardly: Lauren and I are coming close to celebrating our fifth anniversary. The timing is eerily similar...are we fizzling out, too?

"Honestly, Em, I—"

I hold up my hand. "Stop. It's okay. I don't think she's cheating on me." The knot in my stomach loosens a bit, then clamps tighter when I realize I still don't know what's keeping Lauren from me.

Mer opens her mouth to say something, then shuts it without uttering a sound. I steer my stare toward the game, hoping for a distraction from the repetitive thought clanging through my mind: *Why is my girlfriend no longer interested in me?*

* * *

"Em, can you bring another bottle of red out to the deck? Brenna just emptied the sauvignon."

"No problem," I call back to Lauren who's manning steaks on the grill. She'd decided to host an impromptu Sunday family dinner after her soccer game ended. She and Brenna are riding high from their shutout, and Brenna in particular is in a celebratory mood.

I grab a new bottle and the opener. I pause in the doorway, giving myself a moment to appreciate the scene on the deck before me. I love my biological family, but this is an even better family. Mer is sitting next to Brenna, both with full glasses of red wine. Mer's exotic looks clash with Brenna's all-American long blond hair and big brown eyes, but they have clearly clicked, laughing and carrying on as if they've been friends forever. Carly and Jen, who live a few blocks from us, are talking baby-making with Cat, who happens to moonlight as a doula. My best friend, Allison, is next to Lauren at the grill, probably rambling on about one of two topics: her never-ending relationship drama (her on-off girlfriend, Sidney, isn't currently here), or the never-ending employee drama at her coffee shop, Perk. I love these women, crazy and drama-filled as they sometimes are. And I especially love how easily Meredith has slid into the picture.

Lauren looks up from the grill as I hand Mer the new bottle of wine. She catches my eye and teasingly rolls her gray-blue eyes. Yep, Allison must be giving her an earful. I smile back at Lauren. She holds my glance for a moment, and I search her eyes for some hint of love, or passion, or anything other than general camaraderie. Lauren continues to stare at me as she takes a long swig from her bottle of beer. Now that look—I know *that* look. My stomach flutters involuntarily. Yep, that's a good look. Lauren seals it with a wink before turning her attention back to the steaks and Allison's chatter.

Soon the eight of us sit down at our dining room table, since the air has become a bit too chilly to enjoy dinner outside. Sidney still hasn't arrived, and Allison's not talking about it, so I don't bother to ask where she is. Before we left the kitchen, Lauren told me that she'd fill me in later regarding the latest Allison vs. Sidney showdown. She also gave me a quick kiss, and the beer on her breath was more intense than I'd smelled in quite some time.

The talking dies down as Cat raises her wineglass. Her smile sparkles, her teeth impeccably white as she toasts us. "Thank you, Emery and Lauren, for yet again opening your door to your merry band of weirdo friends. We love when you cook for us!"

The table clinks glasses and we dig in. Moans erupt from several mouths as the first bites of buttery steak are chewed. Lauren takes the compliments in stride, simply nodding and grinning.

"So, how's the baby making going?" I ask Carly, who's seated to my right.

"Harder than we'd imagined," she answers, looking across the table to her wife, Jen. "I'm going for the next insemination this week."

"It can sometimes take time to get pregnant," Mer reassures them. "I'm sure it'll happen when you're truly ready for it."

"Oh, I know. I just want to be pregnant so badly."

"You don't hear many lesbians say that," Allison says, poking Carly's arm with her fork.

"Including me," Jen says with a laugh. "This is all Carly. No way am I growing a baby in this body."

"What if Carly isn't able to get pregnant? Would you change your mind, Jen?"

I watch as Carly and Jen exchange a look across the table. Apparently, I'm not the first person to ask them this loaded question. It doesn't look like I'm getting an answer as Carly shrugs and Jen takes a long drink. Lauren reaches over and squeezes my forearm.

Conversation quickly picks up, and Jen starts asking me questions about my new project at work. I fill her in on the basics, feeling renewed excitement about diving into the communication mechanics of a struggling company. It's been over a year since I've been assigned to such a big, company-wide consultation. My boss, Libby, has jokingly referred to it as more of a "rehabilitation" than a consultation, but I'm ready for the challenge. Both Jen and Cat know a few of the people I'll be working with at Whitmore Hill, and they seem optimistic about how those people will react to my team working with them to improve their overall functioning as a company.

* * *

"Be safe!" I call to Allison as she backs down the driveway. As soon as her headlights turn to illuminate the road, I yank Lauren inside. "All right, spill it," I say, closing the door and leaning against it to look at her.

"Allison is pretty sure Sidney is cheating on her with the barista she hired a month ago."

I love that about Lauren: when she has gossip she knows I want, she doesn't make me wait for it. "Oh, that's bad."

"It would be if she had any evidence."

I reach up and cup Lauren's shoulders. Her skin is warm beneath her T-shirt. "She never does. And yet, somehow, Sidney is always caught."

Lauren grins and wraps her arms around my waist. I slide my arms around her neck, my pulse quickening at the contact. "Well, if Allison kept her woman satisfied, then she wouldn't have to worry about what Sidney is or isn't doing."

Isn't that ironic coming from you. I don't have much time to think as Lauren's mouth meets mine and unleashes a kiss that I haven't experienced in, well, a long time. Maybe my best friend's inability to keep her girlfriend happy might actually work to my benefit.

I sink into the kiss as Lauren gently pushes me against the door and presses herself against me. The handful of inches she has on me forces her to bend her head just a bit in order to kiss me, and the friction of our bodies moving together makes me want to stand on my toes. The kiss deepens, our breathing quickens. I run my fingers through Lauren's hair, tugging gently when she nips my bottom lip with her teeth.

Lauren slows the kiss then grabs both of my hands. "Gotta lock the back door. Meet you upstairs," she whispers, her voice heavy and tinged with passion.

I take the stairs two at a time. I make a quick stop in our bathroom to brush my teeth, even though it's pointless to do so as we've both been drinking and have alcohol breath. But I brush anyway, hoping to dissolve the tiny bit of panic sitting in my chest. What if Lauren gets sidetracked by Mer? Or another beer, the basement, her weird no-sleep-with-the-girlfriend routine?

But no—there she is on the stairs. And she's moving quickly. I walk into our bedroom and shut the blinds. As I turn away from the last window, Lauren's there, and she grabs me. She kisses me hard and fast, her hands moving quickly to lift my shirt over my head, her thumbs trailing against my skin. "Bed," she mumbles against my mouth, and we fumble backward until we crash onto the bed. Lauren attacks my neck with her mouth as I pull off her shirt and bra. My teeth find her waiting, hard nipples and I take one into my mouth. Lauren's groan is guttural, and I'm hit with the urge to luxuriate in her body. If I can't remember the last time we were in this position, I better make sure that I remember this time. I slow my movements, sliding my tongue slowly over her nipple. My right hand teases her left nipple, alternately stroking and tweaking. Lauren whispers, "I love you, Em" as I kiss my way across her chest. Her hands move toward my breasts, still covered by my bra. I settle my mouth on her nipple, taking my time sucking and teasing her. In fact, I'm so involved in what I'm doing that I don't notice when I'm no longer being touched. And I don't notice when Lauren's breathing slows, then becomes rhythmic in its slowness. But I do notice the snore that escapes her throat when I move up to reignite our kissing.

CHAPTER THREE

"Emery. Em. Hellooooo."

I drop the pen that is busy aimlessly doodling on the hopefully unimportant spreadsheet on my desk. Concentration has *not* been my forte this morning, or this week; my head is embarrassingly clouded with what didn't happen Sunday night. Or what did happen. Well, what happened and what should have happened but didn't.

"What is this? Hungover Emery?"

"This is Distracted Emery," I reply, forcing myself to smile at my coworker, Caren, who is perched on the edge of my desk.

"Distracted Emery better get her shit together, and soon, because I need Focused Emery's brain to help with the finishing touches for our presentation tomorrow morning."

"I'm on it."

Caren cocks her head in my direction, her wide, pale green eyes assessing me, clearly not believing me. We've worked side by side for the past three years, and she knows me all too well. She's often joked that I know her better than her husband knows her for the simple reason that our job forces us to communicate as openly as possible. If we didn't, we wouldn't be successful in anything we do, as ninety percent of our job is based upon teaching or re-teaching people how to communicate effectively. Apparently Caren doesn't feel the same pressure to communicate while at home, even though her husband is wonderful, as is their relationship. So maybe they don't need to communicate. Yep, that might be a lesbian thing: the need for over-communication.

"Everything okay, Em? You seem a little…weird."

"I'm fine. Really. Just distracted."

"Okay, you know I'm not good at this touchy-feely bullshit. Do you need, like, a hug or something?"

"What she *needs* is caffeine." The familiar booming male voice appears before its owner does. Luke drops into the chair across from my desk and shoots both me and Caren menacing looks. "Is this what we're doing today? Chatting?"

"No, asshole, we're working. Part of working is talking."

"Seems to me you're doing more talking than working, Caren. Not that this is unusual, of course." Luke winks in my direction.

"What's on your face?" I ask, leaning across my desk to get a closer look. "Is that dirt?"

"This is the beginnings of a beard, smartass. Something you would know nothing about."

Caren bursts into laughter. "A beard? You're growing a beard for spring and summer?"

"Are you doing some kind of professional lumberjack thing? Is this the new metrosexual?"

Luke glares at both of us, his eyes betraying his menacing look by reflecting amusement. "I'm trying something new. Again, something you two would know nothing about."

"Oh, right, Emery and I are so stuck in our ways that we never experiment with anything new. You're absolutely right."

He might be, I think as Luke and Caren continue their banter. Before I can stop my thought process, I start coming up with ways I can bring newness into my relationship with Lauren. There has to be something we haven't done. In fact, I know there are plenty of things we haven't done together. Skydiving, mountain climbing, ice skating, tying each other up... and suddenly I remember we just did something new last weekend: one of us falling asleep during an attempt at sex. Look at that: newness abounds.

"You have the agenda done for tomorrow's presentation, right?"

I snap back into the conversation, knowing Luke's question is directed at me. "Yes. It's done. We just need to finalize our break-out schedule for Monday."

The past several weeks at work, which is a thriving little consulting company called Pointworth Leading and Consulting, have been a whirlwind. Luke, Caren, and I were put in charge of the new project to revamp Whitmore Hill, a local marketing firm. The three of us have worked together for years, and we've comfortably settled into our roles that depend upon our individual strengths. Luke typically handles financial matters while Caren focuses on all things related to analysis, whether it's hard data or personality tests. My role is usually centered around communication, both verbal and written. Together, the three of us lead workshops and presentations intended to help every person in every company we work with improve their leadership and communication skills. Our boss, Libby, likes to say that Luke and Caren handle the behind-the-scenes work while I take the stage in the leading role, but the truth is that not one of us could be independently successful without the other two, or three depending on Libby's role, working with us. We work so well as a unit at this point that when the three of us are presenting together, we finish each other's sentences and no one gets insulted, although it took Luke a while to accept the fact that Caren can practically read his mind.

Luke gets up and stretches, his six-foot-three frame dissatisfied with having been crammed into the little chair in my office. "I'm expecting a call from Whitmore in a few minutes. I'll email you my agenda for Monday so you can outline the break-out sections."

I nod. "Caren and I will take care of the final pieces and send it back to you."

"Thanks, ladies. You take such good care of me." With a parting wink, Luke disappears to his office down the hall, probably off to crunch some numbers, as that seems to be his favorite office pastime.

Meanwhile, Caren is still perched on my desk, peering at me with open curiosity. Her dark red hair is pulled tightly off her face, leaving her pale, freckled cheekbones exposed.

I stare back at her. "What."

"Do you, ya know, need to talk?"

Dangerous territory. Caren and I may talk a lot, but we rarely venture into my personal life. Not that we couldn't; she's met Lauren and talked with her many times at events. I simply prefer to keep my work life separate from my home life. On the flip side, I know way too much about Caren's personal life. She generally keeps the discussion professional while at work, but our happy hour habits have exposed many of the dirty details that make up Caren's world.

"I'm fine. Really. I appreciate your concern, but I'm cool."

I can tell she's not convinced, but luckily my office phone rings before she can continue her inquisition. Unluckily, one of Caren's favorite habits is answering other people's phones.

"Emery Larsen's desk, how may I direct your call?" she purrs into the phone, batting her eyelashes at me. "Why yes, she is here. May I ask who's calling? Oh! Hi, Lauren. Sure, here she is." Caren hands me the phone with a raised eyebrow, then leaves, quietly shutting my door behind her.

"Hey there," I say, cradling the phone between my ear and my shoulder as I sort through my email. "This is rare."

"Yeah, I just wanted to say hey."

I make a confused face, relieved that Lauren is on the other end of the phone and not in front of me. Lauren doesn't do small talk during the workday. In fact, I never hear from her unless it's important. "Everything okay?"

"Sure. Yeah. How's your day?"

"It's fine. I'm working with Luke and Caren to put the finishing touches on our presentation for tomorrow. Should be out of here at a reasonable hour tonight." I pause, hearing my rushed sentences and tell myself to slow down. "It's been a busy week. How's your day going?"

"Oh, it's fine. You know, the usual."

"Any new projects on your horizon?"

"Nope, doesn't look like it. Maybe in a couple of weeks."

I make another face, realizing no one can see me but I'm unable to stop my facial muscles from contorting. This is so bizarre. We never do this. All our menial work-talk takes place over dinner, which is precisely where it should take place. "Lauren, are you sure everything's okay?"

"I said everything is fine, Emery."

"Okay, it's just this is a little unusual… you don't normally call me to bullshit in the middle of the day."

"I had some downtime and wondered what you were up to. But you're obviously busy, so I'll let you go."

"Lauren, no, listen, I'm happy you called." I glance at the clock. I need to budget a good two hours to finish everything for tomorrow, but I could slip out for an early lunch. "Want to meet for lunch?"

"I can't today." Her tone, not that it was exactly loving and pleasant to begin with, is distant. But if she claims everything is fine, then so be it.

After a moment, she continues: "I guess…I guess I just wanted to hear your voice."

Interesting. I take that in, expecting to feel a heart fluttering or a warming of my skin, anything. But nothing happens. It's sweet, sure, but something feels very off about this conversation. "That's sweet, babe," I manage, hoping my own tone sounds warm.

"I have my moments." Aha, that's the Lauren I know. "And I realized that I never apologized for, you know. The other night." She musters the tiniest bit of a chagrined tone when she says this.

"The other…oh. Sunday?" I bang my head against my palm. This is not happening now. At work? Classic avoidant Lauren. She knows full well that we can't have a real conversation about *that* right now, but if she'd saved it for dinner, who knows how long the discussion might last. Never mind the fact that I totally could have brought it up any time this week, but Mer's always been around, and Lauren and I have had very little alone time.

"Yeah, Sunday. I guess I had more to drink than I realized, and Mer and I had been talking earlier about how good you and I are together, and I wanted to remind you of how much you mean to me. But it obviously wasn't my best timing."

She's talked to Mer. About us. I sigh inwardly, wondering what exactly they've discussed. "Lauren, it's okay. It happens. I mean, it's never happened before, but it's fine."

"You're not upset?"

"Upset? No, I guess not. Confused, maybe. But I'm over it. It's not a big deal."

"You know I love you, Em."

"Yes, babe. I know. I love you too."

She's quiet. I can easily visualize her leaning back in her desk chair at work, long, sinewy legs stretched out and crossed at the ankles. I left before her this morning, but I picture her in one of her blue button-down shirts that make her eyes glow.

"I better go. I'll see you at home later."

"Okay. What do you want to do about dinner?"

"Mer said she'd cook tonight—one of her mom's recipes, I think. So we can both relax tonight."

"Sounds perfect. Have a good rest of your day, Laur. Love you."

"Love you too. Bye."

Long after I've hung up I stare at the phone. I have no idea what to make of that conversation. On one hand, it's sweet that she called at all. But then, to bring up the Sunday night debacle? In the middle of a workday? That's not exactly appropriate timing, but at least we've finally spoken about it, albeit awkwardly. And the truth is: I don't think I'm really okay with her having fallen asleep on me, or below me, as I tried to rekindle the flame that I'm starting to think has burned itself into ash.

CHAPTER FOUR

The next morning, in spite of my growing anxiety about this massive presentation that Luke, Caren, Libby and I are poised to make in approximately, oh, one short hour, all I can think about is last night, which went a little something like this:

1. I got home at six. Mer was in the kitchen, cooking up a Latin American food storm. Lauren was MIA.

2. Mer instructed me to go for a run, go watch the dogs in the park, something, anything—she seemed to think I needed some outdoor activity. I think she just wanted to ensure I was not in her way.

3. I went for a short run through the neighborhood and into the park. There were cute girls there, so I was happy. I mean, who doesn't like stealthily eyeing cute girls, knowing you have your own really cute girl at home?

4. On my jog home, I started to think about all the things I could potentially screw up during Friday's presentation to Whitmore.

5. By the time I got home, I was in full-blown panic mode, ready to have Caren and Luke both come over to completely redo our agenda.

6. Lauren was in the shower when I went upstairs. I considered joining her, thinking it might be a good way to destress.

7. I joined her.

8. She didn't seem to care. In fact, she seemed even more distracted than I was.

9. She rinsed and left the shower. I stayed and considered drowning myself. But the water felt really good and it was so hot that I started to feel my panic dissolve into numbness. Win.

10. We ate dinner with Mer, who had created an amazing meal. Mer did most of the talking. Lauren barely even looked at me. I drank a lot of wine.

11. I cleaned up after dinner. Mer kept me company, refilling my wineglass along with hers. Lauren disappeared into the basement, claiming she had "work" to do.

12. Mer reassured me that she definitely knows that Lauren is *not* cheating on me. She's just going through some stuff. "Some stuff" remains undefined.

13. I vented to Mer re: my fears and anxieties about the Whitmore project, and how despite being overly prepared for Friday, I feel completely unprepared. She reassured me. I realized she should be Lauren. I wondered what Lauren was doing.

14. Against my better judgment, I refilled my wineglass (for the fourth time? That explains today's headache) and descended into the basement. Finding the door to Lauren's cave ajar, I pushed it open with my toe and stood in the doorway. She looked up at me. I looked back at her.

15. She leaned back in her chair. I shut the door behind me, put down my glass, straddled her right there on her desk chair. I waited for her to stop me.

16. I kissed her. She kissed me back.

17. And then she stopped me: "Em, I think you're a little drunk."

18. I quickly and—thankfully—skillfully removed myself from her lap. "I might be. So what?"

19. She smiled. She stood up and wrapped her arms around me. "You need your rest tonight. I don't want to tire you out before your big presentation."

20. In that moment, I think I hated her.

21. Instead of rebutting, I nodded against her shoulder, inhaling her clean, soapy scent. Then I went upstairs, got a glass of water, and went to bed.

22. I woke up at three a.m. and realized I wasn't alone. Lauren was asleep next to me, her skin cool against my legs. It was the closest I'd felt to her in months.

* * *

The headache, mixed in with a tinge of heartache, follows me into the morning hours. I pop Advil before I leave the house, then stop at Allison's coffee shop before I head over to Whitmore. Allison has spent a lot of time making Perk into her dream coffee shop, and it has paid off; she has a steady stream of regulars mixed in with random customers including a fluctuating college crowd. The walls are painted a pale but sunny yellow, and Sidney, in a time when she was wholly devoted to Allison, helped to refinish the hardwood floors. The tables and chairs are all thoughtfully mismatched, lending a comfortable feeling to the space. There's a bookshelf piled high with both classics (only those I approved with my fancy Masters degree in English Lit, of course) and a variety of contemporary fiction, including an entire shelf devoted to lesbian fiction. Another shelf houses poetry anthologies; Carly and I collaborated on that collection. A coffee table in the middle of the shop is always stocked with magazines, both those Allison subscribes to and those customers donate, or accidentally leave behind. Allison keeps the decor sparse but urban and inviting; several local artists have work hanging on the walls, and a local sculptor crafted a somewhat abstract coffee mug with people dancing on the rim. That takes residence on the floor near the counter, which is overtaken by stainless steel appliances, including Allison's baby, the Astoria, lovingly named Stella.

The morning rush is in full force; even with Allison and two other baristas working steadily, there are about seven people in front of me. I'm idly standing in line, mentally rehashing the previous night, when I'm bumped from behind.

"Oh, I'm so sorry. I forget how big this bag is!"

I turn and shoot a tight smile at the woman behind me who is, in fact, carrying a bag that is excessively large. She appears to be a college student—laptop and books burst from the seams of the bag, she wears rumpled clothing and her short, unruly hair caps a face that holds two very bleary eyes. If I hadn't spent extra time this morning picking out the perfect black and gray pinstripe blazer to wear with my best-fitting black dress pants and making certain that my own sometimes unruly wavy, shoulder-length dark brown hair is pulled back into a presentable knot at the nape of my neck, I'd be worried that I look as haphazard as she does. I know my own hazel eyes are a touch on the bleary side, but a quick swipe of mascara (my secret weapon, used only in emergency situations) helps to keep them looking lively.

"No worries," I reply. I scan my brain to determine if I know her, but I come up empty, relieved to not feel like I have to engage in conversation.

"Tough morning," she adds, grinning at me. "I definitely missed my first class. And if this line doesn't move any faster, I'll be unforgivably late to my second."

I nod, not so much in the mood for small talk. Something behind Ms. Collegiate catches my eye and I gaze past her shoulder at a person standing two people behind her as she continues to fill my ears with unprompted chatter about her class schedule. There's something oddly familiar about that stance, and those eyes, which are focused on a cell phone. I know I shouldn't be staring, but I can't help myself. I also know I could be caught at any moment, but I'm too busy taking her in to care. As if she knows I'm not so subtly eyeing her, the woman turns to her right and I get a profile shot, which doesn't help my identification process. She's dressed professionally in a gray-blue button-down shirt, black dress pants (tailored, but they are definitely men's dress pants), and black Doc Martens. Her dark brown hair, darker even than mine, is cropped close to her head except for the top, which is just long enough to messily spike. Her left ear is gauged with a silver hoop, and she's wearing small, silver and black wire rimmed glasses. As I'm watching, her left hand comes up and aimlessly scratches at a spot behind her ear, and I notice the simple thick silver ring hugging her middle finger. If she would just turn back around and I could get a better look at her face, I think I'd be able to—

"Um, I think your phone is ringing? Also, move up."

I snap my attention back to Ms. Collegiate. I force another smile in her direction before whirling around to face the other end of the line. I grab for my ringing phone as I take the required steps forward: three more people to go.

"Please tell me you're in line for coffee."

"Yes," I hiss. "What do you want?"

Caren snorts into the phone. "Is this the attitude of the day? You better adjust that shit before you get to Whitmore."

"I'm fine. What do you want?"

"Wow, Emery, I don't know what's going on with you lately, but you clearly need to get laid or something of that variety."

I'm about to throw my phone away. This is exactly what I do not need today. Plus, dammit, I need to get Caren off the phone so I can subtly turn around and figure out who that woman is. "Caren? Do you want coffee?"

"Aww, that's better. Yes! I'd love a skim latte."

"Fine." Oops, back to hissing. "I have to go, next in—"

"Wait, what? Hang on, Em." I roll my eyes as my patience flitters off to an unknown land. "Luke would love a mocha. Thanks, girl! We'll see you soon."

I suppress a growl and take the last step before hitting the counter. "Skim latte, mocha with whip, and a house blend. All mediums."

"Good morning to you too, Emery," Allison responds.

"Sorry. I'm sorry. Good morning, and please." I shrug and try to appear embarrassed. This is not my normal interaction with baristas, or anyone, for that matter. Fortunately, Allison knows me well enough to not take my morning moods personally.

"Rough morning?" she asks lightly, taking my debit card.

"No. I don't know. Big presentation today, probably nervous." Ah, yes, here come the clipped sentences and hissing again—sure signs that I have lost all communication skills. And excellent timing when I'm off to give a presentation on the very nature and importance of communication!

Allison raises an eyebrow at me, and again I'm struck by how similar her appearance is to Lauren's. Her hair is shorter and more alternatively cut and she carries a good thirty pounds more than Lauren, but something about their eyes and mouths is uncannily congruent. I suppose that makes me a bit predictable, what with my girlfriend and best friend looking oddly alike. Then again, Allison has never been more than a friend, and never will be because we don't see each other in that way, and Lauren…well, shit, Lauren is basically just a friend anymore, isn't she?

"I'm sure it'll be great, Em. You're great. Relax! You know you're awesome at what you do."

I take a deep breath and nod, then move toward the end of the counter to wait for my drinks. What I'd really like to do is disappear into a portal that will dump me onto a pristine beach somewhere. I can't recall a time in my life when I ever felt this overwhelmed. I will definitely require a getaway once I'm finished with Whitmore.

"Here you go! One mocha, one latte, one house blend. Great picks! Have an awesome day!"

I take the carrier from the overly enthusiastic barista. Her name tag reads "Loophole."

"Thanks. You too." No time to wonder about that level of crazy.

As I turn to catch another hopeful glance at that woman in line, Allison appears next to me and grabs my arm. She steers me toward the bookshelf, inadvertently giving me a solid line of vision toward Mystery Woman.

"That's her." Allison's turn to hiss.

"Huh? Who?" Mistakenly, I think she's talking about my Professional(ly Sexy) Mystery Woman Who is Clearly Gay and Someone I Swear I Know.

"Sidney's new experiment."

No, that doesn't add up. Sidney prefers girly girls, Allison being the exception. "Who are you talking about?" *Look at me, look at me, dammit!* She's ordering. Even from the side, I can tell she has a killer smile.

"The barista."

PSMWWICGASISIK (okay that won't work—let's just call her The Woman) now has her back to me, so I begrudgingly give my attention to Allison, who is clearly in some sort of distress. "Which one?"

"The one who gave you your drinks! God, Em, keep up!"

"Loophole? Seriously?"

"That's not her damn name. It's Maggie." Mid-roll, Allison's eyes light up with fire. "Goddammit! Loophole! She thinks she's the fucking loophole! Oh, my God, I am so stupid."

"Whoa, stop. Do you have proof?"

"Well. No. But Sid is coming in a lot, only when Maggie is working."

"So? That doesn't mean anything."

"Em, look at her. She looks exactly like the last one."

I take another look at Maggie Loophole, who is cute in a feminine, former-cheerleader kind of way. She does resemble the last girl that Allison caught Sidney with, and I do mean *caught with*. But like I was just musing—appearance doesn't dictate attraction. Just because Allison looks like Lauren in some ways doesn't mean that I'd hop into bed with Allison, so even though Maggie Loophole is almost a dead ringer for Sidney's previous indiscretion, it's not a sure bet Sidney will take her to bed too.

"I think you need to calm down."

Allison glares at me, the fire certainly not gone from those eyes. "I think I need to find a friend who will help me spy."

"Okay, crossing the line." I catch sight of The Woman making her way through the crowded café. Her caramel eyes, impossible to hide behind those little glasses, flicker over in my direction, and a smile snags her lips. My stomach flips several times. I know those eyes, and even more importantly: I know that smile.

"Are you even listening to me?" Allison asks. I give her something that resembles a nod, and off she goes again.

Lost in the stream of Allison's talking, I steady myself against the raw surprise at seeing Burke Calloway again. The last time I saw her, more years ago than I can currently recall, I had assumed it would be the last. Not for any good reason, but simply because she was living in Manhattan then, and I was only there for a work conference. I was with Cassidy at that time, a four-year mistake that had its share of the back and forth similar to what Allison is experiencing with Sidney. The last time I saw Burke was at a mutual college friend's apartment— an ex of an ex, or something like that, as Burke and I had not attended the same college, but knew each other through a girl Burke had dated and with whom I went to school. I spent the majority of that night in Manhattan talking with Burke on the fire escape. It was the only semi-quiet place we were able to find, and we spent a couple hours catching up and conversing about an array of things, as we hadn't seen each other for a good three years. I mentioned Cassidy at some point, mostly as a way to remind myself that I did have a girlfriend, and even though our relationship was shit and she was probably with someone else at that very moment, I wouldn't be that girl who cheated on her girlfriend. That's not to say there was even the potential for cheating...it's just, well, it was Burke.

But now? Burke? *Now?* Her presence has completely thrown me off balance. I thought she was still in Manhattan.

"You know, you're really not helping, Em."

I take a deep breath and give Allison what I hope is a sincere smile. "I'm sorry. I really have to go. Coffee's getting cold, and I have a major, major presentation today. I'll call you later. Promise."

With that, I practically run out of Perk, hoping and fearing I would run into Burke in the parking lot. And when I don't, I can't quite tell what I'm feeling.

CHAPTER FIVE

By the time I pull into Whitmore's tree-lined parking lot, I'm certain of two things: the coffee is miraculously still semi-hot, and I'm definitely going to find and add Burke on social media, something I should have done years ago. We weren't even friends, really, back in our college days. We only met because Burke dated a girl named Veronica, who lived with my college girlfriend, Taylor. Taylor and I were together through the second half of our sophomore year, and lasted somewhere to the middle of our junior year. There was no good reason for ending things: we just ran out of steam and didn't want to stay together for the sake of being together. We remained friends, and the amount of time I spent hanging out at her apartment with both Taylor and Veronica was how I eventually met Burke. Since Burke went to college two hours away from OSU, she was around most weekends, but that was it. I'd hung out with her, or at least existed in the same room with her, over the span of eight months. I can't even proclaim that we had deep conversations, or an instant, intense connection. Sure, we'd talked, and joked around. And we realized we had some things in common, like our mutual love for Adrienne Rich and macaroni and cheese, particularly Kraft, and especially on rainy nights.

Regardless of our limited interactions, there had always been something about Burke. Beyond her androgynous sexiness, there was a magnetic pull that made me want to talk to her. Of course, my ability to do so was impeded by Veronica's romantic involvement with her. But when Burke and I surprisingly reconnected in Manhattan, I had her to myself. All of those little personality pieces that I'd previously been exposed to were magnified, and impossible to sidestep. I had realized, then, that I wanted to know her. Know more of her, maybe even someday know all of her. And she was wondrously open. Our fire escape conversation covered so much ground that I found myself curious as to how our friendship would have been different if we'd gotten to know each other better while in college.

I wasn't the only participant in that conversation who seemed determined to keep it going. Once we both tired of the noise and crowd of the party, Burke and I left together, our voices overlapping and mingling in the warm, early-summer air around us. As we walked through the never-silent streets of Chelsea, I felt close to her in a way that I hadn't expected and didn't know what to do with. After all, that evening's interaction was the most we'd ever had, and I couldn't even label her as a friend. She was, then, a mysterious acquaintance with whom I was able to speak freely and openly—someone who shared many of my interests. Maybe she could be a friend someday.

When Burke and I parted ways that night in the familiar grungy 18th Street station, we didn't exchange phone numbers or email addresses. It was almost as if we knew that our intersection was as fleeting as it was unplanned.

In the subway, Burke reached out to hug me: we were both waiting for the 2, but I was heading downtown to TriBeca and Burke was going uptown to Columbus Circle, a trek she sometimes made by foot, she told me, but sacrificed to have a few more minutes with me. Suddenly nervous, I smiled shyly and shrugged when her arms extended toward me.

"What?" she said, and her entire face seemed to smile. "You have an issue with friendly affection?"

I shook my head and laughed at my own awkwardness as I sealed that moment, that picture, into my head. She stood before me, her back to the rush of people on the dingy stairway. She wore dark jeans with perfect authentic rips at the knees, black Doc Marten boots (her signature footwear, it appeared), and a simple gray T-shirt. Even then, I could tell that she was wearing a compression shirt; its outline barely showed through the T-shirt, but I'd felt it when I had brushed against her back earlier in the night. Even if I hadn't felt it, I'd be a little suspicious, because she definitely had not hidden her breasts while in college, and they were noticeably smaller to me now. That night, she was just androgynous enough to carry an air of sexual mystery that would make many people take a second wondering glance.

"We've never hugged before," I finally mustered, my shoulders seemingly stuck in that shrug.

"All the more reason to hug now, right?"

I couldn't turn her down. And I didn't want to. In that moment, even with the humid, metallic subway air clinging to every surface of my body, I wanted to know what it felt like to have Burke's arms around me. I remembered how attractive I'd found her while in college, and how I never understood Veronica's flippant attitude toward Burke. Maybe she would feel awful, I reasoned with myself in the split seconds preceding the hug. Maybe you can know things by a touch as simple as a hug, and I would know immediately that our attempt at friendly-closeness was wrong.

And so she hugged me. Our bodies fit neatly together. She smelled of the city, of gravel and misty sweat. And beneath that, she smelled like citrus and sandalwood. I fought against the urge to nuzzle my face in her neck, which would have been difficult as she's slightly shorter than I am.

Our innocent gesture of "hey, nice to see you again" was quickly and loudly interrupted by an incoming train—mine. Burke released me, that disarmingly awesome smile still illuminating her entire face. She held me at arm's length without touching me at all.

"It was good seeing you again, Emery. Thank you for a great evening."

"Same," I said.

I still felt shy, as though I didn't know how to interact with this Burke, a bit more grown-up Burke, and even more confident than college Burke. And grounded—yes, that was it. She was so grounded, as though nothing could uproot or knock her off course. Recognizing that left me with an odd mixture of intrigue and jealousy.

I waved, then turned and dashed to my waiting train, wanting to stay there and talk more, but not wanting to miss the express line. She was gone when I turned to wave once more—it was as if we both understood it was our next time to say goodbye.

* * *

"Thank you so very much," Caren says as she plucks her latte from my hand. "Roll out the posters and let's get those suckers hung up. T-minus fifteen minutes till showtime."

I oblige silently, not wanting to break my reverie from seeing Burke again. Caren would not understand what it's jolted for me, and I'm not sure I can yet put into words even for myself what I'm thinking and feeling about having so randomly encountered Burke. I don't even know if she recognized me, for shit's sake. Granted, I haven't changed that much since the last time we spoke, but life intervenes and brings with it a revolving carousel of people that we meet and leave. It is entirely possible that Burke didn't remember who I was; after all, it had taken me a good amount of staring and recalling to figure out who she was and how I knew her.

Before I start obsessing about whether or not Burke recognized me, Luke and Libby enter the conference room, toting with them two of the head honchos of Whitmore. Seth explains that he heads up the IT department and Charlotte announces that she is in charge of Human Resources. They'll be our point people for the span of our time at Whitmore, so Caren, Luke, Libby, and I make a point to speak candidly before the presentation begins. About twenty employees will be present for this initial presentation, so that one or two people from each department will hear the rollout. They'll take the information back to their departments and starting tomorrow we'll begin meeting with each individual department. Libby is a fan of this system because it puts the department members in charge of relaying information to their coworkers instead of us storming in and laying down the new laws in town. We're nowhere near that intimidating or powerful, ultimately, but this is a little communication trick that we like to use. Consider it a preview of all the fun communication games the employees will be taught to play.

Luck must be in my corner today: Charlotte's a big talker, so while Caren and Libby get their ears pleasantly gnawed off, Luke and I bustle around the conference room making sure everything is in place. Luke has worked with me long enough to know that I can't do mindless chatter when faced with a big project, so our interaction is pared down to grunts and nods.

By the time we finish, I have just enough time to slip out for a quick run to the bathroom to take some deep, cleansing breaths and steady my pulse. I've been a part of so many opening presentations by now that my words and actions are second nature, but the nerves never fail to pop up minutes before showtime. I mentally run through the agenda even though I know it's sitting on the table in front of where I'll spend most of my time standing, then give myself a once-over in the mirror. The quick glance slips into a longer stare. I like to make sure that I look put together and ready to face a room of strangers. I'm glad I picked this particular outfit to wear today. The clean lines of these pants don't enhance my hips, but they don't hide anything, either. I've always wanted a less curvy body, especially considering my breasts made their appearance by the sixth grade, but I've managed to stay relatively fit over the years. My hair is still in place, and my eyes appear to have regained some of their yellow-green light. While I'm busy assessing myself, I realize that my headache has vanished and I desperately need a bottle of water to tame this sudden burst of cottonmouth. Oh, nerves, how I do not love you.

* * *

Back in the conference room, every seat is taken, and there's a calm murmur of conversation amongst the employees. I smile as I make my way to the front of the room where my coworkers are positioned, noticing that the room went silent when I enter. Do I have toilet paper stuck to my shoe or my ass, or has something horrible happened to my hair or face during my short trek from the water cooler to the room? Luke is grinning at me, which can mean only one thing: these people actually think *I'm* in charge.

Libby gives me her usual nod, signaling that she could care less that I've yet again taken center stage by being the last PLAC leader to enter the room. That's one of the best things about having Libby as a boss: she truly does not need any of the attention that surrounds being in charge. She simply enjoys her job, and loves having us on her team.

Charlotte, too, is standing at the front of the room. We never have the first word; we're always introduced in the initial meeting so that the employees don't feel as though we just decided to come here and tell them they suck and need our help to stop sucking. It's much better to have one of the bosses introduce us for solidarity's sake.

"Hi, all," Charlotte begins. "As you know, we're starting a new initiative here at Whitmore, and to facilitate the changes and improvements we've brought in a team from Pointworth Leading and Consulting."

As chatty Charlotte prattles on about the company's short-term and long-term goals, I take in the people gathered in the room. That tiny boost from the disappearance of their voices as I entered the room is enough to make me feel about five inches taller and two levels more powerful. I look around, careful to keep Charlotte's voice on my radar to not miss an important introduction or segue as this part is completely unrehearsed, and notice a lot of faces I've never seen before. Considering the size and demographics of Portland, this isn't unusual. I do make eye contact with a guy who looks familiar and he nods in recognition. Perhaps his wife plays soccer with Lauren, as the only memory I can connect with him involves the image of grass. I nod back before moving my gaze to the woman seated next to him. And then I freeze. Just then Charlotte says, "I'd like to introduce you to Emery Larsen, head of communication consultation. Welcome, Emery!"

Thankfully, there's light applause, which gives me several seconds. My eyes are frozen on Burke Calloway who is casually seated next to soccer guy, an ankle thrown over a knee. At the mention of my name, she winks at me. Winks!

I take a deep breath and focus on the other members of the small crowd. I dazzle them with my best professional smile and go about introductions, determined not to permit Burke's presence to distract me. There is no way I will make an ass out of myself.

"Thank you, Charlotte, for the kind and enthusiastic introduction." Once I get that out, my mouth goes on autopilot.

"Good morning, everyone. I'd like to introduce you to the rest of the PLAC team that you'll be seeing, perhaps too much of as we take up residence in your quarters." There's a smattering of quiet laughter after that, and I relax.

I introduce Libby, Luke, and Caren, giving each of them an opportunity to speak about their roles in this project. We continue to bounce back and forth as we stroll through our agenda; the only hiccup we encounter is one of Libby's surprise sneezing attacks, which, as usual, both entertains our audience and endears Libby to them. We outline clear expectations and timelines for this group, doing everything we can to make them feel secure and as though they are a part of this process, because they are. Without their involvement, we cannot succeed.

Luke fields questions. There aren't many, but soccer guy has a good one about time management that gets my attention.

"The last thing we want to do is disrupt your work," I tell him. "If at any time you feel that we are impeding your ability to complete your work, please have that conversation with us.

We're here to work with you; no one will be successful if we become a burden."

Soccer guy nods appreciatively. I meet Burke's eyes, and she gives me a slow, easy smile. Yep, she remembers me.

Caren wraps up the presentation, making sure to thank them all for their time, as we know they already don't have enough of it in their workdays. Humor always helps to end meetings on a positive note, and this has been Caren's role from the beginning.

Several people come up to formally introduce themselves. We hear nothing but positive feedback, always appreciated but never an expectation. We have found ourselves in situations where companies don't give their employees a fair introduction or explanation for our presence, and we've been perceived as the enemy. A few of those situations ended up being less than successful, but, as a team, we've been able to do major attitude turnarounds in other similar situations. Right now, though, it seems like Whitmore is genuinely excited to have us here.

When I feel a warm hand on my elbow I know it's Burke even before turning the forty-five degrees to face her.

"I suppose I could lie to you and say I'm surprised to see you." Her voice is low and familiar. "But the truth is, I saw your name in an email my boss accidentally forwarded to the entire IT department."

I'm smiling as I fully face her. "The head of the IT department accidentally forwarded an email? Wow. We have more work to do here than I thought we did."

Burke chuckles, everything about her demeanor close and warm, so much so that I find myself fighting the urge to hug her just to remember how that feels. "Layers and layers of work, yes. You and your team may find yourselves stuck here for a good year."

"I imagine there are worse fates," I say, giving her a crooked smile.

She chuckles again, holding my gaze. Up close, I can see she hasn't changed much over the years; there's a tiny sprinkling of laugh lines beside her eyes, but her skin is smooth and still carrying that tint of a leftover tan. "It's really good to see you, Emery. I'm looking forward to working with you."

"It's good to see you, too, Burke. But I'm sure you'll be sick of me and my meddling ways in, oh, two weeks."

She gives her head the slightest of a shake. "No, I sincerely doubt that."

I don't know enough about her to know exactly what it is about this woman, but I'm worried that if I speak, my words will stumble over themselves. I'm right back in that subway station in Chelsea, wanting to stay and learn more. As if she can read my thoughts, Burke checks her watch and hoists her messenger bag over her shoulder.

"I'm about to be late for a conference call. But hey, I'll see you...?"

"Monday," I fill in, hoping I don't sound too excited or, conversely, not excited at all. I silently curse myself for even caring how I sound.

"Monday it is," she repeats, her smile overpowering her face as she turns to leave. For a moment I'm afraid she's going to wink at me again.

"And who was that?" Caren's voice scratches from an alarmingly close space and I visibly jump.

"Just a friend I knew from college."

"A friend who can make you blush so hard your neck is red?" Caren snorts, enjoying my dismayed and flustered reaction. "Some friend, I bet."

"Really, Caren. Just a friend. Now help me clean up so we can go get lunch. I'm starving."

We work in silence, or at least I do; Luke starts a debate with Caren over data analysis, and I'm able to let them fade into the background noise as I try to reorganize my mind around Burke's reentry into my life. She is, after all, just a friend—and even that? I don't know. She's an acquaintance.

And somehow, after all these years, she is still a mystery.

CHAPTER SIX

"That's great, Em, I'm so happy to hear the first day went well!"

"Me too. It's a relief to have started off so well." I knew my mom would be waiting for a complete run-down, and the best way to give her that was to put her on speakerphone while I was driving home from Whitmore. Also, it was a good way to distract myself from over-thinking about Burke.

"I'm really happy to hear that. I, on the other hand, do not have a kitchen."

I groan for her benefit, stifling a laugh. "I'm guessing dad went ahead and started a new project?"

"I told him if I don't have a stove by this weekend, I'm moving to the beach house. He can stay here and live like a caveman."

"He'd probably enjoy that."

"Of course he would! He could eat takeout for months and be satisfied. That man, honestly Emery, sometimes I do not understand him."

"Isn't that part of the overwhelming joy of marriage?"

She laughs, a true, deep laugh from her gut. That particular laugh is a family favorite, and it generally emerges only when marriage, love, or commitment are brought up in conversation—but only when the topic concerns my parents' marriage, love, or commitment. They've been married for thirty-one years, and my sisters and I have always joked that our parents exist in a marriage of convenience (at one point or another, we've all, including my mom, wondered if our father is gay), one that occurred only because they had conceived a child and felt societal pressure to be married. Our parents' interactions have always seemed more friendly and humorous than passionately loving; however, that level of friendship provided a decidedly stable childhood environment for the three of us.

"Speaking of marriage, has Lauren popped the question yet?"

I'm very happy that I'm sitting at a red light when my mom drops this bizarre bomb.

"What? No. What? Why are you asking me that?"

"I think it's a perfectly natural question to ask! You two have been together for quite some time now, you own a house together, and you're both in your thirties, certainly not getting any younger. Don't you want to get married?"

"I still don't see why you're asking me this question."

"I'm just making conversation, honey. Neither you nor Lauren has said much about your relationship lately, so I was wondering if, perhaps, one of you was planning a big proposal."

I'm stunned by both my mom's needling into this previously unexplored area, as well as my reaction to her poking around. Marriage? Me and Lauren? I don't know that I've ever even considered it. Beyond the marriage issue, I'm perplexed that my mom continues to talk to Lauren behind my back. I know it sounds ridiculous, but Lauren certainly hasn't mentioned their conversations lately. Then again, when would she? We haven't had many significant conversations lately, and I know I'm partly to blame because of how wrapped up I've been with prepping for the Whitmore project, but conversation is a two-way street.

"No," I tell her as I turn onto my street. "No, I don't think either one of us is planning anything. We're fine as we are." Those last words stick a bit in the back of my throat and I hope my mom doesn't notice. "What have you and Lauren been chatting about recently?"

"Me and Lauren? Oh, I haven't spoken to her much lately." I can tell she's lying by the tone of her voice; it gets a little squeaky. "How is she?"

"She's…she's home," I say. Yep, her car is in the driveway. At three o'clock on a Friday afternoon.

I feel worry rising inside of me. Lauren does not cut out early from work. Either she's sick or something's happened. "Listen, I need to go, Mom."

"Of course, honey. Tell Lauren I said hello. Talk to you soon."

I park my car behind Lauren's SUV and I approach the front door, mind already racing with all the possible horrible things that could have brought Lauren home early.

I burst through the door to see Lauren and Mer sitting casually at the dining room table. Instead of work clothes, Lauren's wearing old sweats and an equally old, worn Portland State soccer T-shirt—the kind that's so old and worn that it's unbelievably soft. They stop talking as I enter, and both give me looks of surprise. Right, as if I'm the one who doesn't have flexible hours.

"I might be home early a lot now," I announce stupidly.

Mer wears a smile of amusement, while Lauren wears a completely blank face. Slowly, the blankness shifts into a tentative smile.

"Did something happen?" I continue with my stellar communication skills.

"No, Em, everything's fine," Mer answers. "Come sit with us, we're planning a little dinner party for next weekend."

Silent, I continue watching Lauren, who is avoiding my eyes. I may not be communicating very well, but my champion talker of a girlfriend is not communicating at all. I am so sick of this, I don't even know how to—

"Em, I made reservations at The Olive Tree for tonight. Just the two of us."

My mouth salivates as if on command. I love The Olive Tree. Maybe more than love. It's been a favorite haunt of mine since I moved to Portland. There's not a stitch of Greek in my familial blood, but my mother has been moderately obsessed with Greek food for all my life, so I had many Greek-style meals while growing up. Since leaving home, I've been in an eternal search for the next best Greek restaurant, and after my first meal at The Olive Tree I knew it would keep me satisfied for many years.

This is a date? Sounds like it. "That sounds great, Lauren."

"I thought it would be nice for us to go out. We haven't done that for a while."

She's looking at me now, a soft image of hope spread across her face. I catch myself comparing Lauren's wholesome looks to Burke's darker, more mysterious ones. Stop. This is Lauren, my girlfriend whom I love, and she has arranged for us to go out on an actual date tonight. This is lovely. She is lovely.

"I'm looking forward to it," I finally say, hoping that my internal voice didn't break out, or that my pause wasn't too weird or obvious. "But why is it that you're home so early?"

"I took a half day. I didn't tell you? I swore I did."

No she didn't. Or did she? Am I that distracted by work? "I...yeah, maybe you did. Sorry. I must have forgotten." Mer won't meet my eyes, and Lauren has the good grace to look sheepish.

"I think I'll go for a run to shake off the day." *And* their weirdness.

"Good idea, babe," Lauren says. She stands up, and comes to hug me. Yes, she fits, too. This hug is home. "I want to go do some yard work, so take your time."

* * *

By six, I've jogged, showered, shaved, dressed, and read an article that Libby emailed. My fingers involuntarily move toward my laptop and I give in.

I log in to Facebook for the first time in a week or so, and navigate over to Veronica's page. Her profile picture is one of her usual artistic/sexy self-portraits that she swears are not self-portraits. We were never that close in college, but I know Veronica well enough to recall precisely how vain she was, and likely remains. I scan her page quickly. She's still living in San Diego, with her girlfriend Dianna the graphic designer, and still a real estate agent moonlighting as an erotica writer (published under a pseudonym, of course). The rest of her profile is kind of bland, so I skip over to the best possible place to find the Facebook connection to Burke, if one exists: a photo album cleverly titled "College Daze."

I scan through the thumbnails, keeping watch for references to myself along with Burke. I can't recall any photo tags from Veronica, but that's not to say there aren't any unflattering pictures of me hidden somewhere in this album.

"Oh, that's horrible," I mutter. As if on cue, a picture of me and Taylor pops onto my screen, both of us in baggy sweats and OSU hoodies. We're sitting on the sofa in Taylor and Veronica's apartment, deeply engaged in a video game. I look like a hot mess, as I did for most of college. In the background, though, I spot a familiar face.

I click through the next couple of pictures, which must have accumulated over the course of a winter weekend judging by our apparel and our documented laziness. I groan as another unsightly image of myself skitters over the screen, and then: got it. There she is. Next in line is a picture of Burke sitting on the floor, surrounded by books. She's not looking at the camera and doesn't even seem to be aware of the camera's presence. She's completely engaged in the texts and whatever she's scribbling into her notebook.

No luck, though: no one is tagged in the picture. But comments! There are comments, the second one from none other than BK Calloway: "just another poetry-filled saturday at osu. thanks for the memory, v."

I click on BK Calloway and am swept to a new Facebook profile page. It's private. All I'm permitted to see is Burke's profile picture, which seems to be of her Doc Marten-encased feet standing on a double yellow line. The innocuous details of her life are readily available to the seeking public: Female. Liberal. Single.

Uh-oh. Single. I bite my lower lip. I hadn't been expecting that.

* * *

"This was a really sweet idea, Lauren." I reach for my menu and send my girlfriend a warm smile. I'm still confused about this supposed half-day that Lauren took, but dammit, I am going to have a good, romantic, rekindling date with my girlfriend.

"I thought we could use some time for us. I know Mer hasn't been here for long, but since she is *always* here, I wanted to make sure we had time to spend with just each other." Lauren returns my smile with an equally warm one of her own, and throws in a wink for good measure. She changed out of her sweats and is wearing nice jeans and a simple black button-down. She's also let her hair loose around her shoulders, a rare treat, and if I ignore the slightly weary look in her eyes, she looks happy and gorgeous.

"Speaking of Mer always being at home—does she have plans to get a job or anything?"

"She doesn't need to. But I'm sure she'll get bored and go pick up some brainless part-time job after a while."

Ah, yes, the life of an only child graced with deliriously rich parents, one of whom died many years ago and left his baby a sizable chunk of cash.

"She did start painting again," Lauren adds as she closes her menu and places it gently on the table.

"Oh, that's great! I love her work. Remember the first painting she gave us?"

"The one that you adore and I can't stand?" Lauren laughs. "Where is it hanging now?"

"I have it in my office. I still like it."

"Well, we don't have to like all the same things, Em." She says this lightly, and I can hear the amusement in her voice.

I turn my attention to the menu, even though I know what I'm ordering. I agree with Lauren's statement, but if I recall correctly, she *had* liked that painting at first. After a week or so of it hanging in the living room of our apartment, she'd decided it creeped her out and took it down while I was out of town with my family. She wouldn't explain how or why it creeped her out, so I was relatively sure that was a cop-out to simply not liking the painting. It was a standard abstract painting that incorporated many different hues of blue and purple with, as Mer explained, randomly purposeful streaks of silver throughout. I'd always found it to be calmly inspiring. Or maybe I just like the colors.

After the waitress takes our orders, Lauren reaches across the table and takes my hand. I wait for the expected flood of warmth. I wonder if Lauren is feeling anything.

"So, I wanted to talk to you."

"Okay." I nod, showing my openness to talking. We can't continue to exist in the same places but lack the connection that has kept us together for this long. I want my girlfriend back, I realize.

"I know you were surprised about my being home early today. Honestly, I wasn't expecting you to get home before five, so I wasn't really…prepared."

Prepared? Prepared to see me, after you've been seeing me every morning and evening for the last four plus years? She's not making any sense, so I focus on our clasped hands, wondering when that physical connection spark is going to sweep through my body.

"I've been getting home early a lot lately."

"Why?"

She hesitates. The weary look I'd noticed earlier seems even more pronounced, and for a split second, I'm afraid that she's about to dump me. I arm myself with reasons why she should not do that, so deeply entrenched in my own thoughts that I miss what comes tumbling out of her mouth. Then again, if she is dumping me, I could…what? No. Why am I even thinking like that?

Lauren is quiet. I must have missed something. "I'm sorry, what? I didn't hear you." I brace myself for the dumping.

A flash of something—anger? regret? embarrassment? I can't quite tell—spirals across her face. "I said, I lost my job."

But she can't dump me! We've made it this far; this is just a little stupid bump, we'll get—wait. No. That's not what's happening here, is it?

"You what?"

"Em," she hisses, "are you even listening to me? Like, at all? How many times do I need to tell you that I fucking lost my job?"

"Oh, shit." Embarrassed silence from both of us. We stare at each other as our food arrives, a necessary interruption to our deteriorating conversation. Without any further comment, we both begin stuffing food in our mouths. Anything to fill the space that has been voided by her bomb and my complete lack of preparation for it.

A full plate of baked eggplant with feta cheese later, I pick up the silence and move it to another table.

"It's okay, Lauren. We can handle this."

She doesn't respond. She's concentrating on dragging her knife back and forth over her discarded napkin. She even appears to be pouting.

"Seriously, it's just…it's just a bump in the road. We'll be fine. I'm sure there are lots of jobs available."

"There aren't. I've been searching—" She breaks off. "I've looked."

"Laur? How long have you been jobless?"

"I kind of would rather not tell you that."

"You'd rather lie?"

"Em, I'm not proud of this. Any of it."

"Could you just be honest with me?"

She hesitates, refusing to look me in the eye. "It's been about three weeks."

Three weeks. Really. I gnaw on that for a moment, letting her sweat before I deign to respond. She's been lying to me for three weeks. She's been out of work for three weeks. And I wouldn't know that, since we don't share a bank account. Suddenly, about sixteen red flags pop up around Lauren. They wave boldly in the air surrounding her, begging me to acknowledge their existence.

"We'll work it out," I hear myself say.

Lauren's hand finds mine once again. "I'm sorry, Em."

I shrug. If my mind wasn't a clusterfuck prior to sitting down to dinner, it sure is now. "We'll work it out," I repeat.

CHAPTER SEVEN

Lauren sleeps in our bed that night. Neither of us says much; to fill in the quiet, we tune in to repeats of *Law and Order: SVU* and let our minds drift far from the elephant in the room. Frankly, my mind is filled to its capacity, too burdened to make room for conversation. Between Lauren's confession and Burke's reentry, I barely have room for any of my own thoughts. I know Lauren and I are going to need to have a serious conversation about her job loss and her silence about it, but tonight doesn't seem to be the night to do that. She's emotionally zapped; I can tell by her posture and the heaviness of her eyelids. I chastise myself for not having noticed the physical changes in her over the past three weeks. She looks thinner, too, and kind of pale. My normally happy, energetic girlfriend looks like she has the veritable weight of the world resting on her, and I couldn't be bothered to notice anything but my own angst over the changes in her behavior.

After Lauren falls asleep (and I notice that she makes a point to kiss me and tell me she loves me, something I've missed), I turn down the volume of the TV and burrow deeper into my thoughts. Beyond needing to have that necessary conversation with Lauren, I also need to put Burke aside and not let my curiosity about her negatively affect my relationship or my work with Whitmore. I sigh inwardly at this thought, watching Detective Benson do her sexy authority thing in an interrogation room with a suspected rapist, and wonder which of these tasks will prove to be more difficult: the conversation, or the shelving.

The truth is: I am not very good at shelving things, people, feelings, or situations. I tend to hang on when I shouldn't. A therapist would likely have a delightful time digging into my brain to discover the root of that issue, but I've managed it on my own for long enough to know that habit isn't changing.

In fact, I have such a distinct history of hanging on for too long that it's how I ended up meeting Lauren in the first place.

* * *

When I graduated from college, I landed an amazing internship with a consulting company based in Manhattan. I'd always loved New York, so it felt like a good fit. I quickly learned, though, that the company had several outposts, one located in Portland. As luck would have it, one of my college classmates ended up in the Manhattan office and I headed for Portland. On my very first day, there I was, dressed in every ounce of professional gear I'd been able to muster, and in she walked: Cassidy Shively.

Cassidy was my immediate supervisor, and though there were several interns, she gave me the most attention. At the end of the second week, she asked me to meet her for drinks, and I obliged, thinking it was a good way to schmooze. The internship made no employment guarantees past the end of the summer and I was itching for a permanent position. I figured if Cassidy had taken a liking to me, I just might land myself a job.

As it turned out, Cassidy had already taken quite a liking to me, but perhaps not the kind of liking that would help me get a job. Three drinks each and two hours later, she took me home to bed. I stayed for the weekend. And every weekend after that. Cassidy wasn't even my type, at least not what I perceived as my type. Ten years older, she was a strong, brash woman with a killer figure and long, vibrant red curly hair. She spent her workweeks in expensive suits with unnaturally short skirts and high heels, and her weekends in equally expensive jeans and deep V-neck sweaters…or nothing at all. Allison, who had become my closest friend by then, met her several times, and would only refer to her as "The Vixen." Later, Cassidy became "The Lady Killer," and finally, she evolved into "The Evil Bitch."

Needless to say, Cassidy did not get me a job with her company, which didn't matter because I found one on my own, but she did employ me as her bedmate—and on good days she would even refer to me as her girlfriend. There was love there, too, but the kind of love only aroused when needed. For example, "I'm sorry, Em, you know I love you." Being my first true relationship, I thought I had to stick it out through everything. "Everything" with Cassidy meant, among other things, no sense of commitment or discussion of it (if she called, I showed up; if she didn't, I didn't), being talked down to/treated like a child, and a variety of other women who took my place when Cassidy didn't feel like remembering I existed and was terribly in love with her, and would do anything for her/with her.

Even though I knew Cassidy was seeing other women while telling me she loved me and that I was the only one for her (or, more accurately, the only one who would consistently put up with her lying, verbal abuse, and bullshit), the thought of cheating on her never registered. It wasn't an option. I had done that in the past—my freshman year in college with an irresistible junior who had lured me away from my then-girlfriend who was a senior in high school and clear across the country. I still carried guilt from that and despite how poorly I was being treated by Cassidy, I was determined not to sleep with anyone outside of my relationship. And so I hung on.

It was within the last year of that relationship that I ran into Burke at that ephemeral fire escape party. And just a few months afterward, with Burke mostly out of mind again, Cassidy invited me to an art gallery opening. Her boss had asked her to go on behalf of their company, which was partnered with the marketing firm that had organized the gallery's opening affairs and publicity. Wanting to impress her, I was dressed up in tailored black pants and a revealing, sexy deep purple sleeveless top that Cassidy said she loved.

Cassidy essentially abandoned me as soon as we arrived at the gallery. She claimed she had to go do business, but I was willing to bet that she had spotted another one of her bedmates. I entertained myself with the free wine and the unique, expressive art embellishing the walls. I was so deeply involved with a painting depicting, among other things, a distorted mirror reflecting the image of a crying clown, that I didn't notice the proximity of another person until she spoke.

"You know, I've always had this thing against clowns, but seeing this makes me want to, I don't know, hug a clown."

I laughed without turning to see who the voice came from. "I hate clowns. Always have, always will."

"They are terrifying, but there's something about this painting that makes me feel sympathy for them. It's gotta be hard hiding behind all that makeup."

"But it's a chosen career," I said, finally looking at my mystery speaker. I'd never seen her before but I was taken by her immediately. Wearing dark jeans that looked made for her and a form-fitting white button-down shirt, Lauren stood before me, her blond hair hanging loose at her shoulders. She carried an air of confidence and security, and the way she was looking at me made me feel…wanted. Very, very wanted.

"Would you like another glass of wine?" she asked, gesturing to the empty glass I was clutching.

"Absolutely," I said.

"Would you like to go across the street to have that glass of wine?"

Oh God, did I. I really did. And already four mini-glasses of wine in, I was leaning toward saying, "Hell yes, let's go right now." But that persistent loyalty to Cassidy wrestled itself to the front of my mind.

"Actually, I'm here with someone…" I trailed off, knowing how ridiculous I sounded, because if this woman had been observing me at all over the last hour, she would know that while I had arrived with someone, I certainly didn't appear to be *with* that someone.

She looked around jokingly, even peering behind me. "I don't see anyone," she whispered.

"She's here somewhere, off doing business things." Or not, I thought. Probably not. Either way, I was not making a convincing case for myself, and the truth was I really did want to go to the bar across the street and have a glass of wine with this woman.

"Do you think she'd mind if I bought you a glass of wine? It's not often I meet someone who also hates clowns. My girlfriend happens to love them."

Aha. That sounded like a safe enough opening. "You know, I think I'm ready for that glass of wine."

As we crossed the street, Lauren introduced herself and thanked me for joining her. We drank, we talked. We talked for a long time about many things way past the realm of clowns. She bought me three glasses of wine, the last of which I couldn't finish. We exchanged phone numbers and she told me she'd love to talk about clowns another time. I went home by myself, not even wondering too much what Cassidy was doing.

That was February. Cassidy didn't ask what happened to me that night, nor did I bring it up. I never called Lauren, but she called me a week after we met. We spoke sporadically, but I refused to see her, making up excuse after excuse. She told me she would keep bugging me until I allowed her to see me again. I asked her what her girlfriend would think about that, and she laughed, explaining that she didn't have a girlfriend but she could tell the only way she'd be able to get me out of that gallery was to assure me that she wasn't a threat to my relationship. I didn't speak to her for two weeks after that.

At the end of those two weeks, now mid-March, I told Cassidy I wouldn't answer any more of her (dwindling) calls. Almost immediately, as if by some strange cosmic force, I started seeing Lauren out and about in random Portland haunts. It was always amazing to me how, in this bustling lesbian metropolis, we hadn't crossed paths before the night at the gallery. But now that Cassidy was history, Lauren was everywhere. She respected the fact that I was ignoring her by simply waving and smiling. She never approached me. But I wanted her to. It took me till May to accept the fact that I wanted more from Lauren than just a wave and a smile. The first time I called Lauren, she told me we could date but she didn't do relationships (I didn't know a drop about her past at that point, and wouldn't for some time). In August, she caved and told me she was in love with me. We haven't looked back since.

* * *

The next morning, Mer ushers me onto the deck. She was refilling her coffee mug when I came downstairs in search of water. I'm sure my expression gave me away; I hadn't slept well, and Lauren was, surprise, gone when I woke up. Neither event had improved my general morning appearance.

"You kind of look bad, Em," Mer says. She sits across from me and gazes at me with an open look of curiosity and care.

"Reflects how I feel." Here we go again with the busted sentences.

"If it helps, I know what you and Lauren talked about last night."

"You do?"

"I do…she said you took it pretty well, even seemed okay with it."

Was that true? Was that really the perception I gave her? "I don't know if I'm okay with it."

"I don't blame you. I'd be pissed."

I study Mer as she gently blows the hot liquid in her mug. "Mer?"

"Yeah?"

"You knew."

I'd like to give her credit for the fact that she meets my eyes when she nods, but I'm becoming too angry. "She told you? You knew the whole time?" I run the math in my head. "Holy shit, you knew before you moved in!"

"Em, sweetie, it's not—"

"It's not what? It is! It fucking is! She lied to me for three weeks and you knew the entire fucking time. You both kept it from me."

"It wasn't my place to tell you, Em. I told her that repeatedly." Mer shakes her head slowly, those languid curls framing her face. "I think it's really shitty that she kept it from you for so long. I am truly sorry. I'm also pissed at Lauren for putting me in this position."

I take a deep breath and try to calm down. "Why did it take her three weeks to come clean? And what the hell has she been doing for these three weeks? Fucking around like she was before we started dating?"

"No! I told you, she's not cheating on you. She's been looking for jobs. I guess she's been home more often now that I'm here. And Em, I don't know why she didn't tell you. She never explained that to me but even if she had, that's something she has to answer. Not me."

I sit with that for a moment. Mer is right—this isn't her explanation to give. After all, she's not the one who lost her job (and was she fired? let go? what's the story here?) and lied to her girlfriend about it for three goddamn weeks.

"What can I do to make this better for you two?"

I shrug, the fight leaking out of me. "Nothing, Mer. Lauren and I obviously need to have a real conversation about this."

"Well...she's under the impression that you did. Last night."

I laugh bitterly. "I guess that really says something about the state of our relationship. That conversation lasted about five minutes. I have no idea why she lost her job, nor do I know what her plans are to rectify this situation. We can't afford to be a one-income family."

Family. The word slips from my mouth before I have the chance to censor it. Lauren is my family. We are a family. But a family shouldn't harbor lies.

"I'll help with the house."

"No, you won't."

"Yes, Em, I will. I'm not going to stay here for free. You're doing me a favor, but I'm not a leech."

"But you don't have to make up for Lauren's shortcomings."

"I won't. I can't. That's something you and Lauren need to take care of."

I nod. She's right. Mer can't fix our problems, nor do I expect her to. I'm worried that Lauren does.

"Correct me if I'm wrong," she continues, a note of caution in her voice, "but you and Lauren don't seem to... talk much."

I wish I could figure out when we stopped talking. If I could, I might be able to trace back and find the root of the problem that's rumbling beneath us. "We don't. And she barely sleeps with me anymore."

"I think that coincided with her losing her job," Mer says gently.

She's right, of course. The timing may not be perfect, but Lauren's absence from our bed does link up to her forced absence from her job. "I miss her."

"I think she misses you, too."

"But things are... messy." I want to say "fucked up," but that's a bit too harsh for what we're dealing with. Despite the prolonged lie and the anthills of other issues, I don't yet feel like this relationship is irreparable. Maybe I'm crazy, maybe I love her that much...or maybe I'm hanging on, yet again.

CHAPTER EIGHT

The weekend passes. The Necessary Conversation does *not* take place. It is avoided as much as we avoid each other, whether by chance or purpose. Lauren spends a lot of time doing yard work over the weekend, and I immerse myself in planning for the coming week even though the majority of the work is already completed. I spend Saturday night at home while Lauren and Mer go see a movie then meet a couple of our friends for drinks. Lauren plays soccer on Sunday while Mer and I go grocery shopping, and later I fill the afternoon with running miscellaneous errands, even spending an hour sitting in Perk reading and sipping green tea. While I'm there, I notice that Sidney does make an appearance, and sure enough, Maggie Loophole is working. They don't pay much attention to each other and I make a mental note to tell Allison that she's likely making too much of it.

To her credit, Lauren sleeps in our bed throughout the weekend, and we even have a few minutes of cuddling on Sunday morning. It's difficult for me to enjoy her closeness, though, because I have a layer of anger seething beneath my skin. I want to enjoy her arms wrapped around me. And I want to bask in the feeling of comfort. But it's impossible, and after a while, once I've noticed she's fallen back asleep, I quietly untangle myself from her and get out of bed.

By the time Monday morning rolls around, I find myself looking forward to a full day of work. I usually hate the first week of a new project—it requires serious professional dress, as in straight-up skirts or tailored pants and blazers, and I'm never fully comfortable in that type of clothing. Our team's unspoken rule is that once the first full week passes, we gradually relax the professional dress requirement and move into more comfortable business casual clothing. If we could work in jeans and T-shirts, we'd be happiest, but that doesn't fly with every company. I'm not sure what Whitmore's preference will be, but I plan on putting the feelers out this week. Suits every day are not my idea of comfort, even if I do have a collection that I've carefully curated over time.

Yawning and quietly grumbling (Miss Unemployed is still sleeping, I dare not disturb her!), I put on a DKNY black pantsuit. I cringe as I force my feet into low black heels; this is really not enjoyable. I work my fingers through my hair as I partially blow dry it, then let the rest air dry before I pull it back into a knot.

About to be running late, I skip the emergency mascara, happy that my eyes are lacking the deep circles from the previous week, and grab my bag. On the drive to Whitmore I run through the day's agenda and swallow hard when I realize I'm meeting with the IT department first thing. Seeing as I haven't quite managed to put Burke on that mental shelf, I'm not sure how I'm going to feel when I see her today. Then again, there's surely no harm in getting to finally know her as a friend—a real friend this time.

* * *

Coffee in hand, Caren and I walk into the lower level of Whitmore's office building. It is noticeably darker than the upper floors, but there are windows, and it's clean, airy, and inviting, even if most of its inhabitants are hunched over computers with their backs to us.

Since the IT department is the smallest one at Whitmore, Caren and I decided we'd start there with some basics including the survey we'll conduct today in order to get a read on the department's needs, strengths, weaknesses, and basic wish list. It's an easy day for everyone involved; all the employees need to do is show up, submit their answers, and toss out questions if they have any. Caren and I will field the questions, run analyses on the surveys, and come back in the afternoon to give a few starter techniques before formally introducing any workshops.

I spot Burke immediately even though her back is to me. She's not hunched over her computer but instead engaged in animated conversation with a younger guy holding a pile of spreadsheets. I observe them laughing and talking easily, and wonder if maybe we won't have that much team building to do in this particular department. Then I recall Burke's comment about Seth, the head of IT, accidentally sending the entire team a confidential email and realize, no, there is definitely work to do here.

Caren and I set up camp in the middle of the room. She's chatting my ear off about a new band her husband discovered and how they're touring and will be in Portland soon. I nod along at appropriate times, relieved when Caren runs out of things to tell me. I sneak a quick look at my cell phone before we begin—there's a text from Allison: *Tried you at work. Where are you? Call me, have news.* I shoot back a quick reply telling her I'll call her in a bit. I can only imagine what this "news" is.

"Good morning, Emery."

I slide my phone back into my bag, and turn to face Burke. "Good morning to you."

She points to my coffee. "So, you don't have loyalty to a particular coffee shop?"

"I don't. Starbucks called my name this morning, and I couldn't resist."

Burke holds up her own Starbucks cup. "I know the feeling. What's your poison?"

"Breakfast blend with soy milk. I like to keep it simple."

"So you're a fan of the medium roasts?"

I tilt my head toward Burke, wondering where all this coffee talk is coming from. "I am… Does that say something significant about my personality?"

She laughs easily. "I was a barista during college. There's no textbook correlation between coffee choice and personality, but I have enough experience with blends and people to make a couple educated claims about you."

I feel myself start to blush. I'm about to ask her to tell me more when Caren touches my arm and gestures toward the clock.

"Maybe I'll tell you later," Burke says. She winks at me before she takes a seat with her department.

* * *

Once the meeting ends, the IT ants scatter back to their hills and dig back into their technological engagement. The meeting went well—there seems to be a true camaraderie in this department, and it's obvious they all respect their boss, Seth, the infamous accidental email-forwarder. They also have a great collective sense of humor evident even in the short period of time that Caren and I had their undivided attention. I couldn't help but to watch how Burke interacted with the group, impressed by her ability to pay attention without being distracted by the people around her. She appeared to be a model student. I hadn't even gotten too flustered by the amount of times I'd caught her eye.

"I'll get a head start on these surveys if you want to check in with Luke and see if he needs any help with the finance department," Caren says as we leave the IT basement. "Libby's worried that's going to be our tough spot."

"Why's that?"

"She mentioned something about 'unethical usurpations in management.'"

"So...they got a new boss recently, and don't like said boss, nor the way said boss was hired?"

"You got it."

We're both surprised to see Luke sitting in the first-floor conference room/our new home base. He shakes his head at us as we enter.

"Don't even ask. It was not pretty. And judging by the results from these surveys, it's going to take a hell of a lot of action to make anything remotely better."

"Maybe we should have sent Em with you this morning," Caren remarks as she settles in across from Luke. I mentally acknowledge the fact that I'm glad we hadn't thought of that before now.

"Yeah, it might not be a bad idea for you to come back with me this afternoon," Luke says to me.

Which means I won't be with Caren, or the IT department. Not that it matters. It doesn't matter! "Of course."

Luke nods and the two of them silently descend into the surveys. I slip out of the room and call Allison.

"Em, Sidney swears she saw Lauren at the unemployment office last week. I told her she's crazy, that Lauren must have another sexy twin, but she is adamant that it was her."

I could lie. Or I could be honest. "It may have been her."

Allison's quiet for a moment. "What are you saying, Em?"

"Lauren lost her job. Three weeks ago."

"Three weeks ago? Why didn't you tell me?"

"Why didn't she tell me until this weekend?"

More quiet. "You're kidding me."

"Wish I were."

"Why did she wait so long to tell you? How did you not know?"

Good questions I'm still struggling to answer for myself. "I don't know, and I don't know. Honestly, Allison, I had no idea. I know that sounds ridiculous."

"Why did she hide it from you?"

"I don't know. We haven't exactly…discussed the circumstances." I brace myself for Allison's response, which is bound to be borderline hysteria.

"Emery, what the hell! She lies to you for three weeks and you don't *bother* to ask what happened or why she lied? Are you serious right now?"

"Allison, I don't know what to say to her."

"That you're pissed at her for lying! That you demand to know why she lost her job! Fuck, Em, come on! This is ridiculous! Stop babying her."

I'm not in the mood to be lectured by my best friend, or anyone, for that matter. I am, after all, completely aware of the fact that I avoided talking with Lauren this weekend because I'm fearful of what I'm going to find out.

"I know I need to talk to her. And I will. But I'm not ready to."

"Are you angry?"

"Very."

"I'm sorry, Em. I don't want to make it worse, but I'm really not happy about how Lauren is handling this."

"Well, neither am I, and I'm the one who has to intimately deal with the repercussions, so…trust that I'll handle it, okay?"

"I've gotta head back to Perk. Call me later if you want to talk."

I drop my phone to the table and stare out the window. I've got to have this conversation with Lauren, and soon.

* * *

I accompany Luke to his second check-in with the finance department and spend most of the meeting grinding my teeth. The climate here is a far cry from the IT department and I can't imagine how much work it's going to take to get this group on track. It doesn't seem as if they were ever on a track to begin with. It's amazing Whitmore isn't struggling financially with the amount of negativity and petty bullshit that permeates this group. They must at least be good at what they do.

"Painful, huh?" Luke says as we make our way back to the conference room.

"Wow," I muster, still shaking my head.

"Think I need Libby for this one?"

"Yeah. I do. At least to start."

Burke is standing down the hall, talking with a woman I recognize from Friday's meeting. Seeing her makes me feel...a little funny inside.

I wonder if she was waiting for me. And then I wonder why I would even wonder that.

In the conference room, Luke gives Libby a call and puts her on speakerphone; I perch on the table next to him and throw in my own observations of the damaged finance department. She agrees that she needs to come in and give Luke a hand.

Shortly after the call, a knock sounds from the open door. Burke leans in the doorway.

"Hey, come on in. Burke, this is Luke. Luke, Burke."

They shake hands, and Luke quickly excuses himself and leaves the room. I'm still sitting on the table, feet resting on the chair in front of me. Burke sits next to me, establishing the perfect amount of distance between us.

"I heard you got snared away to F-squared this afternoon," she says.

"F-squared?"

"Professionally, we refer to them as F-squared, or Fragmented Finance. Outside of the building, though, F-squared generally means Fucked Finance. I think it's a fair assessment of that department."

I laugh. "Professionally, I am forbidden to agree with you."

"Oh, of course. I would expect nothing less."

Burke sends me a smile that ignites tiny sparks in my limbs, leaving me tingling. From a smile. That perfect distance now seems compromised, but I'm not sure which way I should move.

"So, medium roast."

I exhale quickly, not having realized I was holding my breath. "Go ahead. Lay it on me."

"Experienced baristas would say a preference for medium roasts means predictability, or safety. They're always available, so you like to have what you want when you want it. They are also characteristically smooth, which indicates you like comfort. They're a good middle-ground on the blend spectrum and I've found that most medium blend-lovers are comfortable with gray areas. Not so reliant on everything being black and white, so to speak—perhaps they even embrace the gray at times. But at the core of your coffee-drinking self, you appreciate the stability of what a medium roast delivers. Adding the soy milk, though, that's a whole different level of analysis."

I try not to gape at Burke, thrown by how close her fun and games personality analysis hits. I scramble for something to say.

"I'll need some more time to think through the soy element," she continues, her voice low, her face seeming closer to mine now.

"Take your time," I manage. I sit up straight and take a breath. If I could physically shake myself right now, I would.

"No rush," she agrees. "After all, you could be stuck here for years."

CHAPTER NINE

The workweek tumbles by in a flurry of official meetings, impromptu check-ins and the initial rotation of the first workshop, centered around each department's survey responses. Aside from the finance department, the survey results were similar across the board. I don't think Burke was correct in her assumption that I'll be stuck at Whitmore for years but regardless of the fact that most of the employees seem to generally like each other, there is quite a bit of work to do in the leadership and communication areas. Luke has a real mess on his hands with the finance department; even after having a few one-on-one conversations with people from that department (and there are only ten of them), we were unable to find a positive place to start. Libby and Luke have been spending the majority of their time working with and around the finance department, so Caren and I have found ourselves spread pretty thin across the other six departments. It's becoming one of those times we wonder if we should add another person to our team.

Running around nonstop all week, barely stopping to eat or think, I've had several run-ins with Burke. She's always ready with that slow, easy smile, and something entertaining and/or adorable to say, but she's not flirting with me. It's more like we're getting to know each other again. I've spent more time this week talking to Burke than I have Lauren. Maybe it's just that the former has proximity to me for at least seven hours every day, or perhaps it's that the latter has only shown up for dinner and bed. I haven't exactly sought Lauren out to talk to her, but I find myself anticipating every next run-in with Burke.

Either way, even I know this is probably not good.

Late Friday morning, Caren and I are back in our conference room at Whitmore, trying to plan a leadership workshop for the product development department. Neither of us seems to be able to summon our working brain cells; Caren spends most of the time dragging her pen across a blank sheet of paper while I ramble in half-sentences and stare blankly at the screen of my laptop.

"Why is this so difficult today?" Caren asks, seeming genuinely surprised. "We usually do this stuff in our sleep."

"It's been a long week." I stretch my legs out in front of me, grateful to be wearing comfortable khakis and a lightweight navy blue V-neck sweater. Caren is dressed similarly, though in a definitively more feminine manner; I'm beyond excited to see that our Time in Suits has expired. "We have other workshops we could use. No one is expecting us to come up with something brand new."

"I know, I know. This company is so different from the others we've worked with. We've never had to guide a product development group before. I mean, isn't leadership moot to them? Don't they *need* to be independent?"

"They also need to be able to take initiative. That's this department's fatal flaw."

We lapse back into silence, the only noise coming from beyond our glass bubble. I watch people come and go across the main lobby, noting that many of them are in jeans. My gratitude for khakis is renewed; if I were sitting here in a suit seeing these people in their jeans, I would be silently seething and envious of their comfort.

"So, I'm going to ask again. Who's the hottie from the IT department?"

By again, Caren means daily. She's not going to lay off until I give her a better answer than my standard 'friend from college.'

And yet, I delay the inevitable, still unsure of how to talk about Burke. "Why are you so curious about her?"

"Because she's around a lot. She comes to you. She seeks you out."

"Not true."

Caren snorts. "Really? Then why is she approaching us right now?"

I whip my head up. Burke is walking our way, looking unbearably cute in dark jeans, those standard Doc Martens, and a plaid button-down shirt with the sleeves rolled up to her elbows. As she enters the conference room, I can see the edge of a tattoo on her right forearm, something I don't recall noticing years ago.

"Well, I'm off to meet with Charlotte," Caren says loudly, "which will claim me for hours, I'm sure. See you later."

"I'm starting to get a complex," Burke says from the doorway. She is an excellent doorway-leaner. It does nothing to temper the sexuality she oozes, which I seem unable to ignore. "Every time I come in here, someone leaves the room."

I laugh, then shake my head. "Don't take it personally."

Burke raises her eyebrows. "I'll try my best. So, I was thinking about taking a long lunch, and I wondered if you'd like to join me."

I struggle to find a reason to say no, but I have none: Caren is in a lunch meeting, and so are Luke and Libby. For the first time all week, I have no lunch plans. I can't say no to her. And the truth is, I don't want to. All week, I've been wanting to continue every conversation we've had, however small or insignificant.

I stand and grab my bag. "Let's go," I say brightly.

* * *

Our walk to Lunchbox is short but offers us the opportunity to enjoy a couple minutes of the spring-heavy air. I'm grateful for the comfortable quiet, happy that Burke has given me the opportunity to sit down with her and talk like normal adults who are becoming actual friends.

Lunchbox is cute and cozy, with a hole-in-the-wall quality smattered with a contemporary hipster feel. It's precisely the kind of place Lauren would avoid, and the place I would want to explore. The menu is scrawled on a wall-sized chalkboard. All the tables and chairs are mismatched, and the environment reminds me a lot of Perk. Other than us, only two other tables are occupied. A steady stream of customers is coming in and picking up to-go orders, and the service looks to be speedy. Only two people are hovering near the counter, waiting for their orders.

Burke sits down across from me. I thank her for inviting me to lunch, and she grins.

"I just wanted to sit down and chat with you, outside of the work environment. We haven't seen each other in years."

"Not since New York," I say before I can stop myself, worried suddenly that she won't remember that night.

"You know, I've been back to that apartment a few times since that night, and I have to say, the fire escape has never been the same."

A wash of warmth sweeps through my entire body, and I'm certain that my cheeks have raised an intense blush. I do what I do best: deflect the conversation. "So, how long have you been back in Oregon?"

"A couple of years," she says, swirling her straw in her cup. "I got the job at Whitmore as a fluke, really, and decided it was time to grow up, which meant moving home."

"You grew up in Portland?" Check one: something I never knew about her.

"I was born in Newport. Both of my parents are professors, so we moved around a lot, and landed wherever one or both of them had an adjunct gig."

"So how did you end up in Manhattan after you graduated?"

Burke looks at me questioningly, but she's still smiling, so I'm pretty sure she's not annoyed by me. "You're awfully inquisitive. I don't remember this side of you."

"Guilty," I admit, raising my hands in mock defeat. "Years of working with people and their communication skills have turned me into a question machine. Feel free to tell me to stop."

"No, I don't mind. I like that you're interested." And there goes the rush of butterflies in my stomach. "The Manhattan question, though…that might be one for the next time we have lunch. Or, actually, a time or three after that."

I'm saved from my lack of a witty response by the arrival of our sandwiches. We eat in silence for a few minutes, enjoying the delicious sandwiches.

"So," Burke says, wiping her mouth with a napkin. "How long have you been with PLAC?"

"Coming up on seven years, which seems inconceivable."

"Why inconceivable? What are you, thirty-one?"

I raise an eyebrow. "I'm not sure how I should feel about the fact that you nailed my age on your first attempt."

"Amazed, I'd think. The fact that I can remember such a tiny detail about you for so many years—that your birthday is exactly nine months after mine—*is* pretty impressive."

She's right, of course, and I remember as soon as she says it. That so-called tiny detail is one of the many that revealed itself that night on the fire escape. And I remember too: Burke is an Aquarius. In another degree of my weird nerdiness, I had innocently looked up her astrological sign after that night, and couldn't help but to notice that our signs, Aquarius and Libra, are noted to be compatible. Not that that means anything.

"I am impressed," I tell her. "My own parents have been known to forget my birthday every couple of years."

"You're kidding," she says, a note of incredulity creeping into her voice.

"Sadly, no. But it's become a matter of joking in the family. They've also forgotten my sisters' birthdays as well, and have occasionally mixed up the birthdays, so I've gotten birthday cards in December and singing phone calls in the middle of June."

Burke laughs, a hearty, full laugh that lights up her face. I love how she has a mix of feminine and masculine features that mix seamlessly. Not many people can pull that off, but Burke does it flawlessly.

"At least your parents make an effort to remember *someone's* birthday, even if it's the wrong kid," she says. "Gotta love family dynamics. I'll tell you all about mine some other time. If I remember correctly, you did not grow up on the west coast, right?" Burke seems awfully comfortable in the role of inquisitor too.

"Correct. Born and raised in Pennsylvania, moved to Oregon for college. I needed to break away from home, as much as I loved it."

"I completely understand that."

"But you grew up in Oregon, went to college here, are still here…?"

"Ah yes, but there are a good six years that are unaccounted for in Oregon time."

"How mysterious," I remark, aiming for casual.

"You're not going to press me with a question about those years?"

"Not at the moment. I'll give you some time to make sure your story is straight."

"Oh, Emery. If there's one thing you need to know about me, and never forget, it's that my story is always straight."

For some reason, that confident statement makes me weak in the knees. Maybe it's because I thought I could trust Lauren to always give me a straight story, but now…now it seems as though that's not a priority for her. Was it ever? I'd like to believe so, but judging by how difficult a time I'm having moving past this three-week-lying jag, I'm not sure anymore.

"That's an admirable quality," I finally say to Burke, who is watching me closely.

"It's one I choose to live by," she says quietly.

We stare at each other for a moment, both of us seeming to be caught in a simple moment of pleasure, of awareness, of common ground. I clear my throat to break myself out of the reverie, and make a pointed look at my watch.

Before exiting, Burke turns back and waves goodbye to the man working the counter.

"Come here often?" I joke as we emerge onto the quiet side street.

"I do. And I'm hoping you'll come back with me."

I nod, not trusting myself to speak. Because honestly, I'm a little afraid of what I'd hear myself say.

CHAPTER TEN

It's now been a full week since Lauren's job-bombshell. The Important Necessary Conversation still has not taken place, and I'm finding myself a bit worried that neither one of us is going to be strong enough to force the conversation. There are layers of hurt, guilt, and anger, and while I don't want to make Lauren feel worse about having lost her job, I wonder if Lauren doesn't want to make me more angry by bringing it up again. We're at an impasse, and we've spent the week in moderate silence. To her credit, Lauren has been doing more around the house—she's cooked dinner every night, and even told me to go relax instead of cleaning up after dinner.

Tonight, we're hosting family dinner night and come six o'clock, the warm spring air has taken a turn back in time, and the skies are heavy with rain and late-winter temperatures. Our houseguests are stuck inside with us, but everyone came armed with alcohol, appetizers, and empty stomachs. Mer is busy in the dining room shuffling food around the table while engaging Carly, Jen, and Brenna in conversation. Cat is stuck at home, meeting a last-minute deadline for her freelancing job, and we're all moderately surprised to see Allison arrive with Sidney, who acts as though she hasn't been missing in action for over a month. Sidney slinks into the kitchen to see if Lauren needs any help, effectively shooing me out into the bustling dining room with the rest of my friends. Lauren's attention is rightfully focused on the food she's cooking, but she's been short with me all day, and I'm tired of it. I'd stayed in the kitchen because that was what we agreed upon, but I'm relieved when Sidney tells me she has it under control.

Mer gestures to my wineglass and I allow her to fill it halfway. I'm not interested in acquiring any kind of wine-induced buzz tonight; I have a hunch that it will not help my cluttered mind. Trying to focus on my relationship with Lauren and our attempts to put up a unified, happy front to our friends has been draining, and it's only been a half hour. I hope she'll be able to relax once dinner is finished; otherwise, I could be in for a long night.

I notice that Carly's drinking water with lemon, not her usual IPA. I nudge her with my elbow and ask quietly, "Big news?"

"I wish. Still nothing."

"Oh, Car, I'm sorry."

"Me too." Her eyes fill with tears and she squeezes them away. "It's hard not to think there's something wrong with me, you know? Why else would it be taking so long?"

"There's nothing wrong with you. I'm not a baby-making professional, but I'd have to think the old fashioned way makes it a little bit easier."

"Are you suggesting I go have sex with a man?"

I laugh and rest my hand on Carly's forearm. "Not at all. I'm sure the insemination will take, and soon. So forget my horrible idea."

"This process is getting expensive," Jen pipes up, having joined us. "It's worth it, but I'm really hoping this next one will take."

"And that's why I decided to stop drinking ahead of time," Carly explains. "I figure it can't hurt."

"Hopefully we'll have better news next month," Jen adds, her arm protectively around her wife. "Little baby X is making us work awfully hard."

I lean in and wrap my arms around my two friends, lovely women who will make amazing parents when they are finally given the chance. As they join in with the conversation around us, I take a quick mental step back, and realize how much I don't want what they have. Or, more accurately, I can't picture myself having with Lauren what Carly and Jen already have, and are working toward. It just doesn't fit our relationship. I'm not sure married + kids fits any potential relationship I could land in, but the simple thought of it is so far out of my domain that I sometimes can't believe I have friends who are married and trying to get pregnant.

"Dinner is served!" Sidney calls from the kitchen. Her announcement sends Mer and Brenna into a flurry of clearing the table of appetizers. Allison and Jen go to refill their drinks, and Carly and I go about setting the table.

Shortly, we're all seated around the table, each of us salivating over bowls of Lauren's Choked Pasta—penne tossed in olive oil with garlic-sauteed chicken, artichoke hearts, sun-dried tomatoes, roasted asparagus, and paper-thin slices of browned garlic. A container of shredded Parmesan cheese makes its way around the table, and silence falls upon us as we all dig in. Lauren made up this recipe years ago, and has tweaked it over the years by adding and subtracting various ingredients. It's a group favorite, and soon the silence is trumped by delirious moans from happy mouths, then the chatter slowly begins again.

As I happily and unabashedly stuff my face, I survey the group seated around our dining room table. These are some of my favorite nights, all of us enjoying food and drink, filling the air with a wide range of discussion. We've all known each other in some degree for over ten years—some of us college friends (me, Allison, and Carly; Mer and Lauren), some of us through sports (Lauren and Brenna), and some completely random (Lauren and Cat met years ago while waiting in line at a local greenhouse; they'd hit it off immediately, which we all still find weird, considering they are completely opposite in personality aside from their love of yard maintenance). And of course, Sidney and Cat are long-time friends, which is how Allison and Sidney met, and Sidney is a huge part of the reason Allison returned to the west coast after having moved back east after college, which I'm selfishly grateful for even though their relationship is, essentially, a shit show.

Now, though, I can't help but to notice that Sidney is paying a lot of attention to Allison, who is trying to act nonchalant about it but is clearly pleased. No one can figure them out. I'll admit that I encouraged Allison to move out here to be with Sidney while knowing that Sidney is notoriously unattached, and prefers it that way. Allison seemed okay with a low-key relationship for a while, but she soon started pushing the monogamy issue, and that's when Sidney started her string of non-monogamy. Watching them now, I can see the love Sidney has for Allison, but I can't imagine how Allison can trust her anymore.

After dinner, everyone piles into the living room and argues about what game to play. As usual, the top contenders are Cards Against Humanity and good old Scattergories. Amidst the friendly arguing, I sneak into the kitchen for a moment of quiet. It's not often that I feel overwhelmed by the presence of my friends, but I'm having a hard time handling Lauren's continued clipped responses to me. The passive-aggressive mood between us needs to be addressed and ended; it's making me miserable. It's making me not want to be here.

I lean against the counter and close my eyes. I'm so stuck in my head that I don't notice that Allison has also snuck into the kitchen and is standing next to me until she quietly says, "So, do you want to talk about it?"

I exhale slowly and softly. I know Allison is referring to Lauren, or Lauren's job loss, but a piece of my brain starts bringing up thoughts of Burke. "I don't know," I say honestly.

"Neither of you looks happy. But I have to be honest, Em— Lauren is putting up a better front than you are."

"Aside from how she's speaking to me, you mean?"

Allison shrugs. "Well, yeah. But that hasn't been obvious to anyone else. I'm guessing you haven't had that important talk yet?"

"We haven't." I shrug and sip from my wineglass. "I guess neither of us is sure of what to say."

"Or you're both avoiding something that's going to be difficult."

"I'm really mad at her, Allison." A small pressure lifts from my shoulders after finally admitting that, obvious as it may be.

"I think you have every right to be, Em. But you need to give her the opportunity to explain herself. More than that, you need to stop avoiding it and *talk* to her, Ms. Communications Expert."

At that moment, Lauren appears in the kitchen. She looks at us with a slightly concerned expression. "You guys okay?"

Allison squeezes my arm. "Sure are." She moves to leave the kitchen, giving Lauren's ass a friendly swat on her way out.

"You don't seem okay," Lauren says as she comes over to stand next to me.

I shrug. "I've got a lot on my mind."

"Anything you want to talk about?"

"Yes, but not right now. Not with a room full of our best friends."

Lauren nods, and puts her arm around my shoulders. "I think I've been a little short with you today. I'm sorry, babe. I was anxious about having people over and didn't know how to handle the whole no-job thing."

Her honesty lifts something inside of me, and I decide to meet her on her level. "Why didn't you tell me that earlier? I could have helped you work out a way to handle it." I bump into her and she tightens her hold on me. "You know, talking about difficult things is kind of my specialty."

"And yet we haven't talked about the difficult things that we need to talk about," Lauren says as she kisses the side of my head.

"Well, Lauren Cabrian, you haven't exactly made yourself open to conversation lately."

"I know. Trust me, I know. Mer has pointed that out to me on numerous occasions."

"So…what are you afraid of?"

She's quiet. I realize I haven't put my arm around her waist, as I always do when she puts her arm around my shoulders, and do so. She feels different somehow. I wonder how disconnected we've become, how emotionally distant from each other we actually are.

"I'm afraid of you being disappointed in me."

I want to ask her if she was fired, or if she was laid off. That answer holds a lot of weight and until I get it, I don't know how to continue this conversation. But nagging at the back of my head is the fact that we are entertaining at the moment. I'm not surprised that Lauren has chosen this moment to begin the conversation; it's classic Lauren, really, bringing up an important piece to discuss at a time when we can't get into any kind of huge discussion or argument because there are other people around.

Even though I know I should wait, I can't anymore. Besides, she started the conversation. So I allow the question to rush from my lips: "Were you fired?"

"No." She answers with no hesitation, no warning sound in her voice. A simple answer: no. "They were making cuts, fifteen total. They tried to spread them out. My boss tried to save me. But my position came up, and that was it."

I do feel some relief, but it's compromised by my continued anger with her having held this information from me for weeks. I might have understood the withholding had she been fired, but layoffs happen, and they're out of an employee's control.

"Okay. Thank you for telling me."

Lauren tightens her grip around me and kisses my head again. "I know there's more to talk about, but can we do that tomorrow?"

"Yes. Of course."

Lauren turns and faces me, then palms my chin. She searches my eyes for a moment before closing her own and kissing me, full on the lips. I return her kiss, but the pangs of anger and fear are gnawing close to my surface, and I can't enjoy the moment of closeness.

"Ready for some games?"

"Yeah, I'll be out in a second. You go ahead. I'm going to get a bit more wine."

I take my cell phone out of my pocket. I'd felt its vibration while Allison and I were talking, but I didn't want to be rude and check it then.

My heart trips a bit when I see the name on my screen. My fingers fumble over the touchscreen of my phone, hurrying to expose the message.

How do you feel about Thai? Great place near Lunchbox. Join me for lunch Monday?

Yes, Burke, I happen to love Thai. And I would love to join you on Monday.

I just have to have a slightly less difficult talk with my girlfriend, my partner, before then. And I have to hope really hard that I don't come out feeling hopeless because if that's the case, then I definitely cannot have lunch with Burke on Monday.

CHAPTER ELEVEN

When I get to Whitmore Monday morning, I'm running later than I'd planned. I didn't have time to pick up coffee, but it turns out I didn't need to. When I hustle into the conference room, I find Caren sitting by herself, presumably waiting for me, and next to her stuff on the table is a large cup from Perk.

"Oh, you're a lifesaver," I breathe as I throw my bag into a chair and grab for the cup. The first sip is delicious and exactly what I need to get me moving. I shut my eyes to fully enjoy the decadent sip of caffeine move its way down my throat and slip itself into my veins.

"Nope, not me. I didn't buy you that coffee." Caren gestures toward a slip of paper that was sitting beneath the cup.

In tiny, impeccable capital letters: *Thought you might need this. Sorry I couldn't deliver it in person—meeting at 8. See you for lunch. -B*

I avoid Caren's gloating stare for as long as I can. I hate when she's right. But more than that, I really hate when she's *proven* to be right.

"Friends," I say pointedly.

"Liar," she replies.

"I'm not cheating on Lauren."

"I didn't say you were. All I said was she seeks you out. And, frankly, I think the lovely lady has a thing for you, my dear. Not that I can blame her, of course."

I sit facing Caren, preparing myself for her lecture. "She doesn't have a thing for me. We're just getting to know each other again after not having spoken for a long time."

"Ooh, so there is past drama! I knew it!"

"No. There is not."

"Then why haven't you spoken for so long?"

There's no good answer for that; even the truth sounds weird. "We just…lost touch. I guess we never were in touch to begin with."

Caren rolls her eyes at me. "Don't be intentionally confusing. It's not going to make me stop asking questions. So just tell it like it is, Emery. What's your deal with her?"

I tap my fingers against the coffee cup. "The last time I saw her was in New York. I was there for a conference; she was living there. In completely random fashion, we ran into each other at a party. We talked a lot that night. But then, we went our separate ways."

"I don't get it."

"There's nothing to get!" I exclaim, perhaps a bit too defensively. "We were nev—"

"No, stop." Caren holds up her hand in front of my face, and I swat it away. "I don't understand why you didn't stay in touch. No phone numbers? Emails? Not even Facebook?"

"Nothing. It didn't come up. We just parted ways. Like I said, it was random. I certainly wasn't expecting to see her that night."

Caren studies me, her crystalline pale green eyes boring into me. I'm sure she's seeing something that I haven't even realized yet, but she won't tell me. That's Caren's style; sometimes I truly believe she can see right through me, but she's always let me figure things out without intervening, both in my personal and professional lives. That's something that I love about her, and also something that I don't get from, say, Allison, who likes to tell me what to think and do.

I gulp down a hot swallow of coffee when I realize that whatever this is with Burke is the first time my professional life has collided with my personal life. Sure, there was the Cassidy situation all those years ago but this is different. I've never had to deal with this before, and I'm not sure I know *how* to deal with it. However, there's not anything to deal with right now. We're just friends. Acquaintances. Friendly acquaintances who are getting to know each other again.

"You had no idea she worked here?"

"None. I didn't even know she was living in Portland."

"You're that out of touch with her?"

"Yes. Caren, what do you think I'm not telling you?"

She continues her probing look. "Do you want me to be real with you right now?"

"Yes."

"I think you've deliberately stayed out of touch with her because you're afraid of what might happen if she is in your life."

I stare back at Caren, simultaneously wanting to hug her and shove her out of her chair. I try to respond, to dispute, anything—but my mouth stubbornly refuses to open.

"Were you with Lauren when you saw Burke in New York?"

"No."

Caren raises a meticulously groomed eyebrow. "Okay, that may have just ruined my theory."

I debate not telling her the other side, but my mouth betrays me: "I was with Cassidy then."

"Oh. Ohhh. Okay. Then my theory stands."

"Don't be too proud of yourself."

"So you agree with my theory?"

"No. I don't know. I haven't given it much thought at all."

"I can tell that much is true." Caren leans in and taps her manicured middle finger on Burke's note. "But, Em, you might want to start thinking about it."

"Lauren and I are having problems," I blurt out. Shit. My internal organs are churning; I've never had an anxiety attack before, but I'm pretty sure this is what it might feel like. My head feels a little spinny, and breathing feels unnatural.

"I wondered about that."

"She lost her job. She was laid off. She didn't tell me for three weeks. She's been looking for a new job, but she told me yesterday she's not even getting callbacks. We haven't had sex for a long time, and I feel so far away from her I don't even know how I feel about her anymore."

Caren lays a warm hand on my shoulder. "Breathe, Em."

"I am."

"No, you're really not. Take a deep breath."

I do as she commands, and feel a piece of pressure fracture off and disappear. If only it were that easy to erase all of my confused feelings.

"Do you love her?"

"Lauren? Yes. Of course I do."

"Em, are you still in love with her?"

Uh-oh. "Um."

"Yes or no?"

"I don't know," I admit.

"That's probably a no, sweetie."

I shake my head in disbelief. Me? No longer in love with Lauren? It doesn't seem possible, or plausible. She's everything I've ever wanted in a woman. Isn't she? "We hardly even talk anymore."

"She was never a big talker to begin with, though, right?"

"Right. It took us a week to talk about the fact that she's jobless. It took me an hour into that conversation to even mention the fact that I'm mad at her for waiting so long to tell me. She didn't seem to care about me being mad."

Caren leans back in her chair, her determined but sympathetic gaze never leaving my face. "How honest were you with her?"

"In yesterday's talk?"

"Yes."

I pause and think back. It wasn't an easy talk. In fact, both of us avoided eye contact through most of it; I'd stayed curled up on one side of the sofa while she sat on the opposite end. She gave me the run-down on losing her job, what she'd been doing for the past handful of weeks—which finally explained why she'd been sleeping in the basement, because she wasn't sleeping much at all, and she didn't want to disturb my sleep. She also told me she'd been looking for jobs ever since the day after she lost hers. I could see that she was frustrated, and even embarrassed. Once she finished spilling everything she'd been holding back, I did my best to politely explain to her how it made me feel, what I was worried about, and enumerated all the highly employable skills she has. I did tell her I was angry about her having withheld the information, but as I told Caren, Lauren didn't have much of a reaction to that. In fact, she didn't have a reaction to much of anything I'd said. Naively, I'd been thinking she would show signs of regret, or being upset for having contributed to my negative feelings. But there was nothing of that sort, which didn't exactly encourage me to continue to tell her what else I was feeling.

Now, sitting in Caren's thoughtful stare, I shrug. "Perhaps not as honest as I should have been." To my horror, I feel tears stinging the inside of my eyelids. I absolutely do not, and will not, cry while at work. I shut my eyes tightly and wait for the burning liquid to slip back into its ducts.

"Em, I think you need to be honest with Lauren. Really honest. Don't try to protect her feelings just because she's in a bad spot right now. The longer you don't talk openly with her, the harder it's going to be to reopen that line of communication."

I smile and open my eyes, relieved that the tears have disappeared. "You'd think I'd know that, considering my career."

"Seriously, Queen of Communication. But it's easier to communicate professionally than it is to do so personally. You know that as well as I do."

I nod slowly, my fingers working their way to Burke's note. I'm not about to tell Caren, but I'm ready to admit to myself that

I'm having an easier time communicating with Burke than I am with Lauren. That's not shocking, though—Burke and I don't have any of the romantic, financial, committed entanglements that Lauren and I have. Things with Burke are easy because whatever we are as friends is just that: easy.

* * *

Since I'm running a workshop in the afternoon, my morning is clear of obligations. I take advantage of that rare situation and drive over to PLAC to get some peace and quiet. The other team that is housed in our bank of offices is up in Washington for two weeks, so I know I'm guaranteed to have time to myself.

I drop into my desk chair and heave a sigh. What I'd really like to do right now is go to sleep. The intense conversation with Caren has zapped me of energy.

My eyes wander across my desk and its fine layer of dust. I swipe at it aimlessly, moving the particles around rather than getting rid of them. I reach toward the framed picture of me and Lauren that sits next to my phone. Allison took it at Carly and Jen's wedding four years ago. The newness of us is visible in our posture, our smiles, even the way we're not looking at the camera. We hadn't been together for a full year at that point, and we had just moved into our apartment. Lauren's expression in the picture is one of intense happiness; she looks full of life and excitement, her mouth caught in a laugh instead of a simple smile. She has her arm wrapped solidly around my waist, and I'm half-turned into her, my left hand resting on her chest, right arm around her back. I'm looking at Lauren and about to laugh, she's looking toward the ground and laughing. I can't remember what was so funny, but the love between us is evident. In that moment, we were the only two people that existed.

I pull my hand from the frame. I know that love still exists between me and Lauren, but it looks and feels so different from what's seen in that picture. I would love to be able to go back to that spot, right now, and have Allison snap the exact same picture of me and Lauren. I cringe, knowing that such an outward pouring of love and affection would not be nearly as evident. I wonder if it could be seen at all.

I open my laptop and busy myself with double-checking the slides for the workshop that afternoon. I've done this particular workshop so many times, I'm sure I could do it in my sleep, but I'm a big fan of being prepared. Besides, this afternoon's workshop is with the finance department, and I cannot be too prepared to face that.

I've so completely distracted myself with tweaking a role-playing element that I don't notice the time slipping by. And if my cell phone didn't ring at 12:05, I don't know when I would have bothered to check the time.

I grab for it blindly, answering as I'm inserting new lines into the role-play.

"So, I either botched the soy milk to coffee ratio and you're avoiding my coffee-preparation inadequacies, or someone else drank the coffee I left for you because you aren't coming to work today."

Burke. Coffee. Note. Lunch. Oops. I take a deep breath to steady myself and mentally switch gears out of work mode. "How about C, none of the above."

"Tell me more."

Her voice resonates through my body and I clutch the phone harder against my ear while telling my body to stop reacting so easily. "The coffee was perfect. So perfect that I finished it too quickly and have been mourning its absence for two hours."

"Lucky for you, I think it can be arranged that you receive more of that coffee."

"That would be lucky." Oh, God, am I flirting with her? Is this flirting? What the hell am I doing? "I'm not at Whitmore right now." Smooth, Em, way smooth.

Burke laughs; I guess she's getting used to my inability to transition in conversations. "I've gathered that much. Everything okay?"

"Yeah, absolutely. I just needed some time at my real desk."

"Ah, so you're a few miles away. Well, lucky for *me*, good ol' Charlotte is always ready to join me for lunch."

My heart drops clear into my stomach. Charlotte? No! Not Charlotte! I'm supposed to have lunch with Burke! Oh, right, I ruined that by deciding I needed to come back to PLAC in order to clear my head and get some work done.

I hurry to recover, not thinking before I speak. "I'm that replaceable, huh?" I stop myself, barely, from banging my head against my desk.

"I imagine not, but I don't want to disrupt your work."

"I could wrap up in about ten minutes. My workshop's not till one thirty."

"But Charlotte will be so disappointed, Emery."

"Oh, I'm sure Charlotte has had plenty of lunch dates with you."

Another laugh, this one as easy and full as the previous. "That she has. All right, you've won me over. How about we meet at Hillside Park in twenty minutes? I'll pick up food from the Thai place on my way."

"Sounds good. Picnic tables?"

"See you there."

* * *

I purposely leave almost immediately to arrive before Burke. I scope out the mostly deserted picnic tables, and choose one doused in sunlight. It may be a beautiful, blue-skied day, but the temperature is barely pushing seventy in the shade. In the sun, though, the unexpected early spring warmth glides over my skin, begging to be let in.

As I wait for Burke, I try to shut down my nerves. She is just a friend. A week ago, I couldn't even say that; then, she was just someone I once knew, sort of. But now, she is definitely a friend, albeit a friend I'm still getting to know.

She pulls into the parking lot and comes to a stop next to my car. Of course she drives a Jeep Wrangler, and of course it's painted a deep black that reflects everything it passes. She saunters toward me, bags of food in hand, easy smile on her face.

"Hey there," she says, putting the bags down on the table. "Hungry?"

"Famished. I forgot about breakfast."

"I think we can ease your hunger pains with this spread." Burke starts laying out the food, and my mouth waters. It smells delectable. She looks incredible, dressed in khakis and a blue and white tiny-checkered button-down, again with her sleeves rolled up to her elbows. I spot the edge of the tattoo again, and have to stop myself from reaching out to touch it, or expose more of it. Now I can see that it looks like the edge of a wave.

"Vegetable spring rolls, chicken satay, drunken noodles. I didn't want to risk a shellfish allergy, so I went for the chicken with the noodles."

"No allergy, but chicken was the right call." I go straight for the noodles, and try to retain some manners as I ease the chopsticks into my mouth. I nearly groan; the chili sauce is absolutely perfect.

"Good?" Burke asks quietly. I can hear the amusement in her voice.

"Beyond good. Thank you so much."

We eat quietly for a few moments before I ask Burke how her weekend was.

"Good. I met with my realtor on Saturday morning and closed on a loft."

"Congratulations!"

"Thanks. I'm excited about it. I've had my eye on this building for a while."

"Which building?" Allison and Sidney live in a gorgeous loft close to Perk and their building is highly sought after.

"Belmont Street Lofts."

I nearly choke on a bite of spring roll. Belmont Street Lofts are basically down the street and around the corner from my house. This may be a *little* too close for comfort.

"Ever been there?"

"I haven't. But I'm familiar with them." Suddenly, I don't want Burke to know that we're going to be almost-neighbors.

"You'll have to come see it. I have a great view of Laurelhurst Park. The loft itself is so open and modern. I'm looking forward to getting some paint on the walls."

I catch myself before I offer my admittedly extra good painting skills. "Yeah, I'd love to see it. My friend Allison, she owns Perk—she and her girlfriend tried to get a loft there a few years back, but settled for one a couple blocks away."

"Allison…blonde funky asymmetrical-cut?"

"Yep, that's her. She's there nearly every day; she's a bit of a control freak."

"I would be too if I owned a place like that. She usually has good baristas, though."

"Ah, yes, but surely they don't measure up to your coffee-making skill. Maybe you should inquire about a part-time job?"

Burke playfully points her chopsticks at me, and lightly jabs me in the shoulder. "Funny."

As I watch her I wonder if she ever appears unruffled; there's this distinct calm air that surrounds her, and while she's not unemotional, she seems peacefully happy all the time. I have no idea what that feels like but when I'm with her, everything inside of me feels calm and (mostly) under control.

"How long have you known Allison?"

"We met in college."

"You two weren't together, were you?"

"Oh, no. Never. Just friends."

"So the woman you were with when we saw each other in New York—are you still with her?"

I could take a few pointers from Burke; she can seamlessly transition in conversations. So seamlessly, in fact, that I'm somewhat dumbfounded when I realize she's asking if I'm single.

"No, I'm not." I wait for my mouth to catch up with my head, patiently wondering when *No, Cassidy and I are long over, but I've been with my partner, Lauren, for almost five years* is going to come out. Nothing happens.

"I think about that night often."

I look at her with open curiosity and surprise, my need to be upfront about my relationship momentarily eclipsed. "The fire escape?"

Burke looks at me for what feels like the first time in hours. We study each other openly, that precious feeling of calmness slipping away, replaced by a quiet growing attraction. Burke's eyes are the unusual color of dulce de leche, not hidden by her glasses today. Beneath her stare, I feel exposed but protected, as though she is only searching for the parts of me I am ready for her to see.

"Yes, the fire escape," she finally says.

"I do too."

She smiles and looks away; I let out the breath that had been stuck in my throat as she says, "It was so unexpected, seeing you that night. Unexpected but really cool."

Cool, huh. Cool. Cool is better than *nice*, I guess.

"I'm not very good about keeping in touch with people but I've always regretted not making an effort to stay in touch with you, Emery," she continues.

Cool is way better than nice. Cool is good. "It does seem odd," I venture, "what with the plethora of technology and social media that we never found each other on Facebook or anything."

"Did you really just use the word 'plethora' in a sentence?"

"Self-confessed vocabulary geek, yes."

Something passes over Burke's face, but she keeps it to herself. "I'm impressed. And here I thought you only loved poetry. Adrienne Rich, specifically."

This woman's memory is impressive. "I can't believe you remember that. That was—"

"College," she finishes. "I remember."

As much as I do not want to end this lunch, I know I'm going to be pressed for time shortly. "I'd love to dazzle you with more of my impressive vocabulary, but I need to get to Whitmore." We pack up our trash and leftovers, which Burke insists I take.

I open my car door and lean in for my wallet. "How much do I owe you?" I ask as she walks up to me.

She closes her hand over mine. "Next time is on you."

Her hand stays on mine for that terribly important extra second. *Oh shit*. "Thank you, again," I manage, hoping my voice isn't betraying my rattled nerves.

"Hey, good luck this afternoon. I'm sure you'll blow them away."

"If I can get them to listen to me without screaming at each other for five minutes, I'll consider it a success."

"I'm sure you'll have their undivided attention the moment you walk through the door."

"Not likely, but I can hope."

Burke shakes her head while grinning, and I can practically read her mind, though I know it's dangerous territory. "Let me know how it goes. Or, call me if you need me to come up and kick some ass for you."

"Excuse me, Burke Calloway, I'm no princess in an ivory tower. I can handle my shit," I say, puffing up.

"I have no doubt about that, Emery." She winks at me. "Just know I'm there if you need some rescuing. I'll see you later."

CHAPTER TWELVE

With the incomparable assistance of Luke and Libby who have somehow gotten the finance department to at least listen to them without interrupting every five minutes, I manage to get through that afternoon's workshop without being scarred and/or thrown out on my ass. It's oddly important to me that Burke knows I can, in fact, handle my shit. She has no idea how much I'm not handling my personal shit, but that's beside the point. Professionally, I have Whitmore on lock, and I'm proud of it.

I do not, however, have the repeated replay of that day's lunch with Burke on lock. It keeps running through my mind. I've analyzed everything we said and reprimanded myself multiple times for not telling Burke I'm in a relationship. Then again, she didn't come right out and ask me if I'm single—she only asked if I'm still with Cassidy. For Burke, Lauren doesn't exist.

I suddenly find myself determined to show Lauren that she very much exists, and I do love her. My conversation with Caren has been bouncing in my head for the duration of the workday.

I check my phone before I exit the building, anxiously hopeful that Burke's texted about the workshop, but my phone is blank.

On my way home, I stop at the local market and pick out a lively bouquet of seasonal flowers. I text Lauren, explaining that I want to make dinner tonight. She replies quickly with a simple *Ok* and I scurry through the market to gather ingredients for homemade turkey burgers and sweet potato fries. It's not the most romantic dinner I could come up with, but one I do well, and Lauren has always said she loves my turkey burgers.

At home, I notice Mer's car is gone. That wasn't part of my plan, but her being out of the house might help Lauren and I reconnect. I haven't gotten past making dinner, but I'm hopeful our relationship will take its natural course over the evening. I refuse to think about the fact that it hasn't seen its natural course for a long time, so long that it may be on an entirely different course now.

Lauren looks up from the dining room table as I walk inside. She's camped out with her laptop and a half-empty beer.

"Flowers?"

"I thought they might cheer you up."

"They're nice, Em."

Okay, not exactly the reaction I was hoping for. "Yeah, I just…I saw them and thought of you, so, here."

"You bought me flowers?"

What the fuck is wrong with her? "Yes, Lauren, I bought you flowers." I stop before I say something rude.

"I don't think you've ever bought me flowers before." She gives me a weird look.

"Maybe not, but I did today. So, I hope you like them."

"I do. Thank you." There's an odd note in her voice, something that sounds almost like anger, but that doesn't make any sense to me.

I stand there looking at her looking at me. Neither of us makes a move for a hug or a kiss; Lauren doesn't even get up to take the flowers and put them in a vase. This is off to a great start.

"Okay, well. I'll put these in water. You hungry?"

"I'm getting there."

And we are getting nowhere. "Okay if I take a quick shower before making dinner?"

"Sure. Let me know if you need help with dinner."

I retreat into the kitchen and yank down a dusty vase from a high shelf. The dust speaks volumes. When was the last time someone purchased flowers for someone else in this house? I'll be damned if I'm not going to enjoy these gorgeous blooms, even if Lauren feels the need to act like a spaz about them.

After shoving the dinner ingredients into the refrigerator, I head upstairs and hop into the shower. I linger there, taking care to shave and scrub, hoping the steam will help clear my head. I towel off and stand naked in my closet after having lathered my entire body with lotion. I now suspect that no matter what I choose to wear, Lauren is not going to look at me with any more desire than she did the damn flowers. I settle on an old pair of her Portland State faded green sweatpants and a gray tank beneath a white tank. I forego a bra, silently thanking my mom for perky genes. Having been with an athlete for this long, I'm pretty confident she'll respond accordingly to this decidedly laid-back but sexy outfit.

I return to the kitchen without saying anything to Lauren, who is, as she said she would be, still at the dining room table. I notice she has a new beer bottle in front of her and her expression is no less stressed than it was twenty minutes ago. I'm not going to let that deter me; I'm not sure I can do anything to help Lauren feel better, but I'm determined to try.

I'm cutting up sweet potatoes when Lauren comes into the kitchen. I feel her eyes on me, maybe even sweeping me up and down to take in my ensemble.

"Mer is out for the night. She has a date."

I snort. "A date? Really?"

"I know, that's what I said. But, yeah. She met some guy, an artist, at one of the galleries downtown."

"Well, good for her. I'm surprised it took her this long to... never mind."

Lauren laughs and moves closer to me. "I know. I am, too. Maybe she's actually learning to be cautious."

I turn and give Lauren an 'are you serious' look, surprised to see she's moved so close to me. "I somehow doubt that."

"You never know," she says, her voice quiet. At the pace of a snail, her hand reaches out and strokes the bare skin of my arm. "Em."

"Lauren."

"Thank you for the flowers. They really are beautiful."

"You're welcome."

Her eyes light on mine. "Thank you for the thoughts behind them. I'm sorry I wasn't more grateful when you gave them to me, I was just…I don't know…I don't want you to pity me." That last part comes out in a rush.

"Babe, I don't pity you." I lay the knife down on the cutting board and turn to her. "I do feel bad for you, but only because I don't like seeing you so…lost."

"This is hard, Em. I didn't expect it to be. But I feel like I'm letting both of us down, and I hate that feeling."

"You're not letting me down. This was totally out of your control."

"Maybe if I'd worked harder, or gotten involved with more projects, maybe—"

"Lauren, stop." I rest a hand on her cheek. Her skin is soft and cool beneath my fingers. "It's not your fault. Hear me."

"I do," she mutters. "I'm really sorry about all this. I can't believe I haven't found anything yet."

"You will. I believe it. You have to believe it too."

Our eyes meet again. Lauren's gaze falters, and it slides down my face to land on my nipples, which have noticeably hardened beneath the thin layers of the tank tops. "I'm so sorry, Em," she whispers.

I pull her to me, and lock her in an embrace. She wraps her arms around me and holds on tightly. I try to lose myself in that hug, scrambling for the fractured feelings I have for Lauren, and for us. I can feel by this simple touch that I do love her, and that I am attracted to her. It's that "in love" part that I'm no longer certain about, and it's not coming to me now. I'm so focused on trying to find it that it takes me a couple seconds to realize that Lauren's hands are no longer gripping me, but instead are slowly massaging me, working their way from my back to my sides, to my ribs, and yes, there they go, to my waiting, hard nipples.

I inhale sharply as her hands solidly close over my breasts. Almost instantly, Lauren's mouth is on mine, her kiss hot and needy. I return the kiss with hopefully as much passion as is suddenly surging from Lauren—passion I've missed, passion I'd worried was gone. I try to lose myself in the kiss, but find I can't.

Her tongue slowly works its way into my mouth, and our kiss deepens. I pull Lauren closer to me, but she resists, turning us and pushing my back against the kitchen counter. One hand moves to my nipple, even harder now, and rolls it gently between the pads of her fingers. I softly moan into Lauren's mouth, which doubles the intensity of her grip. My other nipple is taken captive too, and in spite of my inability to mentally lose myself to this moment, my body is ready to give itself up.

Lauren breaks away from my mouth to pull my tank tops off; they go sailing across the kitchen. As she kisses her way across my collarbone and down my chest, skimming over the tops of my breasts and heading straight for my waiting nipples, I move my hands under her T-shirt. Her small breasts are waiting for me beneath her sports bra, which I quickly maneuver over her breasts, setting them free. For a fleeting second, I think about how much easier this would be in a horizontal position, but I'm not about to risk losing the moment.

Lauren pulls my nipple harder into her mouth, her teeth grasping it. I push back against the counter, audibly moaning. I need her inside of me. Her hands are working their way down my waist, over my hips, and they gently slide my/her sweatpants down over my bare ass. Lauren doesn't make me wait; as she lifts her head up to mine, her fingers glide over the wetness emanating from me. I arch my back involuntarily, causing her fingers to press harder against my clit. Both of us exhale loudly, some mixture of a moan and a groan, and Lauren rubs her thumb over my clit. We rock together, her thumb building pressure and speed, and I fumble my hands past her breasts, down her body, and yank down her shorts and briefs without ceremony.

"Oh, Em," she groans as my hand meets her arousal. She's wetter than I can remember her ever being. I slide two fingers inside of her. She bucks against me immediately, her own fingers moving to push inside of me. I gasp at her movement, feeling my body constrict and then release, opening for her touch. Our fingers move to their own rhythms, both of us working to find the other's cadence. As Lauren reaches further into me, bending her fingers toward my center, I clamp my teeth down on her exposed neck and push harder into her.

We fuck each other there in the kitchen with a practiced pulse, one that has not outgrown us but has slightly escaped from our routine. As soon as I start rotating my thumb over her clit, Lauren comes in a rush of heat and moans, her body bucking slightly against mine. Her movements instantly slow inside of me, but retain enough pressure to bring me, quietly, over the edge.

"I'm so sorry, baby," she whispers, her tightness still clenching against my stilled fingers. "I am so, so sorry."

I ease out of her, and wrap my arms around her. She does the same, and we stand there silently in our kitchen, holding on to each other, each of us battling unique fears of disappointment and loss.

* * *

Lauren insists on helping me finish dinner, since, as she says, she's the one who interrupted it. We work together amicably; Lauren takes over the sweet potato prep and I work with the turkey burgers. She notes that we have ingredients for guacamole and whips up a batch while the fries bake and the burgers grill.

We eat together on the living room floor, backs up against the sofa, food spread out on the coffee table. We laughingly argue over which to watch: *Modern Family* or *House Hunters*, and

I win with *Modern Family*. Lauren drinks another microbrew and I steal sips when she pretends to not be looking. During a commercial break, Lauren leans over and kisses me, then whispers, "Nice touch with the lack of bra and underwear."

Lauren insists on doing the kitchen cleanup, and I slip out the front door to get the mail. The night air is clean and filters through my lungs, allowing me my first true deep breath of the day. I perch on the front steps for a few moments, enjoying the cool evening.

In the dark quiet with the brightly lit house behind me, I admit that tonight didn't fix everything. I hadn't truly expected it to, but I was hoping I'd feel steadier about me and Lauren than I actually do. Sure, we talked, and yeah, we definitely had sex, but I'm still feeling like something is missing.

And what scares me is that the something missing isn't something little: no longer being in love with someone is not what I would consider…little.

CHAPTER THIRTEEN

"Oh, thank God you're here," Allison hisses as I walk into Perk on Wednesday morning. "Did you get my email?"

She grabs my arm and pulls me back into her office. "I'm about to throw Sidney out," she announces as soon as she shuts the door behind us.

"What happened?"

"You didn't read my email?"

I shrug in confusion. "I didn't see any email from you. When did you send it?"

"Like two hours ago."

I make a face at her and reach into my bag for my cell phone. "I was sleeping two hours ago." Sure enough, there's an email from Allison in my Gmail account. "Oh, okay, hang on. I'll read it."

She slaps at my hand. "Forget it. Read it later."

"What the hell is going on with you?"

Allison practically growls as she paces the small office, which is cluttered to the point of total disarray. I don't know how she gets any work done, let alone how she's able to pace without tripping and falling. What frightens me even more is the idea that she might actually interview potential employees in here. I shudder at the thought, thinking not for the first time that Allison might benefit from some of my professional tough love.

Since she's not forthcoming with actual words, I press harder: "Is it Loophole?"

"It's every fucking loophole possible!"

"Okay, listen to me. If you want my help right now, you need to calm the hell down and talk to me like a human being, because I am not Sidney, and I am not your punching bag."

Allison stops in her tracks and stares at me. She's used to being the one to land these verbal punches. "Is that how you talk to people at work?"

"When they act like uncommunicative freaks, yes. Yes, I do. Now sit your ass down…somewhere…and explain." I check my phone again. "And stick to the facts, because I don't have much time."

"Sidney told me she cheated on me."

"Again," I can't help but to interject.

"Yes. Again."

"With Loophole?"

Allison buries her face in her hands and shakes her head, her sun-bright blond hair swishing back and forth. "Nope."

"I might remind you that I don't have time for guessing games."

"Fuck, Em, it was with Cassidy."

I should be surprised, or I should at least be able to act surprised. One would think I would have *some* sort of reaction to this, but frankly, I don't, and that's mostly because this isn't the first time I've heard Allison say this. Is it weird that my best friend's sort-of girlfriend keeps cheating on her with my ex-girlfriend? Yes. Definitely weird, but in a city that teems with lesbians, it's not that far-fetched. Beyond that, I have absolutely zero feelings of any sort for Cassidy, and haven't for a long time, so anytime Allison brings her up I'm able to react appropriately.

"Um, again?" I say lightly, knowing this is a sensitive subject.

After all, Cassidy is the woman Allison previously caught Sidney with in their bed. She's also the woman Sidney spent a long weekend with in Seattle while telling Allison she was visiting her parents.

"I know! But this is it. I'm done."

I've also heard this before. "So, you're going to throw her out?"

"Yes." Hmm. No wavering, that's new. "I mean, I think I am." That's more like it.

"You don't have to decide anything right now." This conversation is so disappointingly familiar that it's practically scripted.

"Here's what I'm thinking. And yes, I'll keep it short; you can read the details in the email." Allison takes a deep breath and looks at me, her expression betraying a tiny bit of insecurity. "I'm going to tell Sidney that I think we should be non-monogamous."

I bite my tongue, hoping I don't accidentally inform Allison that Sidney already appears to be under the impression that they were never monogamous. Instead, I nod, not trusting my words.

"It could work, right? She gets to do whatever she wants, but so do I."

"Is that really what you want?"

"I don't know. But I don't want to lose Sidney. I know that sounds crazy and pathetic, but I really do love her, Em."

"But are you in love with her?"

"Yes." Again, no hesitation. I'm struck by the fact that my best friend feels more confident about her feelings for her perennially cheating girlfriend than I do for Lauren. I don't know which one of us is more ignorant in that respect.

"Well…" I pause to look at my phone, buzzing in my hand, "if that's what you think will work, then go for it." I watch as Burke's call drops into my voice mail.

"I don't know that it will, honestly. But I'm willing to give it a shot. What the hell is it about the fucking Evil Bitch, anyway?"

I wish I had an answer for Allison, one that could help her see not only why I hung on to Cassidy for so long, but also why

Sidney seems incapable of staying away from her. Sure, the sex is good, but it's not mind-blowing. It's something about Cassidy's personality and her seeming lack of need for other people. She is the unattainable, and women like me and Sidney spend too much time trying to attain her. I can only hope that Sidney will eventually see, as I did, that there is simply no attaining that woman. On the flip side...maybe Sidney and Cassidy are perfect for each other; Cassidy's reputation is not exactly one of monogamy, either. But I'm not about to bring that up right now.

"There's just something about her," I offer, hoping it will suffice for now. "You remember my struggles with her. I'm sure Sidney will come to her senses eventually." I tell myself I didn't just lie, I just kind of...made a statement that probably won't ring true any time soon, if ever.

"And there's not something about me?" Allison looks hurt— not from my words, but from her girlfriend's inability to return the love Allison so wholly gives.

"Oh, sweetie, there are tons of somethings about you. Trust me." My fingers are itching to tap into my voice mail. "Listen, let's get together this weekend. Just us. We'll get unhealthy takeout and watch shitty movies."

Allison nods, and opens her arms to hug me. "I'd love that. Friday night?"

"Friday it is." I hug her tightly. "In the meantime, try not to drive yourself crazy, okay? Remember that you can only control your actions, not Sidney's."

"Yes, oh wise one."

I tell Allison I need a minute to check my voice mail, then I'll meet her in the café and pick up my coffee, which I am pretty much dying for by now. I tap in my code and listen to Burke's smooth voice—she's asking if I want her to pick up coffee for me.

I quickly save the voice mail and call her back, hoping she hasn't already gone out of her way.

"Well, good morning," she answers.

"Good morning to you. Sorry I missed your call, I was dealing with a friend crisis."

"This early in the morning? Wow, you must be a damn good friend."

"So they say. Listen, I'm actually at Perk right now, so why don't I get coffee for you today?"

"That would be great." She gives me her order of a medium latte with skim milk, extra hot, then thanks me.

"Right place, right time. Besides, I think I owe you."

"Oh, we can discuss how much you owe me later." She chuckles, a deep, sexy sound vibrating in her throat.

I fully expect the phone to slip out of my hand and crash to the hardwood floor.

"No witty response for me?" she says.

"I think you knocked the wit out of me with that one."

"That's a first."

"Indeed."

"Hopefully not a last."

I close my eyes and not so gently rest my head against the bright yellow wall of Allison's office. This woman is killing me, and I'm beginning to think she is not oblivious to that fact. "Hopefully not," I finally reply.

"Maybe your wit is just a bit slower in the morning?" I can hear, in the background, the sound of a car door shutting.

"Let's not forget I'm also currently uncaffeinated."

"Well, I am, too, which might explain my slightly unprofessional chatter here. I hope I haven't offended you."

"No, not at all," I tell her, confused by her semi-apology. "Not at all," I repeat.

"Good," she says, and I find myself wishing she were standing in front of me. I remind myself that right now, it's absolutely safer that she is *not* standing anywhere near me.

"Well," I say.

"Emery?"

"Yes, Burke?"

"I'm really thirsty," she whispers.

I let out a laugh. "Okay, okay. I'm on it. Coffee coming your way, ETA ten minutes, give or take a few depending on traffic."

"Thank you. I anticipate its arrival…and yours."

* * *

After I put in my coffee order with Allison, I make a quick detour to her private bathroom. My black dress pants and simple white button-down shirt fit well, and the shirt is designed to lack the first few buttons, thus exposing my collarbone and some skin below. My mom actually bought me this shirt last year, telling me "a little decolletage never hurt anyone." She's got a slight obsession with getting me to wear more feminine clothing; sometimes, I let her win.

I tug the shirt down a little lower, and tuck my loose hair—wavy and down for once—behind my ears. It frames my face and diverts a bit of attention away from the glimpse of my cleavage (which is rocking it today, thanks to my best bra). I didn't dress up for Burke. Nope. But it *is* possible I put a little more effort into my appearance today. I shake my head at my reflection before hurrying on my way.

Burke's back is to me when I make my way into the IT basement. Seth, her boss, spots me first, and gives me a friendly wave. Seth's proven to be a really nice guy, but we have a lot of work to do regarding his management skills, of which he is definitely lacking. At least he's been receptive to the workshops. The IT department is resolutely the most balanced, adaptable department at Whitmore. Every time we've met or worked with them has been a pleasure so far, and I anticipate nothing less for future engagements.

If there's one person who has consistently embodied the awesomeness of the IT department, she sits before me, deeply focused on a string of characters littering the screen of her computer. I take a small step closer to her and catch a whiff of her scent, heady without being overwhelming, and downright sultry while being clean. That scent *is* Burke...at least, what I know of her.

"Are you going to say hi, or just stand there and hold my coffee hostage?" she says, that unmistakable rumble of quiet amusement floating through her voice. She doesn't turn around, her eyes still trained on her screen.

"Have you suddenly developed a sixth sense?"

"If seeing forms and shadows in the reflection of my computer screen equals a sixth sense, then yes, I do believe I have."

Now she turns around to face me. Her gaze is steady, not particularly cautious, but undeniably fastened on the length of my body. I'm paralyzed in that stare. I don't want her to look away.

"Now, about that matter of you owing me." Burke breaks the silence after she takes a long sip of her latte; she's moved her prolonged stare up to meet my eyes.

Her voice shatters my trance; I give myself a mental shake and move to perch on the edge of her desk. "I'm listening."

Burke rotates her chair to face me. She always prefers to have direct eye contact during most conversations. Another sign that she probably does not need my team's help. Come to think of it, she'd be a great replacement for Seth. I tuck that thought into my back pocket to revisit when I'm not so captivated by her.

"What are you doing Friday night?"

"Nothing."

"Good answer, though I admit I'm surprised by that."

"Surprised? Why's that?"

She leans in close to me and drops her voice. "I know I haven't finished my coffee yet, so my neurons aren't all firing, but Emery, really—how does a woman like you not have plans on a Friday night?"

I push the tips of two of my fingers against her shoulder and nudge her back into her seat. "Watch yourself, Burke Calloway. We are in a professional environment."

"Shall we go outside to finish this conversation?"

I pretend to get up. "If it's that bad, then we probably should abort the conversation at this point."

Her hand wraps around my wrist and tugs me back to my perched position. "Not needed. I'll keep it quick and nice, promise."

"I'm listening," I repeat.

"I have an extra ticket to see Chris Pureka on Friday night. Show's downtown, starts at seven. I was wondering if, professionally, you'd like to go. With me. You've been working so hard, and doing a fantastic job at it, that I'd like to take part in rewarding you for that hard work."

If there was any common sense in my brain, it's gone. Burke is asking me to go with her to a concert, and I can't think of saying no even though I'm well aware of the potential for danger in us being out, together—and though she's mocking the whole professionalism thing right now, this is definitely not a professional engagement.

"I would like to go." Clearly, segments of my brain are not connecting; I'm acting on impulse. An impulse that won't shut up and is demanding that I sit up and pay attention to what is sitting right in front of me, asking me to spend more time with her.

A smile erupts over Burke's face. "Excellent answer. I have a late meeting with a client that day, so how about we meet at the venue? Maybe grab a late dinner afterward? With complete professionalism, of course."

Crisis of potential awkward 'pick me up at the house I live in with my girlfriend' situation averted. I should feel a level of guilt at having accepted Burke's invitation to this professional date, but I can't find it.

I stand and say, "I'm looking forward to it." And I am. More so than I should be, considering the circumstances.

"As am I." We hold each other's stares and smiles. "Off to teach people how to speak nicely to each other?"

I roll my eyes and give her a callous grin. "My work is never done."

I leave with a wave. As I walk through the basement, I'm aware I'm being watched, but I don't dare turn around to see whose eyes are trained on my retreating form.

CHAPTER FOURTEEN

The finance department implodes on Friday. And it's ugly. Even with both Libby and Luke in the conference room with me, we have a hell of a time wrangling them back under control. There's yelling, accusations, and one complete emotional breakdown by the woman we were hoping would step up and apply for the newly reopened management position. It gets so bad that Libby has to make a dash for Charlotte, who comes in armed with the CEO.

Krista Whitmore is a rather intimidating woman whom I've met previously—at a softball tournament, a couple soccer games, and several professional events, including a fundraiser for the LGBTQ+ Community Center. She's not exactly closeted, but she's not completely out, either. She seems to run interference between the lines of sexual identity, but those who know, know: this woman dates only other supremely attractive women. She's seriously gorgeous with long, thick brown hair that cascades down her back in loose waves, round pale blue eyes, porcelain skin, and a toned but voluptuous figure. In the community, I've found her to be an engaging, genuine woman with a quiet sense of humor paired with a kind heart. Professionally, she doesn't tolerate any bullshit and can be a bit of a bulldozer.

So when Krista enters the conference room that Friday, the room falls into silence. I'm standing at the front of the room, still in disbelief and disgust at how these people handle themselves. Krista simply looks around the room, forcing every single employee to make eye contact with her before she speaks.

"Go home, all of you," she orders. Her tone intimidates me and I'm not even her employee. "Now. I want all of you back in this conference room at eight a.m. on Monday."

The bedraggled department exits the room in single file, no one daring to look up at her.

As Luke, Libby, and I hurriedly pack up, anxious to leave the scene of the disaster, Krista candidly explains that she knew this department would be the most difficult to handle, and she apologizes for not having intervened sooner. We assure her that we've seen worse, and we certainly have, including office supplies and chairs thrown across a room. Luke once had to dive under a table to avoid getting hit by a stapler. Krista bites back a laugh after that story, and apologizes to us again, assuring us she will handle the finance department on Monday morning.

Luke and Libby head for other meetings. My afternoon is clear, the first time in several days I haven't had to rush to a workshop.

Krista clears her throat. "I've been getting great feedback on your presentations, Emery. How do you feel it's going?"

"Overall, I think we've been successful," I tell her. She totally intimidates me in the work environment. When she's in her softball uniform, not so much. But right now, her intoxicating curves tucked into a deep navy blue skirt with a delirious slit up the thigh, topped with a tight pale gray dress shirt? Whew. Total intimidation. Even if I'm attracted to not-so feminine women, I am not immune to the oozing sexual prowess of women like Cassidy and Krista.

"I think so too." We walk down the hall together. "I'm glad your team came aboard. I asked for that, you know."

News to me. "Why's that?"

"Other local companies told us you have a great balance within your own group and it seems to spread within the companies you work with."

"Thank you, that's great to hear."

"Plus," her voice lowers and she leans closer to my ear, several tendrils of her hair brushing against my shoulder, "it's always nice to have family around." She laughs softly, and gently bumps her shoulder into mine.

I know veritably hundreds of women who would kill to be in my place right now; Krista is certainly not flirting with me, but that proximity, that slightly more than friendly closeness, is precisely how she lures women in. Not that she needs to lure, of course, because women drop at her feet like flies, but a little luring never hurt anyone.

It's barely registering on my radar, though, because I've spotted Burke near my conference room/makeshift office, and the look on her face is not one I've seen before. It reads as jealousy, but there's a layer of concern mixed in. She continues to watch us as Krista takes hold of my elbow and stops me in my tracks.

"Libby's told you about the New York trip, right?"

"Yes."

Krista tucks her hair behind her ear, expensive and intoxicating perfume wafting my way. "Level with me, Emery. Whitmore is able to send one non-managerial employee from each department. I have a working list but I know how closely you've been working with my staff and I'd like to hear who you'd think would benefit from the conference."

Before I can out-think myself, I rattle off six names, one from each department. I'm left with the IT department. My head is saying *anyone but Burke* but the rest of me is screaming *BURKE BURKE BURKE YOU IDIOT BURKE*. The clear and present danger of me being in New York City with Burke for an entire week is palpable. But my mouth is apparently no longer connected to my head: "And from IT, Burke Calloway."

Krista's expression doesn't change, but her body shifts and her eyes flicker to the right to settle on Burke who continues her open observation of us. "All good picks, many of which were already on my list. Thanks, Emery. Enjoy your weekend. You deserve a break after this afternoon."

With that, Krista vanishes in the opposite direction, and I walk over to Burke. She graces me with a smile, and uncrosses her arms from their rigid position over her chest. "Was Ms. Whitmore giving you any trouble?" There's an edge to her voice I haven't heard before.

"Not at all. Just checking in to see how things are going."

"Good." We stand and awkwardly stare at each other for a moment until Burke snaps out of her weirdness. "I'm about to head out for my client meeting, but I wanted to stop by and tell you that I'm looking forward to our professional engagement this evening."

"I am too," I tell Burke. She reaches out to shake my hand.

I clasp my hand in hers. Firm grip. Even shake. Unbearably soft and strong fingers. "How professional," I muse.

"Nothing but. Till this evening, Ms. Larsen."

"Till then, Ms. Calloway."

* * *

At four o'clock, Libby orders me, Luke, and Caren to stop working and meet her at The Station, a bar near PLAC that we frequent on Fridays, rough days, or any necessary day in between. I try to beg out, but when Libby orders you to drink, you have a drink. Luckily for me, my three teammates seem hell-bent on getting drunk, already having claimed a designated driver in Caren's husband, who won't be out of work until eight. Their plans for intoxication increase the rate at which they begin drinking, and so it's easy for me to have one drink, half of a second, animatedly discuss the F-squared implosion, listen to gossip about Krista Whitmore, and quickly take my leave as they're readying to order their third round.

I'm home by five thirty, and when I hit the front door, I realize I haven't told Lauren I'm going out tonight.

"Hey, Em. How was work?" Mer and Lauren are both relaxing in the living room, both with laptops out.

"Not bad. What are you two up to?" I inquire.

"Oh, the usual. Man searching, job searching."

Lauren snorts. "Hopefully you know which one of us is doing the man searching."

"I can only assume," I say, leaning against the stairway. "Any luck for either of you?"

Lauren's face darkens immediately, and Mer tries to divert the conversation. "Luck is relative. You hungry, Em?"

"No, not yet." Say it. Do it. Now! "I'm actually just here to change. I'm going back out, just for some drinks and a late dinner. It's a work thing."

Lauren barely nods, her attention focused on the screen in front of her. Mer shoots me a weird look, but doesn't press for more information.

Upstairs, I throw on the outfit I'd planned on my drive home: gently worn jeans that fit me perfectly, a faded olive green V-neck, black Vans, and a black zip-up hoodie. I stare down my reflection in the mirror. *This is me*, I think. I wonder if Burke will remember this laid-back side of me, the part of Emery that doesn't like to be in anything other than comfortable clothes. All she's seen since we reunited is Professional Emery, and while I know that Professional Emery dresses well and looks good, I'm so much more comfortable in this skin.

Plus, I think as I grab my phone, keys, and wallet, and make my way out of the house calling a goodbye to Lauren and Mer, *this is definitely* not *a date outfit.*

* * *

Stage 12, the cozy venue for the concert, is lit by a single spotlight on the outside, but I've been inside for enough concerts to know that the interior is far dimmer than the exterior. I check my watch as I walk toward the front doors: just on time. A text comes in from Allison: *What time/whose house?* Shit. We had plans tonight. I groan inwardly, feeling like a terrible friend. I send a quick reply: *Don't kill me. Work thing came up. Call you tomorrow.* I hang by the storefront next to the venue, hoping Allison replies quickly and doesn't hate me. *Asshole. Talk tomorrow. YOU OWE ME.* Oh, do I ever.

I look up from my phone and see Burke leaning casually against the brick façade of Stage 12. She watches me approach, an indiscernible look on her face. She, too, is wearing jeans, and another long-sleeved button-down, this one a rusted red, navy blue, and iron gray tiny plaid print. I don't need to look further down her body to know she's wearing her Docs. Her dark brown hair is messy and tousled, as if she's just rolled out of bed.

"Hey there," she says. "You look great. So," she says, leaning in closer to me, her butt still pressed up against the wall, "what do you say we drop the professional curtain?"

Shivers cascade through my body. If Burke Calloway can have this effect on me by just speaking to me, I can't even begin to imagine what she could do with her touch. How's that for unprofessional thoughts?

"Shall I take your lack of an answer as a silent acquiescence?" she pushes.

"I'll give you a trial period," I manage. "If you can prove to me that you can be politely unprofessional during the concert, then I'll extend the trial period through dinner."

"And what happens if I fail this little exam?"

I shake my head. "I don't think you're prepared to face those consequences."

A dark glimmer passes over Burke's eyes, a darkness that infers something I'm not ready to see there. "I accept, though in the future I'd prefer if you could neatly outline the so-called consequences for me." She winks at me and puts her hand on my lower back to escort me inside the venue. "You see, Emery…" Her voice is dangerously close to my ear. "I sometimes like to break the rules because the ramifications of doing so are often more alluring than the benefits of playing by the rules."

I playfully push Burke away from me and thrust my pointer finger close to her face.

"Strike one."

She laughs gamely, and shrugs. "Maybe you should explain the consequences."

"Or maybe you should trust me and behave."

Burke bites the top of her lower lip, a gesture that makes me wish I were her teeth. We stare each other down as we stand next to our reserved table. Finally, Burke nods.

"Okay. Your rules tonight, Emery."

* * *

After the concert, we head out for food. Our walk down the street to a pub that offers great microbrews and glorified bar food is quiet. Both of us seem to be in a slight trance, and I'm not totally sure if it's from Chris Pureka's intoxicating voice. We maintain a comfortable space as we walk. A good thing—I'm becoming more and more worried that if something, anything, were to happen, I wouldn't be able to stop myself.

Seated in a dark booth near the back of the pub, Burke seems to relax. Her playful and teasing smiles return, and we're both able to converse normally. We order some food to pick at and share, and I'm surprised when we both order water.

I start to ask Burke why she didn't order a beer, but she preempts me by asking, "So? A-plus?"

"Trial periods don't earn grades."

"Pass/fail situation?"

"Yep."

She cocks her head slightly to the right. "And?"

"And...you have passed, although your first strike remains on the table."

Burke nods, a satisfied look on her face. "Now what?"

"Why didn't you order a beer?"

"You really have a talent for maneuvering the conversation, you know that?"

"Communications major, I might remind you."

"Is that what they teach you? How to avoid questions and determine the direction of conversations? Oh, and they must spend a lot of time on non sequiturs, because you truly have those mastered, Emery." Burke delivers this with one of those teasing smiles; had she not done so, I'd be concerned that she thought I was trying to control every conversation we have.

"Amongst other valuable techniques, yes. I'd say it pays off, wouldn't you?"

"Absolutely. Star student."

"So? The beer?"

"And persistent," she adds. "I have no earth-shattering reason for not ordering a beer. I simply don't want one right now. Why didn't *you* order one?"

"I want a clear head tonight."

Burke studies me. "Emery."

"Burke."

"Brace yourself for strike two. I am so happy that our paths have crossed again."

I can handle that. "So am I."

"There's more. Continue bracing." That teasing smile has faded, and in its place is a serious mouth that I am finding impossible not to kiss. "I don't like to live my life with regrets. And in many ways, I think I've successfully lived without regrets for a long time. But now, since you've come back into my life, I realize how much I regret not having had you in my life for all these years when I so easily could have made the effort to be in touch with you."

Real, pure emotion stings the back of my throat and ensnares my heart. "Burke, I—"

"I'm not done. It's this last part that you should really be ready for. Are you ready?"

I nod, unable to find any words.

"I want you in my life, Emery, and I fully intend on making that happen."

I stare at her. *Say something.*

"I will make it happen, whether or not you're okay with it." The teasing smile returns, lighting up Burke's entire face.

I give myself a moment to formulate some kind of witty reply to level the speaking ground. "Are you referencing torture strategies? Is there a special dungeon in your new building that I should be aware of?"

"Would you like to come over and find out? I move in tomorrow."

"Depends on what type of torture we're talking about."

"Why, Ms. Larsen, I do believe you've just earned a strike."

"No way! That was an innocent question!"

Burke leans back in the booth and eyes me with, oh fuck, I know that look. That's hunger. That's want. That's *I'd rip your clothes off right now if we weren't in a public place.* "I'm finding it hard to believe there's much innocence about you."

I hear myself replying before I'm aware of what I'm saying: "I suppose you'll have to stick around and find out how right or wrong you are."

Burke lets out a full, loud laugh. I slap a hand against my forehead and shake my head. Burke reaches out across the table and covers my right hand. Her fingers wrap solidly around mine and squeeze with gentle pressure.

"Strike two, Emery. Looks like we're even."

"Okay." I take a long drink of water and watch our hands separate, reminding myself we're in a public place downtown where *anyone* could see us. "Let's get back to safe ground. Tell me about your family."

"Safe enough. Mom and Dad never married. They seem to like it that way. I'm the precious baby of the family; the oldest is Baylon, then there's Blake."

"Baylon, Blake, Burke. That's a pile of gender neutrality."

"Exactly. Mom would love you. She chose the names for that exact reason, but for the record, Bay is male and single and also gay, Blake is female and in a long-term relationship with a guy named Ryan. They have two daughters, Aislynn and Kenna, and they are the light of my life."

"Are they all local?"

She nods. "Everyone. We're all scattered around Portland, so we meet for family dinners often."

"I'm jealous; my parents are up in Washington, and my younger sister is in northern California. I wish they were closer…well, maybe my dad and my sister. My mom can stay in Washington."

"You don't have a good relationship with your mom?"

"I do. I mean, most of the time, yes, I do. But she can be a bit of a nag."

"I wish I could say I understand, but I don't. My mom has been hands-off my whole life. I almost wish she'd nagged me every now and again. She is one of my best friends, though, probably because of how much she let me figure life out for myself."

Burke has a bright look of happiness the whole time she talks about her family, the trips they've taken, the variety of places they've lived, and the left-of-center traditions they've created over the years. I've always found it an alluring characteristic—women who not only love their family, but are close to them and speak highly of them.

She asks, "So, it's just you and your younger sister?"

"Actually, no, I have an older sister. Helena. She lives in New Hampshire."

"That's right, you're born and bred East Coast."

"Guilty. Straight from a wealthy, Stepford-ish Philadelphia suburb. My parents moved to Washington after I came out here for college; I guess they got tired of keeping up with appearances too. My little sister was in high school when they moved and she was furious for a long time. I think that's why she lives ten hours away from our parents now."

"Is that a family trait?"

"What?"

"Clinging to resentment, acting out through it?"

Whoa. That's an unnervingly correct statement about my family—my dad is the exception, but my mom, sisters, and I all do that very thing in various degrees of intensity.

"I'm not sure how you nailed that so quickly, but yes…it does seem to be a habit."

"I hope I'm never on the receiving end."

"I don't see how you could be." And right now, I truly don't.

"I know it may seem so, but I'm not *actually* perfect, Emery."

"Hang on there, tiger, I was not inferring that I think you're perfect."

"And why on earth not?"

"I don't know you well enough to make that assumption."

"I think we need to change that."

Dinner and conversation over, we walk to my car. I fumble with my keys. Burke smoothly reaches in and takes them.

"I don't want to shake your hand," she says, her voice low and calm over the blur of city traffic.

"Be professional," I manage to get out. Futile as it may be, I said it, the tiny latch holding this evening together.

Burke coyly grins at me before wrapping her arms around my waist. My arms slide around her neck. With her Docs on, she is almost exactly my height, close enough that I press the side of my face against hers to prevent my lips from seeking hers. She holds me tighter. The slow circles she's drawing on my back with her thumb are causing my entire body to thrum with arousal. With an aching slowness, her hands drift down to my hips and grip them firmly. I wait for the first touch of skin to skin under my T-shirt, but it doesn't come.

She uses the leverage of her hands on my hips to push us apart. But I want her. So badly. I can't remember the last time my senses were so overwhelmed by someone, or by the anticipation of someone.

"Thank you for tonight, Emery. I can honestly say there's no one else I would rather be with."

I can only nod, hoping she understands I feel the same.

A darkness shadowing her eyes, Burke traces the contours of my face. "You are beautiful, Emery." Her words are so hushed they nearly get lost in the sounds of the city around us.

The pad of her thumb separates my lips. My heart thumps, and I watch Burke's lips part. The tip of her thumb catches a spot of wetness under my top lip, and she draws it out onto first my top lip, then my bottom lip, taking all the time she wants in wetting my lips.

And then, without warning, Burke's fingers leave me. "Good night, Emery," I hear through the static in my brain. She turns and is gone.

I drop into my car, heart racing uncomfortably. That was the sexiest, most unbearably incredible non-kiss I've ever had.

"Oh, fuck." I cover my face with both hands. Even I'm not avoidant enough to ignore the truth of knowing exactly what path I'm on. Every step leads me closer to Burke, and sex with Burke. There must be detours, ways off the path, but as much as I can't see them, I know that I don't *want* to see them.

For now, though, I have to calm down enough to drive home.

Home to my girlfriend, Lauren. Who, despite the fact that I love her and have desired her, has never affected me the way Burke does.

CHAPTER FIFTEEN

When I push my eyes open on Saturday morning, a cranium-splitting headache hits me full force. I press the cool heels of my hands into my eye sockets, hoping to alleviate some of the pounding pressure. No help. Blindly, I fumble for the bottle of water I always keep next to my bed. Once my fingers grasp it, I hurry it to my cotton-lined mouth. I force myself into an upright position, grateful that the room isn't spinning, and chug the water. Slowly, my limbs come to life. I draw my knees to my chest and rest my forehead on my knees, remembering why I grabbed that bottle of wine when I got home last night.

The memories and realizations swim through my aching head. I can't deal with any of it right now; I need a shower, comfortable clothes, and a gallon of water. And toast. Yes, toast sounds wonderful.

There's no sight of Lauren when I finally make my way downstairs. The house is incredibly quiet, just as it was when I got home last night. I peek out the front window and see Mer's car, my car, but not Lauren's. My stomach clenches. I can't, and don't want to, believe it, but there's a really good chance Lauren never came home last night, and I have no idea where she went in the first place.

Fresh air will help me clear my head from its disarray of cobwebs, so I open the back door, take a cleansing breath, and find Mer sitting on the deck.

"Morning, hot stuff." She smiles up at me, midnight black hair tumbled around her head in a messy bun. "Wild night with your coworkers?" Her question is innocent, but my guilt is warping it to sound accusatory. I remind myself that I don't have anything to feel guilty about. There was no sex. No kiss. No technical cheating. Whatever's going on internally is a different story, but I have to figure that out before I start worrying about any physical cheating.

"Not really," I tell her. "I seem to have drunk a bottle of wine when I came home last night." The sips went down easily as I tried to submerge my thoughts of Burke.

"An entire bottle?"

"Apparently, unless you or Lauren helped me and I don't remember."

"I didn't come home till this morning so it wasn't me."

I wait for Mer to say something about Lauren, but if she was out all night then she wouldn't know if Lauren ever came home. I gently prod her anyway.

"I thought you guys were going to make dinner last night."

"Oh, we did. There are leftovers, by the way, in case you want some for lunch. Quinten called me as we were finishing dinner, so I met up with him later."

"Is that the new boy?"

"Yes, and he is wonderful. Well, he's funny and good in bed, plus he's got that tall, dark, and handsome thing going on, so he's wonderful for right now." Mer winks at me and hands me the other half of her bagel sandwich, which I had been not so secretly eyeing up. "Have it. Half is enough for me."

I take a big bite out of the sandwich, prolonging having to tell Mer that I have no idea where Lauren is. I'm pretty clear on the fact she didn't sleep in bed with me last night, and I'm certain that she wasn't home when I got home. She also didn't text me, call me, or leave a note.

I bite the proverbial bullet and ask Mer: "Where's Lauren?"

"Oh, the greenhouse again. She was leaving as I got home. She muttered something about flowers, seeds, I don't know, and she left."

I close my eyes for a moment. Okay, so that means Lauren probably came home at some point last night, did not sleep in bed with me, and got up before I got up. The matter of not knowing where she was when I got home is less important now that I'm pretty sure she did, in fact, sleep at our house.

"Things any better with you two?" Such a casual question to ask on the day after I realized that I am definitely not in love with Lauren anymore.

I could lie and tell Mer that things are better, that Lauren and I are connecting and getting along and feeling good. But those words aren't anywhere near my mouth, even if we did have one good, normal night this week. "I don't know, Mer."

Mer leans over and touches my arm. "I'm worried about you guys. You didn't even kiss Lauren goodbye when you left last night."

I stare at her, rooting through my wine-cloudy memory. She's right. I didn't. Then again, Lauren didn't even look up when I left: I'm willing to bet that if I asked her what I was wearing when I left the house last night, she'd say my work clothes, or she'd admit she has no idea.

"I don't know what to say."

"You don't have to say anything, Em. It's okay. I just," Mer shrugs, "worry. I want you both to be happy and I haven't seen a whole lot of happy since I've been here."

"I'm not sure I remember what happy feels like with Lauren." I freeze with the bagel sandwich halfway to my mouth, not sure how that popped right out of my mouth.

"Wow." Mer whistles. "That's a heavy statement."

We sit quietly, my words hanging over our heads. It feels good to have finally said it. I know I should be saying it to Lauren, not Mer, but this is a good first step.

"Love changes over time, but I know you know that. Do you think your love with Lauren has changed too much?"

I take a deep breath. "Sometimes I worry that might be true."

"Oh, honey." Mer holds me and rubs my shoulder. "Em, you really need to sit down with Lauren and have an honest talk with her. Maybe she's feeling the same thing. Maybe she's not. You're going to drive yourself crazy if you don't get some answers, and I know how much of a pain in the ass she can be with avoiding conversations, but you have to push her."

"You don't know what she's feeling?"

Mer laughs. "I know less than you do, Em, you know that. Lauren talks to me about everything but her feelings. It's always been that way."

The sound of a car door slamming jolts both of us. It's not Lauren that comes around the back of the house, but Allison.

"Well, holy shit. You *are* alive." Allison stands before me, hands on hips, fury shooting from her eyes.

"Was there any doubt that I wasn't?"

"Other than the fact that you haven't responded to any of my texts or phone calls since seven last night? Oh, no, no worries. What the hell happened to you? You look like shit."

"I had too much wine last night."

Allison collapses into a chair at the table with us. "Did you and Lauren have a fight or something?"

"No." Quite the opposite, really, but I don't want to get into that with Allison right now.

"So you don't care that she and Sidney went out to The Plank last night?"

That gets my attention. "What?"

"Wait, Lauren didn't tell you?" Allison asks. Her face is etched with confusion and concern.

"Nope. I came home last night and she wasn't here. When I woke up, she wasn't here. I have no idea about any of this."

"It's not a big deal," Allison says quickly. I know she's trying to backpedal because she feels responsible for my feelings; she'll shoot straight with me, which is why I love her, but she has a nasty habit of taking on emotions that don't belong to her.

"Not your fault." Mer and Allison exchange looks across the table as I down more water, then abruptly stand up. "I need Advil."

When I come back to the deck, I recognize that I should say something but I'm at a loss. I can't be mad at Lauren for lying by omission because I'm doing the same damn thing. I'm bothered by the fact that she went to The Plank, one of the local lesbian bars, but I'm more irritated that she didn't let me know she was going out *at all*, and I'm especially unhappy with the fact that she went with Sidney, Ms. I'll Fuck Whomever I Want, Whenever, No Matter What My Girlfriend Wants. The only difference between Sidney and Lauren's previous lives is that Lauren didn't cheat on anyone, she just hopped from bed to bed. Sidney, on the other hand, gets a girlfriend, then continues to hop from bed to bed. A slash of hypocrisy skitters through my chest. I bite my lip against the feeling, reminding myself that nothing has happened. Yet. Dammit, yet.

The only thing I know to do right now is to change the subject. "How are things with Sidney?"

Allison shrugs. "Whatever." Well, that attempt went swimmingly.

"Have you had that talk with her?" I press, trying for gentle but probably missing the mark.

"Yeah, the same day I talked to you. She's fine with it." Allison doesn't exactly sound disappointed, but there's an unhappy note in her voice.

"What's going on?" Mer asks.

Allison nods at my questioning look. "Allison and Sidney are going to give non-monogamy a shot."

One of the things I absolutely love about Mer is that she can play along supremely well; if she were Lauren right now, she'd make a crack about how Sidney must have thought that was the plan all along. Instead, Mer says, "Right on!"

Allison widens her eyes at Mer. "What are you talking about?"

"Oh, girl, give it a shot! You can't tell me you haven't been tempted."

"I love Sidney." Allison shrugs again, but she's dropped her defensive look. "I figure if you love someone, that's the only person you should want to be with.'

Mer jumps in to list all the wonderful things about open relationships, and Allison, for her part, is at least listening and not rolling her eyes. She maybe even looks the tiniest bit interested and curious.

Funny notion, there: 'if you love someone, that's the only person you should want to be with.' What happens when you fall out of love, but still love? What happens when your past creeps up on you, waving its mysteriously alluring flags and tempts you into becoming something you swore you'd never be (again): deceitful? How the hell do you handle a situation where you can't imagine life without the woman you (still) love, but can't stop dreaming about what life could be with the woman you almost kissed last night?

"You can have all the vaginas you want, Allison!"

Allison is laughing; I'm vaguely mortified to reenter the conversation at this point. "What if I only want Sidney's vagina?"

"Be real. There is no one else you've thought about since you've been with Sidney?"

Redness seeps across Allison's cheeks, giving her away before she opens her mouth. "Okay. Fine. Maybe one or two women have caught my eye."

"What's stopped you?"

Allison snorts. "The fact that I thought my girlfriend and I are in love with each other and have a committed relationship."

There's another jab in my ribs.

"Fine. But now? Now you can be free and love whoever you want!"

I open my mouth to ask their opinions on this matter of love, but my mouth closes as Lauren comes around the side of the house, weighed down by a variety of flowers.

A vision of dirt and stray leaves, she gives us all a questioning look. "Having an intervention or something?"

"We're having a rather enlightening conversation about monogamy. Join us!" Mer gestures toward a chair.

Lauren's eyes flicker over to mine, and we look at each other for a moment. I can't read her expression, and I'm sure mine is just as clouded. I wonder, though, why we're *both* having this moment after Mer's statement.

"I think I'll pass. Em, can you help me with another load from the car?"

I excuse myself from Mer and Allison as they lapse back into their debate. I can tell Allison's coming around to the idea, even if it means she's opening herself to the risk of falling for someone else.

I follow Lauren to the car, and wait patiently for her to load my arms with flowers. Instead, she leans in and kisses my cheek.

"What's that for?"

"For looking as adorably hungover as you do right now."

"You know?"

Lauren laughs and begins filling my arms. "You were passed out across the bed when I came home. I tried to move you but you were dead weight, and you yelled at me."

"I yelled at you? Oh my God."

"You told me to back off, you'd cut me if I came any closer." Lauren laughs again. "I think that's the first time you've physically threatened me."

"Oh shit, I'm sorry, Lauren. I don't remember any of that."

"Judging from the empty bottle, I'd guess not."

Both of us armed with flowers and bags of mulch, we make our way back to the backyard. She's gotten an impressive array of plants and flowers for our garden—on my dime.

"And these," she rests her hand on two packets of seeds, "are for you."

I bend down to look at the label. "Snapdragons! You remembered."

"Just for you," she says.

"Thanks, Lauren. That's really sweet."

"Anything for you, Em." She kisses me softly on the lips. "Want to go out to dinner tonight?"

My head is swimming; is this my girlfriend? Is Lauren actually back? "Sure."

"Great. I'll make reservations." She turns to survey the backyard. "I'll be out here if anyone needs me."

I make my escape and return to the scene of my latest crime: my bed. I curl up against my cool sheets and feel around under the pillows for my phone. Sure enough, there are several texts from Allison and two missed calls. Another from my mom. Nothing from Lauren the previous night.

Nothing from Burke either.

CHAPTER SIXTEEN

Later that afternoon, I drag my less-hungover ass out of bed and walk over to the park for some sun and fresh air. Once I'm settled on a bench with a good view of the dog park, I call my mom back.

"Hi sweetie. Your dad and I are in Rockaway for the weekend."

That's news to me. I roll my eyes; she'll complain about not seeing me often enough, and then not tell me that she's less than three hours away. Typical mom-behavior. At her request, I tell her a few tales of my work adventures.

Then, no time like the present. "So, Lauren lost her job."

"Oh, yes, that's right. How's she handling it?"

A wash of cold rushes through me. "Did Lauren tell you she lost her job?" Please say no, please say no. SAY NO.

"Yes, sweetie, she did. Must have been a few weeks ago."

"Are you sure?" I ask, trying to keep my voice level. My leg is already jumping with anger.

"Yes, I know it was on a Monday. She called me in the middle of the day, which I knew was odd, and told me she'd lost her job."

I'm about to spit fury. I cannot believe that Lauren told MY MOTHER before she told me.

"What's wrong, Emery? You sound mad."

I force myself to calm down. "It's been a rough couple of weeks."

"Lauren hasn't found anything yet?"

"Haven't you been talking with her every day to know that?" Fortunately, my mom has become immune to sarcasm, the primary defensive communication my dad uses. Turns out, sarcasm is hereditary.

"Actually, no, I haven't spoken with her since that day I told you about."

That doesn't make much sense, but then again, what does right now? "No, she hasn't found anything yet."

"She must be so frustrated."

"She is. Like I said, it's been rough." I need to get out of this conversation immediately. "Mom, I have to go."

I shove my phone back into my pocket. Tonight is going to be tons of fun.

* * *

Lauren's made reservations at our favorite Italian restaurant in Sunnyside, so I pull on jeans and a long-sleeved T-shirt, pleased to at least be able to wear casual clothes. I'm also relieved she hasn't planned some big romantic, fancy date.

I sit down on the edge of our unmade bed and trace my fingers over the pattern on the comforter. Anxiety is building in my chest. The last time Lauren took me out for a surprise dinner, she dropped her no-job bomb on me. Despite how kind she was this morning, how *normal* she seemed, I can't shake the nervous feeling that another explosion is headed my way. Add to that my complicated feelings about Burke, and... well, it's just getting messy in my head and heart. Because Lauren and I have been together for so long, I feel required to try to make it work. And if Burke wasn't in the picture, I imagine I'd be doing a better job with that.

"Huh," I mumble. That's the first clear thought I've managed in a few weeks. Lauren is worth it—she's not perfect, but no one is. If she's willing to put an effort into our relationship, then I should be too. To her credit, Lauren's been doing more around the house. And she did remember the snapdragons. And now, she's taking me out to dinner. I can see her efforts, lined up in a straight line, waiting for my attention.

I just can't quite figure out why I can't seem to give them my attention. Is it Burke? Or Lauren? Or…is it me?

* * *

"The yard looks great," I tell Lauren after we order. The restaurant is relatively uncrowded and quiet for a Saturday night.

Lauren smiles at me from across the table. She looks tired, but her cheeks are aglow with a day's worth of sun, giving her a slightly impish look. "So how's work?"

"I'll be going to New York in a couple weeks," I announce. Nice segue, self.

"What for? A conference?"

"Yeah. Caren and I are going. We're taking some people from Whitmore too."

Lauren doesn't respond. I look over at her and notice that her eyes have traveled across the restaurant. It's likely she's found someone she used to know; that sort of thing happened a lot when we first got together, and I hated it. It seemed everywhere we went, one of Lauren's former conquests would show up, especially when we were out at a gay bar. Lauren was always good about it, making sure that I was introduced as her girlfriend and being affectionate with me in front of them, but I was bothered by it every time. I had to learn early on that there was no escaping Lauren Cabrian's past, because it was everywhere; *they* were everywhere.

A sharp peal of laughter from the foyer of the restaurant grabs my attention. My gaze fastens on the figure in a gray hooded sweatshirt and a baseball hat pulled low on her head. The lithe figure standing next to Burke is unfamiliar to me, but she's pretty in a conventional way, a kind face topped with a dark pixie cut streaked with deep red, and an open, laughing smile. Judging by their visible easy comfort with each other, I'd say she and Burke are quite close.

Burke looks happy. Her smile is bright as she rests her hand on her companion's arm, and the woman leans into her, laughing along with the hostess. Apparently, something is *very* funny over there. I grit my teeth against the second surge of jealousy that courses through my body and remind myself that I'm sitting here with Lauren. No need for jealousy!

However, I suddenly notice that Lauren's focus is on a woman standing in front of her. They're engaged in what also appears to be a happy, funny conversation. Lauren's smiling in a way I haven't seen in months, if not longer.

Frustrated, my attention diverts again. Burke's noticed me; she's looking directly at me. A mix of recognition, surprise, curiosity, and desire (yes, I recognize it now) laces across her features. She tugs a corner of her mouth into a smile and winks at me. Flustered, I smile back at her. We stay locked in that stare until her companion, pizza box and bag of food in hands, bumps against Burke and nods toward the door of the restaurant. They leave.

My eyes linger on the door for a moment or ten. I can hear Lauren continuing her conversation. I'm about to get up and head for a bathroom break when Lauren finally says, "Rachel, this is Emery."

Game face in place, I spin around in my chair and shake Rachel's warm hand. "Hi, nice to meet you."

A silence creeps over the three of us. I excuse myself and head for the bathroom even though a larger part of me really wants to head for the door and walk the hell home.

I return to find Lauren alone. Lauren is busy rolling and unrolling the paper napkin holder. She doesn't seem inclined to explain Rachel, and frankly, I don't want to ask.

"What did you end up doing last night?" The question pops from my mouth.

"Mer and I made enchiladas, then she went out with her new guy. I met Sidney for a couple drinks."

At The Plank. I fill in her purposeful blank, then decide to go ahead and push her. "That's nice. Where'd you go?"

"The Plank." One point for honesty. "It was pretty crowded, so we didn't stay long." I wait, knowing Lauren well enough to know she's not finished with her slow explanation. "We were at Delirium for a couple hours, I guess."

Delirium. You've got to be fucking kidding me. Lauren and I went a few times early in our relationship, and every single time she was encircled by women she'd slept with over the years. I tried to be cool about it, but even Lauren told me she didn't like it, so we tacitly agreed not to go to Delirium anymore.

"It was weird being there, you know?"

"Why was it weird?"

Lauren shrugs, looking uncomfortable. She shifts in her seat and avoids my eyes. "That part of my life is so over. Maybe I hadn't realized that, or I had, but...I don't know. It was affirming." Now she looks at me, her gray-blue eyes warm and inviting. "I'm really happy with you, Em. I love our life. Last night reminded me of how much I don't want that stuff in my life. I'm content with you, and us."

Stunned, I sit in silence. That was definitely not what I was expecting to hear her say.

Lauren seems to be waiting for my response, but I have nothing to give her. We sit in a strained quiet until Lauren breaks it.

"Do you remember Rachel?"

I shake my head, still unable to bring words out to the table.

"I knew her years ago," Lauren continues. "Anyway, she works for GreenSpace and said I should send my résumé in. She'll put a good word in for me."

"Did you work with Rachel in the past? Or intern with her?" Oh, hi, voice.

"No." Stilted pause. "We used to date. A long time ago."

"Oh." I stuff a forkful of noodles into my mouth to prevent pointing out that Lauren failed to introduce me as her girlfriend this time. The oversight was not lost on me. I'm just Lauren's dining-friend Emery tonight, and my old friend Burke stopped in the restaurant and knocked the air straight out of my lungs with a single wink.

"GreenSpace does a lot of work with the parks, right?" I ask, to make conversation.

"Yeah. It would be different work for me, but it sounds interesting."

"You should go for it." A little encouragement won't hurt, even though I'm pretty sure she's already decided to do so.

The rest of our dinner conversation is fragmented and light. I'm cognizant of the depth that's gone missing between us. Lauren doesn't seem aware of it, and while she doesn't bring up Rachel again, she keeps the conversation centered around easy, non-personal topics. I'm struck by how different tonight is from last night.

When we leave the restaurant, I realize two things: I forgot to mention to Lauren my revealing conversation with my mom, and I still haven't heard from one Burke Calloway.

* * *

"Are you tired?" This comes as a whisper against my ear; Lauren and I are lying in bed, both of us reading. The TV is on in the background, offering little more than low white noise and ever-changing flashes of color and light.

Lauren's hand moves across my stomach before I answer. I close my eyes and savor the feeling of her fingertips delicately stroking my skin. I've missed how well Lauren knows my body. I keep my eyes shut and turn my face to meet her waiting lips. I throw myself into that kiss, willing my body to respond.

Nothing happens.

After a few moments, I pull away from the kiss. "Babe," I whisper.

"Touch me, Em."

"Lauren, I—"

"Come on, baby, I need to feel you."

"I'm sorry," I whisper. "I'm just not there right now."

Silence spears the room.

"I guess I'm not either." She gets out of bed, walks across the room, and shuts the bathroom door behind her.

I flop back onto the pillows. Cold seeps through my body, the inevitable and unavoidable nudging its way into my cluttered thoughts.

When Lauren returns to bed, she shuts the lights off and lies down. I pretend to be watching TV.

"I do love you, Em."

I roll my head and look at her. She's looking at the ceiling, her face a perfect blank canvas. "I know, Lauren. And I love you."

"Maybe we just have too much on our minds?"

Guilt trickles through me. "Maybe." I hesitate. "Do you want to try again?" Part of me does. The other part is afraid to.

Lauren's hand rests on my thigh. "Not tonight."

CHAPTER SEVENTEEN

The air in Whitmore feels tense. I sense it the moment I walk in. I assume something's gone wrong again with the finance department since they have established themselves as the weakest link. Avoiding further investigation, I pop open my laptop in the conference room and realize there's a good chance that early morning meeting with Krista Whitmore and F-squared is still in progress.

Libby's left me a note about changes to the afternoon schedule. My hand freezes over my laptop keys as I read it. I can't believe I forgot that today is the day of the big conference announcement. Today I find out if Burke and I are going to be in New York together. In the same hotel. For an entire week.

"Don't even go there," I mutter. But it's too easy to go there, especially with the way things have been with Lauren. I try to focus on all the good, sweet things she's been doing lately, but how I feel about Lauren is very different from how I'm slowly understanding that I feel about Burke, and I am completely perplexed as to how to deal with this.

In the hallway outside the conference room Libby spots me and motions me to come out. "Emery, I need your help."

She looks frazzled, which is unusual for Libby, who is generally the consistently calm, cool, and collected head of our team. She also looks...different. I eye her curiously, but stealthily. I can't quite put my finger on what's changed about her.

"Did you change your haircut?"

"What? No." Libby's hand flies to her hair. "Why? Is something wrong?"

"No, you just look different."

Color washes from her face. "Great. Listen, I need you to run interference with Luke in his workshop right now. HR is not happy with the new email procedures. I can't believe they're reacting like this—they seemed fine with everything else, I just—"

I put a firm hand on Libby's shoulder. "I'll take care of it. Where are they?"

"Upstairs."

"On it." I look at her again, still unable to figure out what's changed in my normally relaxed leader. "Why don't you go sit down with a cup of coffee? You look like you could use a few minutes of peace."

She shakes her head. "Too much work to do today."

I wrack my brain as I climb the stairs—too much work today? I know there's that big meeting this afternoon, but I also know my schedule is relatively light. How is there such an imbalance? Am I forgetting something?

Upstairs, I see Burke at the end of the hall, talking with Krista. I guess the finance meeting is over. Way over, judging by the way they're looking at each other—it looks like they're mid-conversation, and disagreeing. Burke's arms are tightly folded across her chest, and her face reflects more of that serious self-protection. Krista is bent forward into Burke's personal space. My breath catches in my throat and I'm mortified to realize that I've stopped cold in the middle of the hallway. Their conversation is heated enough that they don't notice me. Burke slowly uncrosses her arms and takes a slight step toward Krista, who doesn't move in reaction. I realize that she's trying to get a point across to Krista—a point that Krista does not look very interested in hearing. Burke's fists are balled at her thighs. I don't think I want to see the way this conversation ends.

I slip into the room where Luke is holed up with the Human Resources gang. And a riled-up gang they are, which is surprising because they've been the easiest group to work with outside of the IT department. Considering there are only four of them, you'd think it wouldn't be so difficult to introduce them to a new procedure.

Luke gives me a look filled with gratitude as I walk over to him. He points to the next bullet point, and I cringe. If these ladies are reacting so poorly to step two, they are going to *loathe* step three. Luke and I quickly decide to split into two teams, which again seems ridiculous considering how small a group this already is. Right now, it seems like our best chance. I scan Luke's notes as he calls the ladies back to attention.

There's a knock before it creaks open. "Excuse me, I'm terribly sorry to interrupt, but I need to steal Emery for a moment."

"Oh, Burke, come in and join us! You'll just love what they're making us do with email." This comes from a disgruntled woman with whom I'm not familiar. I catch Charlotte shooting a death glare toward the woman, but she barely shrinks in her seat.

"Actually, I'm happy with the changes. I think they'll simplify our electronic communication and provide clear standards for all employees."

Disgruntled woman's mouth gapes slightly, and Charlotte sits back in her seat, satisfaction on her face. Luke's shoulders relax as he straightens, bolstered by Burke.

I step into the hallway. Burke smiles at me, but there's something about her expression that doesn't seem right, or familiar. "Looks like an exciting pow-wow."

"I actually just came in. What's up?"

"Are you free for lunch today?"

Hmm. Not what I was expecting. "I believe I am."

"I'll swing by your makeshift office around noon."

"I'll be there."

"I'm looking forward to it." She nods her head toward the room behind me. "Good luck in there. They're all bark and no bite."

I conspiratorially lower my voice and lean closer to Burke. "I think they're just pissed because they can't continue their inner-office email gossip train. You know HR always has the best dirt."

"Hmm, you're probably right. Maybe we should invite Charlotte to lunch so she can fill us in?"

I bite my lower lip, fighting the urge to run the tip of my tongue over the outline of Burke's ear. God, even her ears are sexy. Is that possible? "I think I'll pass on that."

Burke leans away from me. "Why, Emery, I do believe you want me all for yourself." She raises an eyebrow at me.

"Watch yourself, Ms. Calloway. I expect a certain level of professionalism from you."

"Oh, and nothing but." We lock eyes for a moment, neither of us in a rush to return to where we belong.

I playfully shove her away from me. "Don't you have work to do?"

"Always." She takes another long look at me, then shakes her head. "Till lunch, Emery."

* * *

At noon I'm more than ready to leave with Burke. The rest of the meeting with HR did not exactly go well. Luke and Charlotte are meeting with Krista for lunch and I'm grateful that no one asked me to come along.

Burke appears distracted. She fills our walk with looping chatter about her department, but the sentences and thoughts aren't linking. She sounds so preoccupied that I'm tempted to lay a hand on her forearm and tell her it's okay just to be quiet.

Sitting at a table in the back of the café, I take advantage of the fact that Burke has finally stopped rambling. "So, I saw you this morning. Talking to Krista."

Burke nods slowly as she chews her sandwich. "Krista and I sometimes do not get along." She shrugs. "And today is one of those times."

I wait for her to give me more information and watch a frown stretch across her face.

"It's complicated. I'm not proud of it, or happy about it."

"Burke, you don't—"

Her hand reaches over and squeezes my wrist. "Krista is the reason I don't mix pleasure and professionalism. I don't mean that she has enforced a policy against interoffice relationships, I mean that my past experience with her has taught me not to mix romantic relationships with professional relationships."

I was definitely not expecting that. Krista? Burke and Krista? Seriously? My head is already flooding with questions.

But instead of any questions about Krista, the first thought that makes its way to my mouth has to do with me. "Is that why…"

Burke nods, her eyes boring into mine. "Yes. That's why I didn't kiss you."

All the breath rushes from me in a fell swoop. "Okay," is all I can muster.

"Okay?" The teasing lilt is back in Burke's voice.

"Yes. Okay. It's okay."

"For the time being, yes."

Not forever. I check my watch, remembering I have a conference call with Libby and the New York outpost of Whitmore before the big meeting at three. The rest of my Krista-questions will have to wait. "I need to get back."

"Me too."

Our walk back to Whitmore is quiet, but not uncomfortably so.

She wants to kiss me.

* * *

"Have you seen the finalized lists?" I ask Libby, though really, it's against my will. I like a good surprise as much as anyone else. It's just that this particular surprise is causing me quite a bit of anxiety.

"I haven't." She exhales loudly and drops her pen on the table. "I am exhausted."

And she looks it, but I don't tell her that. "Are you and Luke getting a bit of a break when Caren and I are in New York? Or did you jam yourselves with too much work for two people?"

"Somewhere in the middle of that. We'll manage, I'm sure."

I pick Libby's brain for more information about the upcoming conference, wanting to make sure I have everything under appropriate control. This is the first time I'm going off to a conference without Libby there to guide me, and I'm looking forward to it as much as I'm nervous about it. Luke and Caren come into the room, followed by the full boat of Whitmore employees. Burke is deeply involved in animated conversation with two guys from the IT department and a woman from finance.

The room quiets as Krista enters, commanding attention in her sleek black pinstripe skirt suit with a silky-looking, low-cut pale pink shell. There's no ignoring her prominent presence, the sex appeal and power.

"Hi, everyone. Thanks for coming to this mandatory meeting." There's a smattering of laughter. Burke's attention is focused on her hands knotted on her lap. "First off, I'd like to congratulate you all on the progress you're making with our leaders from Pointworth. I've seen some great improvements in a variety of areas and I'm looking forward to seeing a continuation of that."

Krista motions to where I'm sitting with my team. "We're incredibly lucky to have this group working with us, and while I know we've hit some roadblocks with them behind the wheel, I do want to remind you that I'm the one who's handing out the road maps and directions. So quit taking out your anger on these kind people." More laughter.

Krista goes on about some upcoming events, and the product development department gets a hearty shout-out and applause for landing a new and lucrative client downtown. Charlotte steps in to hand out new consent forms about electronic policies, which does not go over as smoothly as we'd all hoped, but by and large most people are respectful if not respectfully ignorant. After a few sparse words from Seth, Burke's direct boss, Krista takes the main stage once more to announce the finalized list for the conference.

"Libby and I spent a lot of time working on this list. It wasn't easy to make this kind of decision, especially since so many of you have ties to our New York outpost and this trip will offer ample time to visit with them outside of the conference. So, without further ado or torture, here we go." Krista smiles broadly at her employees, nearly all of them looking at her with rapt attention, even Burke, though she also looks a little pissed off.

"From Human Resources, Charlotte!" Charlotte grins and waves to her cheering fans.

"From finance, Hank!" An older man with a wonderfully gentle but persistent demeanor, Hank had been my first pick. I'm also angling for him to take the still open managerial position in finance, but he doesn't appear to want anything to do with it.

"From the Research Team, Erin!" Another one of my picks.

"From IT, Alaina!"

A breath I didn't realize I'd been holding forcefully pushes its way from my lungs. I like Alaina. She's sweet, funny, and very smart.

But she's not Burke.

CHAPTER EIGHTEEN

"So."

"So."

The meeting has wrapped up, though a good deal of people remain in the conference room. As soon as Krista ended the meeting, I saw Burke make her way toward me, artfully dodging anyone who tried to speak with her. I wonder if the disappointment is etched across my face as it is on hers.

"Can I buy you a drink?" Burke asks.

"Yes."

"Hank's?" The pub Burke and I went to after the concert seems like a safe choice.

"Perfect."

"Meet you there."

We head out of the building and once I'm in the privacy of my car, I call Lauren. "Hi. What are you up to?"

"Same thing I do every day." I wince at her tone, which is layered with frustration and anger.

"Anything looking good?"

"Oh yeah, everything looks great, Em." And now, sarcasm. Lovely.

"You'll find something soon."

"Yup."

I roll my eyes, suddenly not feeling very guilty about going out with Burke again. "I just wanted to tell you that I'm going out for a few drinks after work."

"Have fun."

"Want me to bring home dinner?"

"No. I'll make the chicken."

"What time? I can be home for dinner."

"I don't really care what time you come home, Em."

Whoa. "What?"

"Go out. Have fun. I'll see you later." She hangs up.

I toss my phone onto the passenger seat and curse loudly. Yes, I know she's struggling, but not caring what time I get home? Really? What the fuck is that all about?

* * *

Burke already has a beer in front of her when I walk into the pub. My ordered IPA arrives a few moments after I settle in, and Burke and I sip silently. Her focus is stapled to her beer glass. I want to say she looks less irritated than earlier today but that's not exactly true. Her features soften with each sip she takes but the hardened energy surrounding her remains.

"I'm, uh..." Burke exhales a small laugh, then aimlessly scratches the back of her neck. "I'm disappointed." She stops there and shrugs, finally looking at me. "I don't know of any other way to say it."

"I don't want to assume..." I trail off, hoping she'll fill in the blank.

"I was looking forward to New York. The conference. With you. I'm truly disappointed that it didn't work out."

"Burke, it's not like you had any control over it."

She tilts her head to the side. "That's not entirely true, Emery."

"How? Krista and Libby made all the final decisions. I was asked just once for any input."

Just as Burke opens her mouth to speak, we're interrupted by someone calling my name.

I whip my head around to find Allison walking toward us. She wears no indication of suspicion, just happiness to see me. Still, my breath sticks in my throat.

"Hey! You're about the last person I was expecting to see here today." Allison squeezes herself right onto my bench. She smiles over at Burke before I have a chance to make introductions. "Hi, I'm Allison."

"Burke. It's nice to meet you."

"Likewise." Allison turns her attention back to me. "Rough day?" she asks, indicating our glasses. "It's a little early for empty beer glasses."

"Something like that," I say. "Burke works in the IT department at Whitmore," I add for explanation. "We were just going over…stuff."

"Stuff," Allison repeats, then rolls her eyes at Burke. "Is Em delighting you with tips on how to communicate better?"

"That she is. It is her specialty, after all." Burke winks at me and I'm relieved to see the Burke I know reemerging.

"Yeah, she's pretty good at telling other people how to speak effectively, but she definitely lacks that skill in her own life at times."

I give Allison a smile that hopefully relays the message that I am seriously contemplating maiming her, if not killing her. "You're so sweet," I say through gritted teeth.

"I think Emery speaks very well," Burke interjects. "I haven't had any problem digging past her layers of words and meanings."

"If only we could teach her to just *say* things instead of spinning around what she really wants to say," Allison says with a fake heavy sigh.

"Nah, that would take all the mystery out of her, don't you think?"

"Enough!" I jab Allison with my elbow.

Allison rubs at her wounded ribs and grins over at Burke. "Oh, I like you. You should come around more often."

"I plan on it," Burke says to Allison, but her gaze is steadily resting on me.

Allison looks back and forth between the two us and the prolonged stare we're caught in. I break it quickly. Allison is observant and I'm not prepared to explain anything to her. "What are you doing here, by the way?" Not my smoothest segue, but definitely not my worst.

"Oh." Allison's expression changes from curiosity to embarrassment. "It's a long story."

"Spill it."

"Em, you're doing a work thing," Allison says pointedly. "I don't think my social life should be a topic of conversation with someone you're working with."

"I'll excuse myself to get drinks. Would you like one?"

"No, but thanks." Allison waits until Burke is stationed at the bar before turning back to me, questions scrawled across her face. "And *who* is she?"

"I told you. Hurry up with your drama."

She glares at me before responding. "So Sidney and I are doing that open-relationship thing."

"And?"

"And…she's already talking with some woman who works here."

"Allison. You're spying?"

"No!" she cries. "No, Em, I swear. I just wanted to, you know, scope her out. Nothing wrong with that, right?"

I roll my eyes. "Sure. Have you met anyone yet?"

"Please, it's been, like, a week. Not even. I don't know how to do this shit. Lauren said she'd go out with me while you're in New York, though."

My girlfriend's going to take my best friend out to find a woman to sleep with because *her* girlfriend sleeps with everyone?

"She said you met Rachel?"

A vision of Rachel standing over Lauren just this past weekend rockets into my brain. "Yes. I did."

"Is she cute?"

"Yeah. She is."

"I guess Lauren thinks we might be a good match?"

"Who? You and Rachel?" I watch as Burke walks back toward us. She gives me a questioning look, and I nod, more than ready for her to sit back down, and beyond ready for Allison to take her leave.

"Yeah. No?" Disappointment flutters over Allison's features.

"I don't know her, Allison. I met her once."

"Oh. Okay." Burke sits down and passes me my beer. Allison, for once, takes a cue. "I better get back to work. It was nice meeting you."

"And you," Burke says, shaking Allison's extended hand. "Hope everything works out for you."

"Oh, it will. Somehow. I hope." Allison laughs. "Talk to you later, Em."

I stare down into my beer as Burke watches Allison leave the pub. "She looks familiar, but I just can't place it."

"She owns Perk."

"That's it. And you two are close."

"She's my best friend. And she's very, very complicated."

"Seems that way."

As Burke and I lapse into silence, I gaze around at the cluttered walls of Hank's. Burke interrupts my perusal of the bar by reaching across the table and gently unballing my fist, which I hadn't noticed I'd been clenching. She traces her fingers over mine, now relaxed and palm up. "I have more explaining to do, Emery."

If she keeps touching me like this, I'm not going to hear any of her explanations, so I squeeze her hand before pulling mine back to the safety of my lap. "I'm listening."

"I don't know how much of this you truly want to hear, or how much I need to tell you, but I think the best way to explain is to start at the beginning. Are you okay with that?"

"Absolutely."

"Krista and I were involved. Back when I lived in New York, she also lived there, and we were together off and on for a few years." Burke clears her throat and runs her finger around the rim of her glass. "Krista was a very, very large piece of my life during those years in New York. I'll admit, Emery, that for a long time I was convinced I would marry that woman. When she decided she wanted to join her dad in the family business, I was ring shopping. Then Krista called me and told me she was moving back to Oregon. Just like that," Burke snaps her fingers, "she up and left in a week. She didn't ask me to go with her. I was wrecked. As much as I wanted her totally out of my life, I kept letting her back in. She stayed with me whenever she came out to New York."

"So you two were in a long-distance relationship?"

"No. But I was spending most of my time waiting for the next time she'd come see me." Burke laughs and shakes her head. "Not once did I even go out with another woman before I moved back here. It's crazy to think—I lived in New York City for seven years and Krista was the only woman I allowed myself to be with."

"You must have loved her very much," I say quietly. I'm still not sure where this conversation is going, but just hearing how invested Burke was in Krista has given me a shaky feeling. It more than explains that interaction I observed this morning.

Burke raises her eyes to meet mine. "Yes. I did love her very much. But that was a long time ago." Burke signals our waitress for two more beers. "Eventually she offered me a job here that I would have been completely ignorant to turn down." Burke shrugs. "I knew it was time to grow up, and much as I loved New York, I also knew I wasn't doing myself any favors by staying there. I took the job and promptly decided I wanted Krista back."

My throat clenches. Yep, that's definitely jealousy I'm feeling.

"That was three years ago. For the majority of my first year working at Whitmore, Krista and I had a torrid affair completely out of character for me. I knew I didn't want to continue that kind of relationship and as you might imagine, the break-up process did not go very well."

"How bad?"

"Pretty damn bad. Let's just say my second year working at Whitmore was utterly hellacious, and I went as far as to accept a job offer back in New York before Krista and I were able to sit down with her father and work things out like adults."

"Oh, wow…her dad had to get involved?"

She shrugs again as a vaguely angry but helpless look passes over her face. "I asked him to. Krista was being irrational. I couldn't get through to her. Krista's father is the only person I know who can influence Krista to do the right thing, and so, here I am, still at Whitmore, still in Oregon, and reunited with you in a professional environment."

I steer the conversation back to the question that's nagging me. "Explain one more thing. How does all of this connect to the fact that you're not going to New York?"

Burke nods and looks at a spot on the table. "Krista knows that we'll never be together again and we usually get along within our working relationship. When we don't, it's ugly. That's generally because she's noticed I'm interested in someone other than her." Burke shakes her head. "I know how fucked up this is."

"She knows you're interested in me?"

"Yes. And she also knows that I'm having a hard time keeping *our*," she gestures to the space between the two of us, "relationship professional."

"How does she know that?"

"Emery, at this point, I think it's written across my face."

"So…you didn't…tell her?"

"I don't need to. She's seen us, she knows I'm very, very much interested in you."

I could let the conversation derail with that statement, but I need to get this completely figured out. "If she knows you're interested in me, but she also knows you refuse to mix work with pleasure, then why would she not send you to New York?" Even as the words leave my mouth, I know exactly what the potential harm is, at least for me and my increasing difficulty in keeping my hands off Burke.

Burke exhales deeply and loudly. "Okay, there's one tiny other thing."

She turns her once again emptied beer glass around in her hand, then sets it down silently. "Last month, I received a job offer from a company based in Brooklyn."

I stare at her, unsure what to say or how to react. The thought of Burke being on the other side of the country…

"Can we get out of here?" I ask.

"Let's go."

* * *

I step into Burke's loft and am immediately comforted. It's a beautiful, open, airy space with high ceilings and oak beams. The walls have been freshly painted antique white and are accented by modern but comfortable-looking furniture. A high-top table and chairs sit outside of the stainless steel galley kitchen. The wall at the end of the loft is almost all windows, and there's a clean shot of Laurelhurst Park beyond the small, but perfect for two people, balcony.

"What do you think?"

"I like it. It seems to fit you."

"I'm glad you think so." She nudges me toward the dark blue sofa in the middle of the room. "Have a seat. I'll be right over."

I do as instructed and sink into her sofa, which is much more comfortable than it appears to be. I have a few moments to take in the two paintings hanging on the wall across from me before Burke sits down.

I point at the paintings. "I absolutely love those. Where did you get them?"

"One-of-a-kind art, I'm afraid. Ariel, a good friend from my New York days, painted them. She kept art as a hobby for many years."

The slightly abstract depictions of the female form go far beyond a skill I'd consider to be a hobby. "That's quite a hobby. Does she still paint?"

"I'm afraid not. Ariel passed away a few years ago. She was an incredible artist and an equally wonderful person." Burke sits back on the sofa and slides an arm over the top of the cushions. "Life works in strange ways."

My traveling eyes fall on a framed picture that sits next to the TV. "Is that your sister?"

She follows my line of vision and nods. "Yes, that's the three of us—Bay, me, and Blake. My parents insisted on taking it when I moved home."

I'm doused with relief to be able to put the pieces together: Burke's companion on Saturday night was her sister. "You make quite a lovely group of siblings." The buzzing of a vibrating cell phone breaks into our conversation.

Burke strides to the kitchen counter to look at her phone, then excuses herself, saying it's her dad, and he only calls when it's important. She disappears into what I assume is her bedroom, and I'm grateful she hasn't yet given me *that* tour. I head for the bathroom and give myself a stern look in the bathroom mirror. My thoughts are tangled and torn up. For as much as I want to stay, I decide to make a quick exit and go home.

Burke emerges from her bedroom at the same moment I leave the bathroom. She apologizes for the phone call.

"I need to get going."

"You sure?"

No. I want to stay. "Yeah, it's been a long day."

I move toward the door and she comes to me, draws me into her arms and presses her lips against mine. I wrap my arms around her shoulders as the kiss deepens and extends. She nips at my lower lip until I part my lips and our tongues meet. One of us groans. When I dare myself to pull back slightly and meet Burke's eyes, I'm reduced to a puddle by the sheer, unguarded passion that is reflected in her darkened golden eyes.

Burke releases me, opens the door and stands in the doorframe. I don't have to look back to know that she's watching every step I take that leads me away from her.

I make it to the next landing on the stairwell before I drop down onto the steps and bury my face in my hands.

CHAPTER NINETEEN

There's no way I can go home after that kiss. I sit silently for a few minutes in my car, trying to determine my next best course of action. I mentally check all of my friends, mutual with Lauren and not, off my list of possible destinations, and simply start driving.

I cruise the streets of Portland in the cloak of night. At a red light, my fingers float to my lips and hover there, not wanting to make direct contact. Burke is still there, and I want to keep her there. The thought of that being our only kiss physically hurts.

Soon I find myself in front of an elementary school and pull into the parking lot. Again, I bury my face in my hands, and let the tears fall. This is not how my life was supposed to be; I am not the type of person who jumps at the chance to kiss someone other than the woman she loves, the woman she lives with, the woman she shares a life with. The thought of extricating myself from the life I've made with Lauren is too painful.

I angrily brush the remaining tears away and lean my head back to stare up and out my sunroof. "You're an idiot,"

I mumble, shaking my head. Yes, an idiot. And an asshole for not being honest with Burke. If I'm honest with Burke about how involved I am with someone else, there's no way she'll want to continue seeing me. If I continue to withhold that critical information and continue down this path with Burke—well, that can only last so long before chaos hits. Either way, I'm going to lose Burke.

And either way, I'm going to lose Lauren.

But the real problem is...I still don't know which part is worse.

* * *

I get home close to ten o'clock. I scrunch up my nose as I enter the house; the unmistakable scent of fresh paint hangs in the air. Nothing looks different. *Weird.*

My stomach twists as I ascend the stairs. The smell is getting stronger, and I realize it's coming from the master bedroom. Lauren is stretched out on the bed, watching TV, beer bottle in hand. She looks up at me as I enter, no readable expression on her face.

"What do you think?" she asks, gesturing toward the walls.

Gone are the relatively bland off-white walls; they've been replaced by a lovely pale sage green color that exactly matches the leaves on our comforter.

"I like it. It's a really soothing color."

"Yeah, it turned out pretty well."

"Mind if I open a window?" I ask and open two of the windows on the opposite side of the room from the bed. "It reeks of paint fumes in here."

I can't look Lauren in the eye. I silently change my clothing and head for the bathroom. An out pops into my mind as I return to the bedroom, taking in Lauren's extended form on the bed. She really is a sight to see, even at the end of a day that has clearly taxed her both physically and mentally. She's wearing soccer shorts and a plain white T-shirt and her hair is damp from a shower, pulled back into a low ponytail. Even relaxed, the muscles in her legs are defined and prominent. The only piece of her that looks any different from four years ago are the lightly shadowed bags under her eyes. They detract from her usually luminous gray-blue eyes.

I wait for my body to jump start at seeing Lauren this way, adorable and relaxed, clearly without a bra. I used to find her irresistible like this. Something about the laid-back jock look always made me need to ravish her.

"Coming to bed?" she asks.

"Yeah, but the fumes are so strong in here...I think I might sleep on the futon in my office."

Instantly, hurt falls over Lauren's face. "I don't think it's that bad, Em. I'm fine."

"Maybe because you've been around it all day? I don't know. It's making me kind of light-headed."

"Whatever." Her attention leaves me with the flick of her head.

"Babe, I'm sorry, I just can't handle the smell right now."

"I did this for you, Em."

"And I'm very appreciative of it, Lauren."

"So much so that you can't be bothered to thank me, or sleep in the same room with me."

Deep breath. I sit down on the edge of the bed. "Thank you for painting the room. I love the color, and you did a great job. I'm sorry I didn't thank you immediately."

"And now you're patronizing me." She stares at the TV and takes a drink from her bottle of beer. "Just forget it."

"No, I won't forget it. Lauren, I'm sorry for not being more...expressive with my gratitude."

"I just can't fucking do anything right for you anymore." The words may be fiery, but her tone is oddly cold, and distant.

That was certainly not the response I was anticipating. "What are you talking about?"

"Well, let's see. I lost my job, can't find a new one. I do shit around the house but you barely notice or care. And you don't want to sleep in our bed with me."

Somewhere in there is also the fact that I wasn't into it the last time we tried having sex. Her words fall over me instead of punching me like they would have in the past. I bite back my retort about how she dodged sleeping in *our* bed for weeks, and the fact that she lied to me for weeks. "I do notice, and I do care."

"It doesn't seem that way." She sits up straighter and draws her body away from me. "I want you to be happy, Em, and I don't think I'm making you happy anymore."

That one slices right through me. "Lauren, you do make me happy. It's just…things have been different lately. Difficult, I guess. Or just different. We're not so…connected anymore."

"And when I try to reconnect, you run away."

"That's not true." My guilt is slowly sliding into anger. "Do you realize how hard it is to have a real conversation with you?"

"Because I don't want to fucking talk all the time? I'm not like you."

"I don't expect you to talk all the time, but Lauren, we have to talk sometimes. We have to have real conversations. Sometimes we have to have hard conversations. We can't be in a relationship where no communication happens." I swallow hard before I take the next leap. "And we can't be in a relationship where we withhold really important information from each other."

"Maybe we need to change some things." How neatly she sidesteps my dig at her.

"Like what?"

"I don't know." Yep, effective communication begins here.

I wait for her to continue then say, "What kinds of things could we change to make this better? For both of us?"

"I think it's good that you're doing things without me."

Well, that's not what I was expecting, but then again, this is a woman who has become nearly a stranger to me over the past several months. "What do you mean?"

"You go out and do things with other people. I think that's good."

"And you'd like to do the same?"

"I have been."

That's right. She has. The image of Lauren and Sidney out at Delirium runs through my mind. "And do you still want to do things together?"

"Yeah."

"Okay, so we continue to spend time apart from each other, but also with each other. What else?"

This time, she supplements her "I don't know" with a shrug. Silence slicks itself between us, and we sit on opposite ends of a conversation that can't unfold on its own. Finally, she says, almost whispers, as if she doesn't want me to hear her, "You are the only woman I've been with that I can clearly see a life with, and I've fucked it up."

"Hey. Lauren. Stop." I rest my hand on her arm. "You haven't fucked it up."

"Look at us, Em. Look at us." She does look at me, and I see the tears lining her gray eyes. "We're getting further away from each other, and I can't find a way to bring us back."

"You're not in this alone. I have responsibility too."

"Yeah, but you at least try. You know? That night, in the kitchen? You made that happen. And I know you tried other times, and I just...I couldn't be what you needed."

"But you tried too. Like last weekend, with the flowers, and dinner, and after..."

"And look how well that turned out." Bitterness edges her voice.

"That was both of us, Lauren. Both of us weren't there."

"God, I don't know, Em, maybe we should...maybe we should just, like, back off from each other for a while."

"No," I say immediately. "I don't want that. I don't want to back off."

"I don't either, but I don't know what else to do. We're not okay. We're not us. And it keeps getting worse."

"So you think space is the answer?"

"Space, time apart, I don't know. Em, I love you like I have never loved anyone before. And sometimes that scares the shit out of me. Lately, it just hasn't felt like enough."

"Love isn't always enough," I say softly, more to myself than her.

"Maybe we need a time-out."

Anger surges through me and I stand up, unable to continue placidly sitting next to this woman that I have spent nearly five years building a life with while she sits there seemingly unmoved by the extreme range of emotions and ideas she's presenting to me. A fucking time-out? "What the fuck does that mean?"

"A time-out, time apart, I don't know. A break?"

"And what exactly do you think that will solve, Lauren?"

"It has to solve something. This isn't." She dismissively flicks her wrist toward the space between us.

"So, what? You want to see other people? Test our boundaries to see what we really want?" Now, the image of Burke kissing me pounds into my head, drawing my breath from me. I could easily go along with what Lauren is suggesting, but I'm terrified that it won't work out either way.

"No, Em, I don't. I just want to be on my own."

"Fine," I tell her, then turn and grab a bag from the closet. "Be on your own. I'll go stay with Allison."

"No," she says, and I hear her get off the bed. She grabs my arms and stills my motion. "I don't want you to go."

"You want to be on your own." My negative energy slides into fear that she'll take it all back. I don't know if I want to end things with Lauren, I don't know what I want to do with Burke. Hell, I don't even know what to do with myself.

"No. Yes. I don't know. But I do not want you to leave this house." Her grip on me is firm, and her body is pressed tightly against mine.

"Lauren, I don't understand what you want."

"I don't either, Em. I don't. But I know that I do not want to lose you, and I do not want you to be living somewhere other than here. With me."

"How do we have a time-out when we're sharing a bed?"

Her grip loosens and I'm able to turn around and face her. She pushes a few stray hairs off her face and her shoulders slump. "Maybe that's not what I want."

I throw my bag onto the floor next to her feet. "Dammit, Lauren! Fucking figure out what you want!"

She stares at me. Lauren and I haven't had many fights throughout our relationship, but when we have, she's been the one in a state of anger while I've generally been the one trying to keep everything peaceful while reaching a compromise. But I'm too pissed off and too confused to care about compromise right now.

"Seriously!" I continue, my rage exploding at her silence. "You're miserable. I don't know if it's me or the job situation, but you're a miserable person, and nothing I do makes you any happier. I can't keep trying to make sure you're okay while trying to handle my own life. Figure out what the fuck you want!"

"You," she says with no hesitation. She pulls me to her and kisses me fully on the lips, her hands moving instantly up my shirt. I gasp at her fingertips clamping down on both of my nipples at once. Lauren spins us around and pushes me back onto the bed, then drops herself on top of me. I move with her, removing all clothing separating us, and try to keep up with her hurried kisses and movements. I can taste the overwhelming flavor of beer on her lips and tongue. The moment she pushes inside of me, I clamp my eyes shut and order Burke to get out of my head. But she's all I can see—Burke kissing me, Burke running her hands through my hair. Burke slowly removing every piece of my clothing, that deeply shadowed cloak of passion on her face, hooding her eyes.

Meanwhile, Lauren fucks me with an intensity and drive I haven't ever felt from her, and it's not exactly pleasant. I manage to twist around and get inside of her in a maneuver that forces her to slip out of me. I push through my pervasive thoughts of Burke and let the mix of negative emotions fuel my fucking Lauren. She hovers in front of me on all fours, her eyes shut too, her mouth open and alternating between gasps and moans. I match the force she showed me and quickly drive her into an orgasm that floods my hand. I'm grateful when she drops onto the bed, still shaking slightly from the power of her release.

No sooner has her head hit the pillow before she's asleep. I realize that it's in my best, non-argumentative interest to go ahead and sleep in here. The open windows have helped the fumes, but it's chilly, so I pull on sweats and get back into bed. I allow the pain and uncertainty to lull me to sleep.

CHAPTER TWENTY

The past week and a half have been the longest of my life. There has been plenty of preparatory work here at the main office to keep me busy, and Caren has been more absent than we'd originally planned for, so I've had to work on some of her load as well. I don't mind the extra work part, but I've essentially been by myself in our corner of the office, and not having someone to bounce ideas off of has been difficult. I actually miss being at Whitmore too. As much as I enjoy having time to myself, this spread of time has not been entirely pleasant.

"New York, New York," I mutter to myself as I skim through my inbox. Great, another email notification for a change in presentation schedules, one that does affect me. I am definitely looking forward to skipping out clear across the country in just two short days, but I've had a perpetual knot in my chest for the past two weeks. Spending time with or without Burke hasn't improved it; trying to talk to Lauren hasn't improved it; focusing on my work hasn't improved it. I'm hoping that clarity will find me in New York—and I'm beginning to think it might actually be a good thing that Burke *isn't* going.

As if guided by their own will, my fingers click over my keyboard and mouse to open my Gmail account. There sits a pile of emails between me and Burke; email has become our preferred method of communication. I forcibly exhale and slap my laptop shut. I could lose myself in those emails but Caren is due back any minute, and work is waiting to be tackled.

I grab for my desk phone the moment it rings, hoping it's Burke.

"Wait till you get a load of this shit."

Oh, good, morning drama straight from Allison's mouth. "What's up?"

"Sidney hooked up with Cassidy again."

"You're kidding."

"I'm not. Can you believe that?"

"Um, actually, yes, I can. Sorry."

Allison growls into the phone. "Yeah, okay, I guess I'm not that surprised either."

"What's the big deal, though? I thought you were both seeing other people? Didn't you have a date this past weekend?"

"Yeah, I did."

"And?"

"And…it was fine. It was good, I guess. I don't know, I still love Sidney even though I'm really starting to wish I'd never met her. Or never fallen for her. Whatever."

"Tell me about your date." I sit back in my chair knowing I have some time to gossip before digging into work.

"Her name's Charlie, short for Charlotte, which she hates. She's really cute. Kinda boyish, totally my type. She works at an architecture firm."

"All sounds good. Go on."

"So, Charlie knows your friend Burke."

I sit up straighter. "She does?"

"Yeah, Charlie's good friends with Krista Whitmore. Thanks for telling me that your friend nailed the hottest woman in PDX, asshole."

"That's not really my news to share. And she didn't *nail* her, they were together for a long time."

"What I meant was, Burke still sleeps with her."

My stomach drops to my ankles. "What?"

"Krista told Charlie all about it. She sounds like a real bitch—whenever Burke tries to start dating someone else, Krista comes back to Burke and they hook up. Apparently Krista doesn't like Burke seeing other people. Did you know all that? I don't know how close you and Burke are, but damn, that bitch has one set of claws in her."

"I knew pieces," I admit. "How well does Charlie know Burke?"

"Not that well, I guess. She mostly knows Krista."

Recognizing that this could be a piece of mangled lesbian gossip-drama doesn't do much to make me feel any better. Burke would have no reason to inform me that she's sleeping with someone else. If Burke truly wanted to date me, then wouldn't she be trying to make that happen instead of passively sitting there, all her "no mixing work and pleasure" claims aside? It could very well be that she *is* still involved with Krista, and isn't pushing anything further with me because she's not done with Krista.

An incoming call on my phone beeps. Burke's work number is displayed on the screen.

"I have another call coming in. Gotta go. Call you later."

"Well, good morning, Emery." Burke's voice slides right through the phone and drips into my ear like honey.

"Hey. How are you?" I try to sound normal through my intense feeling of dread.

"Good. Hey, listen, I hate to do this but I need to cancel lunch today."

I push my head against the back of my chair and close my eyes. Lunch with Burke today was our last opportunity to see each other before I leave for New York.

"That's okay," I tell her even though I'm feeling the opposite of okay.

"No, it's not." Her voice is soft and warm. I can picture her sitting at her desk in the middle of the IT pit, trying to appear nonchalant to her coworkers while she quietly talks to me. "I know the rest of the week is packed for both of us, and I want to see you before you leave. Listen, do you think you'd be able to meet me for a preflight drink near the airport on Friday?"

"I think that could be arranged."

"Excellent. I have to go to another meeting, but Emery?"

"Yes?"

"I miss you."

Some of the tension leaves my body at the simple sound of those words. "I miss you too."

* * *

On Thursday night I find myself standing in front of my closet completely lost as to what to pack. I need to look professional, but I don't need to wear a suit every day, thankfully. On the flip side, Libby reminded me and Caren that we have some meetings with Very Important People who could have an impact on the paths of our careers, so I do have to pack a few suits. Begrudgingly, I grab for two pairs of black heels that I might be able to tolerate for a day's worth of schmoozing.

Thoughts of Lauren peck into my head as I start rooting around for the necessary variety of other stuff I'll need for the next week. Since the bedroom-painting debacle, Lauren and I have been quietly civil to each other. For her part, Mer has stayed out of it. She definitely knows something is going on, but I don't know if Lauren's talked with her about it. I get the feeling Lauren is keeping this to herself because neither of us knows what to say or do; that "time-out" conversation remains unresolved. There have been a few nights where Lauren has slept in the basement again, and two nights that I've spent the night on the futon in my office. I can feel the pieces that hold us together beginning to slide even further apart, and while I'm sure Lauren must be feeling something similar, neither of us has made an effort to push them back into place. Then again, maybe they can't be pushed back. Maybe neither one of us wants them to be.

As if on cue, Lauren enters the bedroom and sits on the bed. She watches me maneuver four suits into my hanging garment bag before she says, "Are you excited for your trip?"

I nod as I start rolling up shirts for my suitcase. "Nervous and excited, but mostly excited. It's kind of a big deal to be going without Libby."

"How many presentations are you making?"

"Eight."

"Wow, babe, that's a lot. By yourself or with Caren?"

I glance at Lauren, curious as to her sudden interest in my trip, also curious as to her renewed usage of a pet name. "Five by myself, three with Caren. She has a couple solos as well."

"Sounds like a big week for you guys."

"It is, but we're ready. I think so, anyway," I add as I stare down at my suitcase.

"So, I have a couple interviews this week."

"Lauren, that's awesome. I'm really happy for you."

"Thanks." She shrugs and leans back on her elbows. "I don't know if I'll actually be offered a job, but it's a relief to at least have an interview. Well, two."

"Did you get one at GreenSpace?"

"Yeah, Rachel came through. The other interview is at a newer engineering firm. It's out in Hillsboro so I'd have a half hour drive, but it's a good position. We'll see."

"Hey, a half hour drive isn't that bad. And if it doesn't work out, at least you'll be back in the interview game."

"Yeah. It's been a while. Mer and I were practicing last night." Lauren laughs. "She's the worst potential boss I've ever met."

I laugh too, just at the thought of the two of them sitting around role playing interviews. I can only imagine the kinds of outlandish questions Mer threw at Lauren. "Remember when Mer had that interview with a gallery in LA?"

"Oh, shit, yes. She was convinced the owner was hitting on her because he kept asking her about form and positions."

"Yes, and then his boyfriend walked in."

Lauren laughs and shakes her head. "Classic Mer moment."

"Did I hear my name, you silly bitches?" Mer pops her head in the doorway. She has paint splatters on her face and neck. "Shit talking, are we?"

"We were fondly recalling when you thought the gay gallery owner wanted to know your favorite sex positions."

Mer walks in and sits down next to Lauren. "Definitely one of my finer interviews. I think I scarred that poor man."

"Or you just gave him new ideas to try with his boyfriend," Lauren muses.

"Hmm, yeah, he was definitely a bottom. All ready for your trip, Em?"

"Getting there. Packing is the worst part."

"Ugh, I'm the worst packer ever." Mer elbows Lauren. "Help your girlfriend."

"No, it's okay," I say quickly.

Lauren grins. "Em's a little OCD about packing. She only trusts herself to make sure she has everything she needs."

I stare down at my suitcase and struggle to figure out what I'm forgetting. "Thanks for the distraction, but can you two please leave me alone to obsess over my packing now?"

Once I'm certain they're downstairs, I grab my phone—I thought I'd heard it beep. One new email.

Hey there,

I'm sorry, Emery, but I have to cancel our preflight drink. Work is always getting in the way these days. Have a safe trip. Good luck in NYC.

-B

CHAPTER TWENTY-ONE

There's just something about New York City streets: the crazed, constant movement, getting lost in the sheer volume of people, the buzz of excitement and possibility, the wild range of scents and even the sudden bursts of steamy air—everything. I love it here. That's not to say that I don't love Portland, but I am, after all, an East Coast girl by birth and heart, and this side of the coast—this city in particular—will always be thrumming through my blood.

Back when I was growing up in Philadelphia, my older sister was notorious for hopping the train in Newark and grinding the tracks up to Manhattan at any moment's notice. It was "the thing" for Helena and her high school friends, a way to avoid boredom, a prime way to escape parents and school. The summer before I entered high school, just a month before Helena took off for New Hampshire, she took me with her on one of her spur-of-the-moment day trips to the city, and I fell in love instantly. Helena knew the city as though it was ingrained in her memory from each trip she'd taken. Wandering through the city with her was the first time I remember seeing her truly happy even with her kid sister lagging behind, stunned by the buildings and people. She took me to Central Park and showed me her favorite thrift stores in the East Village. We ate dinner in a hole-in-the-wall restaurant in Little Italy and I've never again had pasta so perfectly cooked. Before we left (after my mom had called reminding Helena that I was still under their parental rule and I *did* have a curfew), Helena bought us coffee at a café near NYU and we listened to an open mic performance. It's the only time I've felt connected to her as a sister. I didn't want to leave the magic of the city but we caught a train and headed back to real life.

On every subsequent trip to New York I've tried to find that café. It's as though it existed only as a way to bring me closer to my sister, however fleeting, as she soon departed for New Hampshire. I find myself looking for the café again today, and again, of course, I come up empty. So I duck into the first coffee shop I pass on Mercer.

I settle in near the windows with a decadent-smelling large coffee and pull my phone out by habit. I'd sent Lauren a text yesterday morning from JFK; she'd responded with a simple "glad you're safe" hours later. Much like the past couple of weeks...or months...we haven't had much, or anything, to say to each other since then; I spent most of Saturday sleeping off my jet lag, and the majority of today prepping for my first presentation tomorrow morning. Typically, when I'm away for work, I'm on whirlwind trips that don't allow for much downtime and Lauren has always understood that our communication would be sparse while I'm gone. This trip is longer and I do have more free time than I normally do, but the truth is, I'm relieved to be away from her. I need a breather.

On the flip side of my heart, there's no way around it: I am going through serious Burke withdrawal. And even though I *know* it's what needs to happen right now, because I have to figure out what I want and what I'm doing, it still sucks. I wanted to see her before I left. That, at least, would have made the distance a bit easier to bear.

I sip my coffee and turn my gaze to the window. The streets are alive; it's nearing six o'clock, and the early spring air has everyone out and about. Part of the reason Lauren and I opted for the house in Laurelhurst was its proximity to both the park and the neighborhood, giving it that small-town feel which allows us to walk to restaurants and stores. I like to be able to walk to places instead of having to drive all the time, something I adore about New York. When I'm here for work I do my best to walk everywhere. It's like I need to absorb as much of the city as possible so I don't lose my connection to it when I'm clear across the country, living in a polar opposite universe. I snort, realizing how bizarre it is to be so equally in love with New York City and Portland. It nearly explains how split I am between Burke and Lauren.

* * *

"If I make it through a single presentation without openly cursing Luke, I will consider this trip a success."

I pass Caren my glass of wine and she takes a generous sip, shutting her eyes briefly as she swallows. "That bad?"

"Yes, that bad. You know I love the guy, but his methodical detailing of financial reports is mind-boggling. He needs to come with a cheat sheet. I have no idea what half of his abbreviations stand for!"

"And you've tried calling him?" I motion for my glass of wine, and Caren begrudgingly hands it over since the waiter has yet to return with her second glass.

"He's no help, Em. The man is going to get a very hard kick in the ass when we get home."

"Maybe we should ask to have him flown out for the week."

Caren throws back her head and laughs. "Libby would lose her mind. You know it's going to be hard for the two of them to manage without us."

"Usually is. Any idea what's going on with Libby?"

"No, but she doesn't look good, huh?"

I shake my head and tangle my hands in my hair, trying to finagle it into a presentable messy bun. "She seems exhausted. And frazzled. It's so unlike her."

"Yeah...I hope it's not something serious. Maybe the whole Whitmore project is wearing her down. It has been an...ordeal."

"It's been interesting," I add. "And all-consuming."

Caren nods, curling her fingers around the stem of her newly filled wineglass as she gazes at me with open curiosity. "In more ways than one for you, I imagine."

A blush creeps across my face and I try to wave her off, but it's no use. Having worked so closely together for as long as we have, I can't hide much from Caren. A sure sign that something is up with me is the fact that I've been dodging personal conversations with her for the past couple weeks. The jig is up: she's not going to back down until I give her information.

Part of me wants to unload and spill everything. But I don't want anyone to know about Burke because...I guess I want to keep it to myself. Keep it sacred. Keep it whimsically real and tucked safely into my heart. So I start with Lauren, since that's a much safer topic. "Lauren and I haven't been doing very well. We can't seem to make our relationship function the way it used to."

"Em, you know as well as I do that relationships evolve over time. You and Lauren will likely never have what you had in the beginning."

This time I do wave her off. "That's not what I mean. I wish I could say it started with Lauren losing her job and her lying about that, but if I really look at our relationship, there were cracks well before that happened."

"Like what?"

"We don't really...talk. And that's been an issue from the start; Lauren won't hesitate to tell anyone that I'm the talker, and she's the doer. We've never seen eye to eye there, and it used to work, or at least, I thought it did."

"What made that change?"

"Am I going to feel like I'm in therapy throughout this entire conversation?"

Caren laughs and shakes her head. "No. Promise. I'm just prodding you so you don't go off topic and leave me hanging."

"Sure you are. Anyway." I pause for a moment and scramble to find something other than Burke, but I know that's the truth. Until Burke popped up and I realized how easily she and I communicate... "I guess it's just been my interactions with friends, and seeing Allison's relationship with Sidney fall apart. Outside elements have helped me see my own relationship more clearly."

Caren eyes me intently. There's a good chance she knows what I'm not saying, but she'll let me get there on my own. "So other people's relationships have affected yours?"

"Not affected. Just changed my line of vision, I guess. And then the whole lying about losing her job thing. That really damaged us, more so than I've let on."

"But you have told her so?"

"Yes. But the conversation surrounding it wasn't exactly fulfilling."

"How are things now?"

I shrug. Good question; I'm not sure I know how to answer it since I can't seem to figure that out for myself. "Unsteady?"

"Why are you unsure? I mean, Em, you've spent a lot of time with this woman and you haven't seemed happy with her for quite a while. If I can see that, then you must know it."

I fiddle with my napkin before looking at Caren. "How long have you seen that?"

She chews her bite of steak for a long minute, a thoughtful expression plastered across her naturally pale face. "At least seven, eight months."

I'm relieved to know it hasn't been *just* since Burke has been around, but then I'm slightly mortified to hear how obviously unhappy I've been—when I wasn't even aware of it. "Really? That long?"

"Yep. Nothing specific—you didn't tell me about a fight or anything. It was just like, one day you didn't talk about Lauren the same way anymore and from that point on you talked about her less and less."

"We had a pretty awful fight the other night," I say quietly.

"How awful?"

I give Caren the rundown of the "time-out" argument, not bothering to avoid any direct quotes from Lauren. With each quote, Caren's pale green eyes widen more and more.

"Jesus, Em. That sounds like a total mess."

"For all I know, Lauren could be bringing someone home this week and it would be acceptable."

"No, that's not acceptable. You didn't break up."

"I know that, but time-out? A break? Time apart? C'mon, Caren, that screams 'Let me see other people.'"

"True," Caren agrees, "but did you argue with her? Say you don't want that? I don't believe you're okay with the idea of Lauren running around looking for someone to bang while you're away."

I spin my fork around my slowly emptying plate of chicken marsala. "In some ways, yes, I argued. But I wasn't exactly… adamant."

"Because?"

"Because I'm not exactly…innocent in all of this."

Caren nods slowly as she sits back in her chair, a satisfied look on her face. "Interesting. Go on."

I hesitate, not sure how much I'm willing to say. "My interest has been diverted."

"Mmhmm, that's a very polite way of saying you're seeing someone else."

"No, not seeing," I reply quickly, even though I know it's a very thin lie. "Just getting to know."

"Intimately?"

"No more than kissing." Caren doesn't need to know just how diverted my interest is.

Caren leans forward. "Emery. Are you cheating on Lauren?"

I sigh. I can't lie anymore. "Technically, I guess I am."

Her expression suddenly changes, and a smile lights up her face. "Well, this is an interesting spin on things," she says through her smile.

"What are you talking about?" I turn to trace her look across the restaurant, but see nothing. When I turn back around, the seat between Caren and me has been filled.

By Burke.

* * *

If I thought New York streets were magical before dinner, walking through Chelsea after dinner with Burke by my side makes them even more enchanting. Being here with Burke gives me a strange sensation of feeling like I'm home.

"I still can't believe you're here," I tell her, smiling as she wraps her arm around my waist.

"Funny thing, food poisoning. It comes out of nowhere, and whacks you down pretty hard. I feel bad for Alaina but to be honest I'm feeling pretty good about being here."

"You must be feeling rather proud of yourself, too, letting Caren in on your little secret and her telling you where we were having dinner." I gently elbow Burke in the ribs. "I can't believe you didn't tell me you were coming."

"I wanted to surprise you. And for the record, I didn't lie on Friday; there really was a network issue I needed to fix."

"Sure there was."

Burke says softly, her lips precariously close to my ear, "Is it just me, or does this little walk we're taking feel familiar?"

I nearly stop in my tracks when I realize she's right—we're just a few blocks from the 18th Street subway station.

"I thought we could take a little spin down memory lane. You know, we walked this very path six years ago."

"Just think—if only you'd asked for my number that night."

Burke looks over at me. "Things were too complicated then, Emery."

"I know," I say softly. They're not that much less complicated now, but unfortunately I'm the only one who is aware of that minor detail.

"There's just one more thing before we go back to the hotel." Burke stops, pulls me to her. There, in the middle of the sidewalk on 7th Avenue, she kisses me fully, warmly, and passionately. I melt into the kiss, returning every surge of its intensity. Neither one of us seems interested in pulling away, both of us choosing to look past the bold, and reckless, openness of this kiss and its need to take place right here, in a spot where this exact kiss could have occurred six years ago.

Burke finally pulls away, and we stare at each other for a heated moment before, in tandem, we turn and walk uptown.

CHAPTER TWENTY-TWO

As I'm leaving my first and only but troublingly long presentation on Tuesday afternoon, my arm is grabbed from behind. My autopilot response is to shake it off and plow ahead; I'm tired of fielding questions only remotely related to the dazzling information I just delivered. I need fresh air. I need a freaking break. I do not need to be further interrogated or, really, even complimented.

Instead of running away, I steel myself with a ready smile before turning around. It's fortunate I put that smile on: standing before me is Anne Bridges, one of the three founders of PLAC. She is the picture of marketing perfection, dressed in a tailored charcoal power suit and heels that would cause me to fall over dead if I were ever to attempt walking in them. Anne's honey-blond hair is shining about her shoulders, ready to be tossed at a moment's notice. Her smile is probably a thousand times more genuine than what I fear is stapled onto my own astonished lips.

"You're a difficult woman to get a hold of, Emery," she says, quickly and seamlessly steering me away from the stream of people flocking around us. "I've been searching for you since Sunday morning!"

I curse myself for my habit of fleeing immediately from my own presentations as well as those I've attended—an attempt to be away from the crowds *and* connect with Burke as often as possible. Truth is, that's been difficult as we're both caught up in this conference more than either one of us expected. But that's no excuse for seemingly hiding from Anne Bridges. One does not avoid Anne Bridges!

"I did find Caren," she continues, a bit to my chagrin. "She told me I absolutely must catch your presentation on Nonverbals in the Workplace." She leans in as if we're sharing a secret and I catch the distinct scent of Chanel No 5. Of course Anne Bridges wears Chanel No 5. Classic, lofty, and distinguished. Anne Bridges *is* Chanel No 5. "I have to be honest, Emery, your presentation was a hell of a lot more entertaining than most of the drudgery I've observed. I don't know how you captivate your audience so effortlessly, but it was impressive. Some of your fellow presenters should take some cues from you."

Now I'm seriously embarrassed, but for all the right reasons. Getting face-to-face positive feedback from Anne Bridges is practically unheard of. She has a bit of a bulldozer reputation throughout the company and Libby has many stories to tell, none of which are particularly pleasant. I've had just a handful of previous encounters with her, and while I knew she knew my name, I had no idea she paid any further attention to me.

"Wow," I manage, bracing myself against the wall behind me, trembling a bit at this unexpected showering of positive attention. "Thank you, Mrs. Bridges. That's unbelievably kind of you to say."

A manicured hand waves away my idol worship. The flickers of light bouncing off her large but tasteful jewelry nearly blind me. "Kind, yes, but true, Emery. And you know that as well as I do."

Well, clearly this is no time to be humble! I shrug a bit, then say, "I do seem to have a way with people."

Her deep, throaty laugh would turn heads and then keep them focused if they hadn't already noticed her classy and classic good looks. If I have any chance of looking as good as she does when I'm sixty-two, sign me up.

"That's putting it lightly. And we have noticed," she says with a conspiratorial wink. "I checked your schedule; you're free tomorrow after three." Something to learn: the phrasing of a direct statement that should, or at least *could*, be a question, but is presented as a fact, and a fact that is under the control of the speaker. Anne Bridges has that skill on *lock*.

"Yes, I am."

"William and I have reserved a table at Craft at seven. Just the three of us; unfortunately, Robert has other plans and, well, you know how he is," she notes with a dismissive flick of her wrist.

Actually, I don't know how Robert is because I've only seen (not even met) him once, but he appeared to be a friendly man. William, on the other hand, is a bit on the intimidating side. A trickle of nerves starts its way down my spine.

"Sounds great," I say, hoping I sound more confident than I feel.

"Oh, it will be. Have you ever been to Craft?" I shake my head, and Anne's eyes widen. "You will absolutely love it. We will dine on delicious food and have an exciting conversation." She squeezes my shoulder and spins to depart. "See you tomorrow at seven, Emery!"

I lean back against the wall, caught in a cloud of Chanel No 5 and Anne Bridges' exhilarating dust. My mental footing scrambles to steady itself and make sense of that surprise encounter. I knew to expect a sit-down with some of the higher-ups…I just hadn't realized how high-up I'd be stretching on this trip.

* * *

By the time I make it outside, dumping myself directly into the so not refreshing humid New York City air, my head is spinning with possible reasons for and outcomes of tomorrow's dinner meeting. Is it even a meeting? Or just a friendly business dinner? I stretch back over the conversation with Anne and recall her note of "just the three of us," which means that not only will Robert not be joining, but also Caren. Anne made it clear that she'd run into Caren and likely told Caren she was looking for me, so Caren will have questions...

"Shit," I mumble. My head is so jumbled and my body so hell-bent on speeding its way back to the hotel that it takes Burke yelling my name before I stop in my tracks and wait for her to catch up.

She touches my elbow when she reaches me, gently guiding me back into the stream of pedestrians littering the sidewalk. Her touch, though just as simple as Anne Bridges', sends desire scampering through my nerves. "Dare I ask whom you're running from?"

"Was I moving that fast?"

She laughs, and a blanket of comfort flitters over my entire body, slowly easing my muscles from their tense holds. "For Manhattan standards, no. Portland? Yes. So, for you? Sort of." Her hand moves seamlessly from my elbow to the small of my back, and I feel my body lean into her touch despite the thickness of the air surrounding us. "Everything okay?"

"Yes. Essentially." I shake my head against my fragmented speech. "I'm sorry; I'm just a little overwhelmed."

"I have an idea."

"I'm listening."

"Go to your room."

"Okay, Mom."

She rolls her eyes. "As I was saying. Take a long, hot bath. Soak until you can't feel your skin anymore. Get out; get dressed. Meet me in the lobby at seven."

I nod slowly. "I can do that."

"Good. I'll be waiting."

* * *

When I emerge from the tub nearly two hours later, I can, in fact, barely feel my skin, and my thoughts have melted into a fine liquid. I still haven't neatly compartmentalized my thoughts but I'm closer to being able to see things for what they truly are, as well as what they may be.

I don't know what Burke has planned for us tonight, but no matter what it is, I already know that I'm not strong enough or willing enough to dodge her affections. I want her.

Burke is waiting in the lobby, just as she'd said she would be. I spot her the moment I step out of the elevator and am instantly relieved to see that, like me, she's wearing jeans and a T-shirt. The look on her face as I approach her is enough to pop the last balloons of Lauren-related-anxiety. Yep, Burke. I am falling madly in love with Burke, and one look from her can undo me just as easily as it can piece me back together.

I may not understand much about life or love, but that… that I understand.

A couple hours later, we're wrapping up a casual dinner. At my prodding, Burke tells me an adorable story about realizing she was gay while still in elementary school.

I shake my head in disbelief. "I can't believe you knew you were gay at the age of ten."

"I'm telling you, blame my parents. I knew what gay meant from the time I could speak. Bay came out when he was eight!"

"So even though you knew you were gay at ten, you still didn't have a girlfriend until you were nineteen? What am I missing here?"

"I didn't want to be anyone's experiment." Her serious expression connects directly with the honest simplicity of her answer. "What about you? When was your great awakening?"

"Well, I had my first girlfriend at the age of sixteen. We were on and off for three years. But I don't think I really understood that I was gay, then. I just liked her, she liked me, and so it was."

"How innocent," Burke says with a wink.

"It was! Until I went to college and cheated on her, which apparently you're not supposed to do…" I trail off as I realize what I'm saying.

"Yes, typically, relationships are between two people," Burke says calmly. "Unless otherwise negotiated, that is."

A sudden quiet falls between us, and we both avoid each other's eyes. Burke's sudden pull-back is surprising and confusing. I'm struck with the seriousness of the moment and fall into it, thoughts scattering through my brain, until I tune back in and hear Burke say something about a meeting tomorrow.

"I'm sorry, what did you say? I spaced out for a minute."

Again, with all the calmness in the world, Burke returns her credit card to her wallet and repeats what she just said: "We should meet for drinks tomorrow night. I have a meeting with a company in Brooklyn at five."

My stomach tightens. "What kind of a meeting?"

Burke shrugs. Her nonchalance is all at once hot and irritating. "A meet and greet."

My brain files through information about Burke and her past in New York. And then I remember: we were sitting in Hank's. Brooklyn. Job offer. Still on the table. "An interview?"

This time, instead of a shrug, I get something that looks like a wince. "Not exactly. It's an opportunity for me to...scope things out."

"So you can decide whether or not you take the job that's already been offered to you?"

Now she meets my eyes and I'm pushed back against my chair by the intensity she can't hide in them. "Opportunity is a funny thing, Emery. Turns out there's no rules or guidebook that tells you when you should just go for it. So, do you? Or do you let it skim past you yet again?"

The flare of heat between us is sparking and all-consuming; I can't think about anything other than her lips on mine, her body against mine. When she stands and waits for me to follow her lead, I don't say a word. I can barely keep my eyes off her. And when we finally make it back to our hotel, I don't hesitate in punching just one number in the elevator.

* * *

My heart feels like it's beating out of my chest, and my hands are stuffed in my pockets because I know without looking that they're shaking. Burke is the picture of cool, calculated calmness; the casual movements of her body show no nervousness.

Her hotel room is dark, but I can make out the same placement of furniture as my own room. The smell is entirely different, though; I inhale deeply and take in the clean, crisp scent of Burke's skin. The scent slowly becomes more powerful, and the sudden heat on my back warns me of Burke's proximity. I lean back against her, and her arms wrap tightly around my waist. "I think we've waited long enough," she whispers into my hair, then turns me around to face her.

Her mouth crushes mine; our kiss deepens to the point of making my knees weak. Her hands are on my hips, and my palms cup the taut lines of her jaw. She maneuvers me up against the wall and presses the full length of her body against mine. A gasp escapes my lips and my body automatically presses against hers. The firmness of her body begs my hands to travel down. I skim the fibers of her shirt with my fingertips, then slide my fingers over the smoothness of her arms. Burke moves against me, pushing our breasts together. She pulls away suddenly and meets my eyes. Both of us are breathing heavily, our eyelids hooded with undeniable desire.

Burke pushes me to the bed then takes her shirt off. Before I can draw my eyes over the contours of her exposed skin, she is on top of me, reigniting our fiery kiss. My hands reach to pull her head closer to mine. Our bodies move together through layers of clothing as we kiss; when I try to roll over to get on top of Burke, she presses her body harder against mine, making it clear that she will remain on top. That simple move of domination soaks me further, as if I weren't already wet.

Her skin is satin beneath my fingertips. I reach up to her breasts and feel the hardness of her nipples straining against the fabric of her bra. As I grab one nipple between my fingers, Burke moans quietly into my mouth. Soon, her hands have moved from my hair to my shirt and she tugs it off me. The break in our kiss is long enough for us to lock eyes as she moves back to my lips, but Burke cuts the gaze short as she pulls my lower lip between her teeth and my body bucks against hers as my eyes flutter shut.

She removes my bra with a swift one-handed movement, and my breasts spill out to meet her touch. Burke sits up enough for me to pull her bra over her head then slowly lowers her bare breasts to rest against mine. Our breathing ragged, we press harder against each other. Burke kisses the line of my jaw as one hand strokes my breast and the other tangles in my hair. I clasp her naked breasts and my fingers fan out over the insanely soft skin. Her breasts are surprisingly full, her nipples hard but small, and absolutely perfect. My entire body responds with crackling fire to the way her breasts feel in my palms.

"You are so beautiful, Emery," she whispers, her mouth moving to my nipple. Caught between her words and her stroking tongue, I groan and squeeze her nipples between my fingertips. She responds with a guttural groan and increases her tongue's movement over my nipple. Our movements shift from belabored passion to an absolute, silent but *loud*, need to fuck.

Burke strips me quickly and pulls off her own jeans as well. She returns to me with an explosive kiss, one that makes my entire body break out into goose bumps. My hands travel the length of her torso, slip ever so slightly under the band of her briefs. She shifts enough to move my hand away, and I grab her in need and frustration. My hands fall away from her as she shifts and my nipple is again taken captive by Burke's mouth; her tongue draws circles around it before her teeth clamp gently over it. A loud groan escapes my mouth, one that lingers and draws out as her hand finally, with painstaking slowness, travels down the length of my torso.

She rests her cheek against mine, and I stroke the smooth expanse of her back as her finger slowly traces the valleys of my arousal. As her thumb glides over my hardened clit, I jerk against her and again reach to find her own wetness. Burke gently moves my hand away and places it on her breast before looking at me with impossible gentleness and saying, "Emery, tonight is for you." I gaze up at her in wonder, but lose my response in the feel of her thumb circling my clit.

When Burke's fingers slide inside me, my eyes flutter shut. She holds me to her while effortlessly pinning me down and moves her fingers until my back arches and my hips press down harder. Her face next to mine, I feel and hear the sharpness of her inhale and my lips graze the top of her head as her fingers move inside me. I don't want this feeling to ever leave; the feeling of Burke's skin cascading over my own is enough to bring me to the edge of orgasm, and the simplest touch from her threatens to push me over the edge.

Soon, too soon, Burke's pulsing brings me soaring into a crashing orgasm. Burke grabs me to her, her fingers still deep inside me, and kisses me hard. I grasp for her, my hands scrambling for something to hold on to. She slowly slides out of me and takes my hand in hers. I grasp her fingers with a pulsing urgency; this moment cannot end.

"I will never get enough of you," she breathes into my mouth. "I want to have you all the time."

"Please," I manage. "Please do."

Her fingers drop mine, then find their way back down and glide back inside my wetness. I reach down to her hip, forgetting her desire to remain untouched, and quickly slip two fingers inside her. She grasps my hand and pins it over my head, stares down at me. We look at each other in the haze of desire and a look filled with such power that I can see the words "I love you" dancing in her vibrant brown eyes, and I've no doubt that she can see the same in mine, and yet we are silent. Caught in the moment that exposes everything we've been weakly attempting to avoid or hide, in this heated gaze we are fused together and there is no turning back.

* * *

Burke lies next to me, her arm wrapped around my shoulders, pulling me to curl around her side. My fingers lazily move over her breasts, and she touches my hand and interlocks our fingers. Her body fits between the spaces and over the curves of my own; the familiarity of our near nakedness is surprising and intoxicating.

"So…" she says, and I can hear the smile without looking up to see it.

"That was fun."

Burke laughs, shaking my body against hers. She tightens her hold. "Fun's a good word. Yes. Definitely fun."

"You know I want to ask…"

"Of course you do. And I don't have a bigger answer than what I already told you: I want tonight to be about you."

I prop myself up on an elbow and look down at her. She smiles at me, reaches up to run her thumb over my cheek, then my lips. "But I want to make love to you. Now."

"I don't doubt that, Emery." Her look deepens, and a single conflicted emotion swipes over her features. It's gone before I can identify it. "Maybe I just prefer to leave a little mystery the first time."

I mull that over. It *is* definitely Burke-like, and combined with what I now know is her understated but definite sexually assertive presence, it makes sense. I can let it go, but… "Just so you know, I do want to touch you. Very much so."

"I know. I can tell." She pulls my face down to hers and kisses me with that gentle command for control. "Maybe next time."

Against my will and desire to get her to cave and let me touch her tonight, I fall into that kiss and end up on my back, again, with Burke on top of me. Her hands explore the length of my body, stopping to cup my hips, and lingering to stroke that soft spot behind my ankles. Her mouth soon moves, again, to my waiting breasts, and her fingertips find my clit as her tongue teases my nipples. She strokes me softly and evenly, bringing me closer and closer, but not enough to make me explode. With the silent skill of an animal stalking its prey, Burke moves her body down mine, and lowers herself between my hips. After a single, luxuriating gaze up my naked, quivering body, she brings her mouth to my lips and separates them to find my swollen clit aching and waiting for her tongue. I gasp involuntarily as soon as her tongue makes contact with my clit, and her hands draw up to my hips to keep me locked down to the bed. She circles and strokes my clit, her tongue never wavering from its position. My hands clench and grab at the sheets below me. I feel a hot, furious orgasm building inside of me; its first pulses send me shaking against Burke's mouth, and she increases the speed of her tongue ever so much. For a slow moment, I am paralyzed beneath her, and then, suddenly, my world explodes in white-hot fireworks as the orgasm takes me. My body jerks and arches, pushing into the limits of the orgasm, and Burke rides along with me, never moving her tongue from my clit. As I start to come down, she sucks my clit into her mouth and holds it in the wet warmth; my limbs soften and after a few final twitches, I melt into the bed and wait for Burke's body to cover mine once again.

CHAPTER TWENTY-THREE

Sometimes I think I could be content being nothing more than an observer of life. People are fascinating in virtually every dimension; the way they walk toward a counter to get coffee, the way they interact with the barista behind the counter, even the way they settle into chairs, coffee in hand, rubbing the bleary morning from their eyes. It's those little quirks—the way a palm slides gently, almost thoughtlessly, across a cheek, or the fury with which another person digs the heels of her hands into her mascara-smudged eyes—that begin to round out the initial, knee-jerk perception of someone. That's how it is for me, anyway. Much as I'm compelled to judge someone upon first meeting, I've learned to examine the quiet details of a person because that's where the mystery leaks out to reveal a greater portrait of who that person truly is.

Burke is *not* a morning person. When she woke up, she turned away from me immediately and burrowed deeper into her pillow. I put a cautious arm around her and she snuggled back into me with a grunt. That was the extent of her communication with me until she was fed and plied with coffee. Once the calories and caffeine made their way into her system, she gave me a lopsided, sheepish grin and said, "So, now you know I don't handle waking very well…"

The swirling memory of Tuesday night with Burke pings my stomach now, reminding me that I haven't seen her since we parted ways after breakfast yesterday. As the luck of a business trip affair would have it, our schedules have been polar opposites and we both had commitments last night. We've had to muddle through our time apart with strings of text messages. Things actually seem to be…okay. Neither one of us appears to be overreacting, or diving in head first, or nipping at the edges of regret over the affair we've walked into.

Affair. Yes, that's it. I'm having…an affair. The excuse: Lauren said we should take a break. The problem: Burke still doesn't know it's an adulterous affair.

My leg begins its new and annoying habit of jittering under the cloak of the table. Caren is fifteen minutes late for our breakfast catch-up session and I'm starving, not to mention antsy about telling her why Anne Bridges wanted to see me for dinner Wednesday night.

Caren bursts through the door of the café and throws herself into the chair opposite me. "Coffee. Need." She reaches for my mug before I can respond, and I signal the waitress.

As soon as the waitress departs with our order, I blurt out, "I got a promotion."

Caren cocks her head at me for a moment, and I can tell she's trying to digest what just spewed from my mouth. "What?"

"A promotion. I got a promotion."

She nods slowly, the information seemingly making its way past the semi-caffeinated blockage in her brain. "A promotion."

"I'm going to be taking Libby's spot for a while."

Her eyes are wide—with anger or disbelief, I can't tell. "Why are you taking Libby's spot? And I'm not asking that, like, why are *you* taking her spot, I'm asking, why are you taking *Libby's* spot?"

"She's pregnant." I grin. "Totally knocked up. And, even better, with twins."

At that, Caren starts to laugh, and something inside of me releases; I'd been worried that Caren would resent the fact that I was tapped for Libby's position. When Anne Bridges offers you an opportunity like this, you do not decline for fear of what your friends who also happen to be your colleagues will think or how they will react. You say yes immediately and graciously. Which is precisely what I did.

"So, what does this mean for you, exactly?"

I grimace a bit. "Well, I'm your boss."

Caren cackles joyfully, the exact response I'd been hoping for. "Luke is going to flip! Oh, this is going to be absolutely delightful."

"You're not weirded out? Or offended?"

"Oh, honey, not at all. You deserve this, Em. Completely. I'm assuming this is just a stepping stone?"

My cheeks flush in a veiled attempt at modesty. "I'm not sure. Anything else is down the road a bit." I keep the rest of the information tucked away, not ready to tell anyone that this stint in Libby's spot could lead to an even bigger promotion, the kind that takes me away from Portland temporarily...or permanently.

"I bet Lauren is psyched for you," Caren says easily.

I choose my words carefully, putting exact and precise thought into my response before I so much as open my mouth. "Lauren doesn't know. Yet."

"Go on."

"I'm having a difficult time getting in touch with her."

"Due to lack of trying?"

I glare at Caren, even though we both know she has a valid point. "No. I've reached out to her multiple times. Radio silence."

Caren nods as she runs her hands through her mane of dark red hair. "So what's up with that?" Her question is so casual that it somehow comes across as entirely daunting.

I weigh my response. This whole thing with Burke is taking up so much space in my head, I have to let it out to someone. Since Caren already knows that *something* is going on…even if I haven't specifically stated with whom that something is developing… "Well. I'm still getting to know someone else. And it's progressed."

As soon as the words are whisked from my mouth, my cell phone vibrates on the table. Of course, it's Burke: *I'd ask for dinner but I have plans in Brooklyn.*

Shit. I need to see her. Trying to figure out our whole… thing…on my own isn't going so well. I need to feel that connection pass through us and encircle us. I need to know, again. I need to remember.

"Em?" Caren gently prods. "You okay?"

"I think I have to leave Lauren," I say, my words slow and weighted with quiet emotion. "I'm in love with Burke."

"Wow," Caren breathes. There's no expression of surprise on her face or in her body language; she simply looks at me for a few moments. "It's clear that Burke feels the same, you know."

She must have known. All along, she must have known; my God, how obvious has it been between me and Burke? "Is it? It hasn't exactly been said."

"Yeah, Em. Yes. You can see it in the way she looks at you." A smile, cautious, breaks through. "There's this crazy, buzzing energy between you two that is downright palpable." She grins then, and tilts her head at me. "And to be honest with you, honey, I haven't seen you that happy in a long time."

Tears burn in the corners of my eyes. I know Caren's right.

* * *

The next morning, I sit on the edge of my hotel bed, my phone in hand. I am completely exhausted. My body is achy, and after a night full of tossing and turning, I'm feeling like a zombie. I press on Lauren's name and put my phone to my ear. The incessant ringing is too familiar by now.

At the beep: "Lauren, it's me. Listen, I would really appreciate it if you could call me back. I'm not sure what's going on; I at least know you're alive because I've talked to Allison, but honestly, this is a little ridiculous. Call me back. Please."

A distinct fury builds and spreads through my torso. This *is* ridiculous. It's not that I want to explain over the phone, some 2,800 miles away, that I've slept with someone else and that I'm definitely falling in love with someone else. But seriously, how much distance am I supposed to accept between us?

Besides: I got a goddamn promotion, and I would *like* to tell my partner of five years about it.

I need to talk to someone who might actually care about the fact that something pretty amazing has happened to me, professionally.

Of course: professionally.

* * *

I dash down the hall toward Burke's room. I know I have limited time, as she's flying back to Portland today. We'd planned on meeting for breakfast and I know I'm early but I also know that I can't wait any longer.

After several beats, the door opens and Burke stands before me in ripped jeans and a T-shirt, toothbrush hanging from her slightly foamy mouth. She smiles around the toothbrush, and pulls me inside, directly into her arms.

"This is a nice surprise," she says, tightening her hold. "Couldn't wait another fifteen minutes?"

"Waiting isn't my strong suit," I say, and pull away to look into her eyes. Unmistakable heat rises between us. More words tumble together in my mouth, but before any can move out into the air, Burke speaks.

"Actually, this is a fortuitous drop-by." I roll my eyes at her fancy wording, and she laughs, then tugs me a bit closer. "My flight got bumped up. I was about to run up and tell you. I'm leaving here in about a half hour."

My stomach sinks. Once we're back in Portland, no matter what happens, everything will become more complicated.

She brushes her thumb lightly over my cheekbone before disappearing into the bathroom. She emerges moments later with some toiletries that she stows in her suitcase. From her messenger bag, she pulls a worn book.

Burke gently places the book in my hands, and closes my grasp around its spine. I look down and smile instantly. *Dark Fields of the Republic.* I turn the book, running my fingers over its worn, loved edges, and find a page dog-eared. I know what poem it is without even looking; of course she remembers "To The Days" is my favorite Adrienne Rich poem.

"I can't believe you remembered," I finally say, emotion bubbling inside of me.

"Sharing a mutual love for an obscure poem isn't something I could forget," she replies. "And forgive my cheesy segue, but, neither are you, Emery."

The book falls from my hands as I wrap my arms around Burke's neck and draw her mouth to mine. I kiss her hard, days' worth of built-up passion and need seeping out into our fusion, and her mouth presses against mine with similar want.

Our kiss is broken by a vibration in Burke's pocket. Almost apologetically, she pulls out her phone. Distaste crosses her face as she returns her phone to her pocket and turns to her suitcase. A low rumble of unease tremors throughout my body, though I can't pinpoint why. Of course she has to finish packing; she's leaving sooner than expected.

Before I can say something, my own phone vibrates, and I hastily check the screen. An email from Allison; not important. Suddenly, I'm struck with the notion that all Burke and I have is a lust-charged affair far from the restrictions and eyes of our everyday lives. She won't forget me; she won't forget this; but is that all that *this* is? Just a solitary, incredibly passionate night in a different city to tuck in our back pockets?

Burke turns to me with apology in her eyes, her once again vibrating phone in her hand. "I'm sorry, Emery. I need to take this."

"Oh. Of course." I back up toward the door, but she motions for me to wait as she answers the call.

"Hello. Yes, I got the email. I told you I would work on it during my flight." She pauses, tension crossing her face. "Krista,

I hear you. Don't make this into something it's not." My body clenches at the mention of Krista's name, and the tone Burke is using with her. "Listen. I told you, I will work on it. There's nothing else I can do from here, okay? It'll get fixed." Another pause, this one longer, and Burke turns away from me to focus on something outside the window. "Yes. Yes. Fine. I'll be in touch."

"Sorry, work issues," Burke says over her shoulder. She is still staring out the window, phone gripped tightly at her side.

"Are things okay with you and Krista?" The question pops from my mouth without permission, and I regret it instantly.

"Same as always," comes her reply, sharp and emotionless.

My mind, working on its own agenda as always, dashes back to that conversation with Allison informing me Krista digs her claws in whenever Burke moves toward someone else. It's pretty clear that Krista knows something is going on between me and Burke.

"So, dinner when you come back to Portland? I'll cook."

My brain doesn't register the smooth transition in Burke, and before I can help myself, more unfortunate words spill from my mouth: "Are you still sleeping with Krista?"

"Excuse me?"

I shake my head quickly, as though such an action could erase my words. "Forget it; I don't know why I even ask—"

"I can't believe you would even *think* that was true, Emery. After everything I've told you about my relationship with her." She's looking at me now, a sharp stretch of irritation painting her features. I avoid her eyes.

My embarrassment is thick and all-consuming, and surely visible considering the heat I feel in my cheeks. I shrug, momentarily at a loss, and completely unprepared for damage duty.

Burke doesn't say anything more, forcing me to gradually lift my downcast eyes and meet her stare. A picture of utter coolness, now: her arms are crossed against her chest, and her face betrays virtually no emotion whatsoever. She is entirely composed and blank.

I take a deep breath. "I'm not sure where that came from. I apologize; it's really none of my business."

"It wouldn't matter if it were." Not the response I was expecting. It's not my business? Didn't we just sleep together? And aren't there feelings crowding both of our hearts? "You don't believe what I've told you. Instead, you choose to believe what you hear from others."

"It was a question, Burke. The way you respond to her, both in person and on the phone, well, it leaves room for wonder." My ground feels a bit firmer; I know I'm being truthful.

"I find that a bit ironic, coming from you."

My stomach turns and I flash my eyes at Burke. "What do you mean?"

"'Room for wonder,'" she repeats, not moving from her statue-stance. "If you want the truth, Emery, I'm well aware that our involvement will stay right here."

I cross my arms involuntarily in a weak attempt to block myself from the disaster that's sparking between us. This is my chance to come clean. To admit the truth of my situation.

"As much as I do know about you, I'm sure I don't know all that I should know," Burke continues. "I can wager a guess as to why you're withholding information, but to be honest, I'd rather not. I'd hoped you would be truthful with me, but Emery, it's getting harder and harder to wait for you to talk openly with me."

Again, not what I was expecting. Yes, Burke's mad, but she's also still…well, still Burke. She's giving me an opportunity. She's not pushing me, but she's also not shutting down.

And my stubborn, terrified tongue refuses to move.

Finally, in a movement that signifies either defeat or acceptance, Burke returns to her packing. I stand, rooted at the scene of my inability to explain, or even communicate. She knows I'm not being honest with her. We both know it. Nothing can save me but the truth, but it's the truth that will also, likely, ruin everything.

The cascading misfortune of my reality slowly spreads through my body, and by the time Burke is armed with her bags and walking toward the door, I am shaken through and through. Blindly, I reach for her arm as she passes me, and she pauses long enough for me to hold on, long enough for me to feel, again, the surge of her closeness, and just long enough for me to understand that this is just the beginning of the avalanche taking its slide.

CHAPTER TWENTY-FOUR

There's not much a person can do with fluctuating and intense emotions while strapped into the confines of an airplane seat, so I attempt to drown out my brain with music. Not enough. I add a book to the noise.

"Emery? Helloooooo. You alive in there?"

I angle my head toward my seatmate, Caren, and blink, hard, then give her a wide-eyed look. "I think so."

She rolls her eyes at me and nudges me sharply. "You're not doing yourself any favors by sitting here obsessing. Listen, drama queen," Caren says as she sits up and turns to stare me down. "You need to get your shit together, and you need to do it quickly, because this plane is landing in less than an hour."

She grabs me and forces me to look at her. "Em, I'm serious. You have a disaster on your hands. You need a plan. You're the Queen of Communication, so just pretend this is another broken company to fix."

I swallow hard, my throat suddenly dimpled with spiky saliva droplets. "Well. When you put it that way..."

"I don't care how you want to put it, Em. You need to deal with this in a way that will not ruin too many lives." She pauses, seeming to consider her words, and lines of confusion cross her face. "I mean, lives are already ruined, but you know what I mean. So figure it out."

She tunes out my protests and drops back into a world behind her earbuds, leaving me to begin to deal with my mess.

An hour or so later, Caren and I walk toward baggage claim. She starts to ask a question, but I stop her with a wave of my hand.

"I need some time to wrap my head around everything." It's a weak excuse, but it's all I've got right now. I fumble with my phone and turn off airplane mode, hoping I'll find a text or an email from Burke. Nothing. It seems ridiculous, now, with my feet back on Portland soil. How was I expecting to carry on an affair in a town like this, with eyes and ears connected to Lauren at every turn?

* * *

To say that I am unprepared to face Lauren when I get home is an understatement. So, imagine that unpreparedness magnified by about a thousand when I find roughly ten cars parked in and around my driveway.

Caren snorts. "Is this a welcome home party?"

"What the fuck," is all I can muster.

Caren twists around in her seat and eyes me. "You really don't know what's going on?"

"No idea."

Luggage in hand, I start making my way to the front door. Whatever's going on inside is already in full swing: all the lights are on, and the combined sound of voices and music floats beyond the front door to greet me as I climb the front steps.

Yes indeed, there is a party going on and no one seems to have noticed that I just walked through the door. I'm the least interesting thing in this house right now.

I shake my head with a relieved laugh and start for the stairs. It looks like I can escape and pull myself together, an unexpected bonus. Then I'm grabbed from behind.

"Gorgeous! I've missed you so much!" Meredith envelops me in her tight embrace. I breathe in the familiar comfort of her patchouli-scented hair.

"Hey, Mer. Missed you too."

"I can't wait to hear all about your trip! But, oh!" She grins wickedly at me, and turns around to tug on the arm of a classically tall, dark, and handsome man behind her. "This," she says with a flourish, "is Quinten."

Quinten smiles affably at me and extends a very strong hand to shake mine. "Nice to meet you. Meredith has told me quite a bit about you."

"All good I hope." I laugh to conceal the suddenly nervous edge to my voice. I may be home, but I'm suddenly feeling like an alien here.

"Of course it was all good," Meredith says, her own laugh tinkling like a fucking wind chime. She swishes around Quinten, gazing at me intently from under his sturdy arm. "You look tired, Em."

"Right. I feel a little tired after flying across the country and landing in a different time zone." I don't try to conceal the edge that's charging my voice.

"Why don't you go upstairs and—"

"Why don't you explain to me what's going on in my home right now?"

"Em! You're home!"

Allison materializes out of thin air and grabs me into a hug. "Upstairs. Now," she grunts against my ear.

I force a smile at Mer who looks concerned and a little pissed from my outburst, and follow Allison upstairs.

In my bedroom, I drop my array of bags into a lumpy mess on the floor then drop myself on the floor next to the bags. I slump over, catch my face in my hands, and take a few deep breaths before I realize that Allison has been talking this entire time.

"Wait," I interrupt her, holding one hand out. "Quiet, please. I need a minute."

"I have to pee anyway," she says, and escapes into the bathroom.

I exhale another heavy breath and force myself to look around the room. It hasn't changed. It's just me and my changes that are making everything seem off-balance and brashly new.

Allison comes back into the room, wiping her damp hands on her jeans, and sits on the edge of the bed. She cocks her head at me, and a look of concern drifts across her features. "What's wrong with you?"

I bite my lip and shake my head, not wanting to get anywhere near what's wrong with me. "Just tired. Long trip, long flight, and this," I point toward the floor and the party below, "lovely surprise."

"Yeah, I emailed you about it. Didn't you get it?"

"I don't remember. Honestly, Allison, this past week is such a blur. What's going on?"

She smiles, but there's something slightly off about that smile. I know instantly she's hiding something. "You should ask Lauren about that."

"I would, if she had, I don't know, greeted me at the door. I didn't even see her downstairs."

"Oh," Allison says lightly, "she's here. Life of the party tonight."

"Please don't bullshit me. Tell me what's going on."

That awkward smile again. "Nothing's going on. I mean, I don't know anything for sure, just what—"

The door swings open and Lauren walks in. I wish I could say she looks happy to see me. It's more like unsurprised. Blank. Aware, at least. But not happy.

"Hey. Mer told me you came home."

Allison clears her throat and bolts for the door. Lauren still looks completely nonchalant.

"Yep. Hi. I'm home." I stand up and meet Lauren eye-to-eye. Her indifference shines unsteadily toward me. I wonder how much she's had to drink.

"That's good," she says, and I instantly smell the alcohol on her breath. "You were gone a long time."

"A week," I reply, unsure of how to navigate this conversation. Apparently, she is too. "But I guess it seemed longer since we didn't talk much…at all."

A cocky grin slides across Lauren's lips and lingers there. She shrugs and takes a step back from me. It occurs to me that we haven't even hugged. "That's what we do when you're away, Em. We just sort of…" She spreads her hands out between us, her shoulders still hunched into a half-shrug. "Do our own things."

"Generally our own things involve a couple conversations, Lauren. Not total silence." I turn from her and reach for my suitcase, lug it over to the bed.

"I've been really busy. You know, looking for a job?" I glance back at her and see a steely fire in her eyes that I haven't seen in a very long time, if ever. "Which, by the way, I got."

This stops me in my tracks. Genuine happiness (or is it relief?) flows through me, and I face Lauren, who looks less arrogant and simply happier. She gestures toward the floor and the slight noise emanating from downstairs before she continues. "Which is why our friends are here. Celebrating. Mer put it all together. I guess she didn't tell you?"

"No, I haven't heard from her. A heads-up would have been nice." I bite back the rest of my bitchiness and give Lauren what I hope is a very happy and proud smile. "Congratulations, Lauren. I'm really happy something came together. Is it the place in Hillsboro?"

"No, actually, it's GreenSpace. I'll be working with—"

"Rachel," I blurt.

Lauren gives me a weird look. "Well, yeah. Rachel works there. I'll be working with the public parks department. Gonna be a big change, but I'm really looking forward to it."

I smile against the irritation building inside of me. I'm happy Lauren got a job. Really, I am. But did it *have* to be with one of her ex-girlfriends? A nagging little voice inside of me pipes up: *like you have room to be a jealous bitch right now.* I shake my head in reaction to my thoughts, but Lauren catches it, snorts and crosses her arms across her chest. "You could maybe pretend to be happy for me, Emery. You know I've had a hard time looking for a job."

"Of course I know that, and I told you I'm happy for you. And I am."

"Yeah, that sarcastic smile on your face seems really happy."

I drop my forced smile and glare at Lauren. "Listen. I'm very happy for you. I just had an extremely long and busy week, followed by a long flight."

"Yeah, I know, Em. Your job and your busy life are so fucking important." Lauren rolls her eyes. "My new little job can't measure up to how big your job is."

"Lauren, stop. I didn't say that, and that's not what I mean or how I feel."

"But all you want to do right now is bitch about how tired you are. You can't even be happy for me."

"I *am* happy for you! I'm also tired, yes, and I was looking forward to coming home and seeing you and having some quiet time and—"

"Oh, so you're pissed that Mer threw a party for me? Because she's so happy about my job and she wants to show appreciation for me?"

"I DON'T GIVE A FUCK ABOUT THE PARTY!" I grit my teeth against my own yelling, then blow out a hard breath. "Stop being such a baby! Fuck, Lauren!"

"No, that's just it, Em. You don't give a fuck about the party, and you don't give a fuck about me."

That one stings. And hard. I scan Lauren's face. All I see is anger and frustration. And alcohol.

"That is not true. Do not go there," I say as evenly as possible. "I care about you very much. And the party is fine. I just wish I'd known about it."

"Maybe if you'd checked your goddamn precious phone while you were off being so fucking busy and important, you would have known about it."

"I checked my phone every fucking hour, Lauren!" My voice splinters off the walls and surrounds us in a cloud of heat. "Every day! And I called you, texted you, emailed you—I even checked your fucking Facebook to see if you updated anything. NOTHING, Lauren. I got NOTHING from you while I was gone." Hot, frustrated tears build in the corner of my eyes. "Did it ever occur to you that I needed to talk to you? That I had my own news to share?"

"If you were checking your phone so often, how'd you miss Mer's email?"

"She didn't email me! And don't change the goddamn subject!"

Lauren stares at me for a moment. It's as if I can watch her backtrack into my last bit of conversation. "Why did you need to talk to me?"

"Because I got a fucking promotion!" For some reason, the tears start spilling down my face, but now that I've started, I can't stop. "I had this big sit-down with the heads of my company and they gave me an amazing opportunity. They promoted me. I had such an intense week, I wanted to share it with you, but I couldn't get to you and tell you about this, this fucking incredible and unexpected change in my career, and I just wanted to tell you—"

"Nice, Em." The steel is back, in her eyes and her voice. "Here I am, busting my ass trying to find a job and celebrating the fact that I got one, and all you want to do is dance around in your fucking ego parade and remind me of how *amazing* and *incredible* you are and how you're so damn good at your job." Lauren takes a deep breath and blows it out slowly through pursed lips. "Real. Fucking. Nice."

"Oh, fuck you, Lauren. Fuck you. You just missed the whole goddamn point." I throw my hands to my sides in disgust and frustration.

"No I didn't. You only care about your career. All you wanted to do was rub it in that you got promoted and I still didn't have a job. So you call—"

"You didn't answer your fucking phone!" I scream. "If you had just answered your fucking phone!" My fight catches in my throat. If she had answered…what if? Oh, God.

"WE WERE ON A TIME-OUT!" Lauren yells. "There was nothing to fucking talk about!"

My breath leaves me completely, and I drop onto the bed, staring at her. Nothing to fucking talk about, indeed. And a time-out. The fucking time-out. As if we are petulant, unruly children who cannot be managed. A fucking time-out.

I can think of a thousand things that needed to be talked about, *need* to be talked about, but it turns out there are no words.

Finally, Lauren shifts and glances at me before turning and walking to the door. "I'm going downstairs. To the party. You know, the one my best friend is throwing for me because she's happy for me. You can stay up here or come down. I don't really give a fuck."

When the door closes behind her, all I can do is stare at it.

* * *

Fifteen minutes later, I'm finger-combing my freshly washed hair and staring blankly in the mirror. A steaming shower helped to calm me down, but I'm still feeling packed with irritation. Lauren's outburst came seemingly out of nowhere. Throughout our years together, we've had maybe six fights, and none of them have come close to what just happened.

A soft knock at the door and Mer walks into the room.

"Hey," she says softly. "I wanted to make sure you're okay."

"I'm sorry about earlier," I tell her. "I wasn't expecting to come home to a party."

"I know, and I'm sorry I didn't tell you about it. I meant to, but then Lauren said she would take care of it and I guess she didn't."

I bristle immediately. That's definitely not what Lauren said, but Mer doesn't need to be dragged into the middle of this. "No, it's fine. Really. She deserves a celebration."

"So do you, I hear." Mer steps in and gives me a big hug. I linger in her arms, letting her warmth seal my broken pieces. "Congratulations, Em. You work so hard, you truly deserve that promotion."

"Thank you," I mumble into her shoulder. We stand in silence for a couple beats, neither of us ready to navigate the elephant in the room. Meredith's smile is tentative, which is unusual for her, and it does little to help my budding anxiety regarding Lauren.

"Come downstairs?" she finally asks. "There's lots of food and you've got to be hungry."

I nod and, somewhat against my will, follow Meredith downstairs into the noise.

In the gentle hum of voices and music and laughter, my friends suddenly realize that I'm present and I easily fall into a conversation with Carly and Brenna. Allison slips me a beer and I sip it slowly, not wanting to get anywhere close to Lauren's level of intoxication. Lauren keeps her distance from me. I can tell by the way she's sitting, all hard angles and closed-off posture, that she's still pissed off, and I would prefer to avoid having an all-out battle in front of our friends.

After a while, Jen joins our conversation and I drift out of it, realizing that Lauren is no longer holding court in the dining room. My breath catches slightly in my throat when I find her, neatly tucked into a corner of the living room, just inches between her and Rachel.

I study them for a moment, trying to ascertain what I'm looking at. Lauren looks calmer, and has leaned back against the wall with her foot against the wall, shoving her knee out at an angle. One hand is curled around her drink, the other hangs loosely by her thigh. Her smile is easy. Familiar. Warm. Engaged. And she doesn't take her eyes off Rachel the entire time I watch them.

Rachel's grin is wider than Lauren's, and her body is angled just enough toward Lauren that it looks like an invitation. A lump rises in my throat. I know that stance. The lump gets bigger as Rachel reaches up to brush long strands of her dark hair off her face and Lauren's eyes watch every single movement her hand makes, including its slow descent past her chin, back to her hip.

"Quit staring," Allison grumbles from next to me. She grabs my elbow and pulls me back into the kitchen.

I shake my head as if the motion will actually clear the image from my mind. "What..."

"I emailed you. You didn't read it?"

My head continues shaking.

Allison sighs. "Em, listen. I don't know what's going on with them, but it's something." She looks at me, waiting.

"Is she cheating on me?"

"I'm pretty certain she's not. Not yet."

I bite my lip and stare past Allison, my wheels spinning and my limbs preparing for flight.

It would have been so much easier if Lauren was cheating on me.

CHAPTER TWENTY-FIVE

When I was younger, my parents made sure we took at least one vacation every summer. This was "mandated bonding time," a way to ensure that their three daughters remained as close as they possibly could in spite of the thirteen-year age gap between my older sister and my younger sister. But those trips weren't just about sisterly closeness: my parents, too, did everything they could to focus their attention on us. My dad spent hours building sandcastles with me and hours in the ocean with Jaelle. Helena preferred to sit next to my mom under the umbrella and read. I guess my parents did something right, and I'm willing to bet those vacations were part of it. After the whole cross-country uprooting thing, my parents made sure to localize us with that beach house in Rockaway—a summer retreat for us as a family, a way to keep us close and family-minded. Conveniently located a short two hour drive from Portland and maybe three hours from Aberdeen, any of us could escape there when the going got tough in our personal lives.

And so it is that I wake up from an emotionally-induced nap on Sunday afternoon to the sound of the slow ocean breezing in through the window of the second-floor, beach-facing bedroom I always claim as my own whenever I'm at the Rockaway house.

Sighing deeply, I rub my fists against my gritty eyes and roll over to hug the pillow. The sun has come out after a morning of mist and rain, but my mood prefers the crap weather to this blast of brightness. It's much harder to dwell in a pool of self-pity when the sun is out.

I reach over and pick up my phone. Lauren doesn't know where I am. Allison does but also can't be relied upon to keep her mouth shut. Meredith doesn't. I haven't heard anything from Burke since we parted ways in New York. Aside from a lone text from my younger sister, probably to verify that I'm still alive, my phone is empty of notifications. Seems that Lauren, after calling me thirteen times between last night and around eleven a.m. today, has finally given up. I drop my phone onto the carpet, unsure of whether or not I'm happy about the lack of contact from, well, anyone I expected to contact me by now.

As if on cue, a slight clank of kitchen noise rings out from downstairs. I groan and press the pillow over my face, willing the scene downstairs to change. While I don't intend to actually suffocate myself, it is a nice alternative to facing the music and explaining the dance to the one person I'm worried simply won't understand.

* * *

Fifteen or so minutes later, having put on a clean shirt and attempting to make myself look mostly presentable, I find myself standing in the entryway to the kitchen.

"Hi," I mumble, staring at my bare feet.

"Hello yourself," my mom responds, her back still to me. She's dressed in her casual beachwear, for which she has an entire closet: loose chambray pants and a brightly colored striped sweater. Her light brown hair, streaked with gray, is shorter than the last time I saw her and curls around her ears. "Sit down; I'm sure you're starving."

"I'm not."

"Well, you're not going to waste away on my time. Sit. I'm almost done throwing together this fruit salad and you *will* be eating some."

No point in arguing. I drop heavily into a chair and prop my chin up on my closed fist.

"You should have called me sooner," she says as she deposits the bowl on the table and hands me the serving spoon.

I cringe, recalling the night before. I'd found myself completely overwhelmed in my own home. And so I did what any logically-thinking adult would do: ran upstairs, packed a bag, snuck out the back door, and drove the hell away.

"I didn't know what else to do," I mumble into my spoon. "This stuff isn't easy to talk about, you know."

"I'm not blind, honey, nor am I oblivious to what goes on in my daughters' lives."

I look up, surprised by the authoritative tone in her voice. My mom isn't the soft and cuddly type, but she's not usually one for bluntness, either. Despite requesting lots of communication, she's definitely not a meddler, so sometimes it seems like she doesn't really know what's going on in our lives. Silly me.

"I can tell you haven't been happy for a while," she continues, offering me a small smile that goes along with her softer tone. "I was hoping you and Lauren would be able to work it out, that it was just a bump in the road, but...I think I may have been hoping that so you'd be spared heartbreak."

"Mom, geez," I manage before the tears start falling again. "I just—I don't know what to do about any of this. I have never been this confused in my life."

"Is there someone else?"

A bitter laugh escapes from my mouth before I can stop it. "On which end?"

"Oh. I didn't realize."

I wave away her embarrassment. "Sorry, that wasn't fair." I take a deep breath and stare up at the ceiling to stop my tears.

It's time for me to come clean, and this is a good place to start. "I cheated on Lauren, Mom. Flat-out cheated on her. I met someone, fell for her, and slept with her. I know it's the worst thing I could have done."

A beat of silence stretches between us before my mom says, "Well, really Emery, it's not the *worst* thing you could have done."

"No? Lying and cheating and starting an affair when I do truly love the woman I've been with for five years? That's not the worst thing?"

"I don't think so," she says gently, leaning toward me. "The worst thing would be lying to yourself and to Lauren and staying in a relationship where you aren't truly happy. That, I think, would be the worst thing."

My mouth gapes in response. It's not that I've been living my adult life thinking that my mom is, like, old-fashioned or whatever, but hell if this isn't a surprisingly evolved comment coming from her. As I'm digesting this, my phone buzzes on the table. Allison. I push the phone away, not ready to deal with all of that.

"You're thirty-three years old, Em—"

"Thirty-one, Mom. I'm thirty-one."

She flicks her wrist and shakes her head. "Oh, I know that. Thirty-one, fine. Anyway, you're young! You made a commitment and you stuck with it while you were in love with her, right?" I nod. "Feelings change, honey. Not every relationship is meant to last no matter how badly you think it should, or want it to."

"How are you being so cool about this?" Part of me is still in shock that I'm having this conversation with my *mother*, of all people.

"Because I've watched my friends stay in loveless marriages, Emery. I've seen divorces happen twenty-some years in when it's clear two people never should have married in the first place. Sometimes, even if we really, really love someone, it just isn't meant to be. And if someone else catches our eye while we're committed to a person, then, well, I just think that relationship needs to be looked at pretty closely to see what's really going on there."

We're interrupted by the sound of wheels on gravel, followed by the slamming of a car door. My insides freeze. I'm not ready to face Lauren. My mother, of course, looks entirely nonchalant as she stands up and walks toward the front door.

"Oh," she says, "I wasn't expecting this. Hi, honey!" she calls out cheerily.

The answering voice, thankfully, does not belong to Lauren.

"Allison?" I peer through my fingers and catch sight of her hugging my mom, smiling at me over her shoulder. "What are you doing here?"

"Uh, hello, best friend in crisis." She casually drops into the chair next to me, and gives me a rough one-armed hug. "I couldn't let Maryann handle this on her own."

My mom scoffs from the kitchen where she's getting Allison a glass of water. "Don't forget that I gave birth to this child, Allison. I think I can handle her pretty well."

"Oh, you can, but I knew you'd need reinforcements for the kind of drama she's sucked herself into."

I glare at Allison, who grins delightedly back at me. "And what all about my drama do you know?"

"Just that you're in a relationship you clearly don't want to be in anymore, and I'd say the same for Lauren, but neither one of you is willing to admit it, so you're both acting stupid."

My mom and I exchange a look. For not knowing the explicit details, Allison isn't too far from the truth. My phone buzzes with an incoming email. Hope soars through my body, praying that it's Burke's name I'll find in my inbox. Nope. Not Burke.

Lauren.

And it's brief, not that I expected anything more:

Em — I have no idea where you are. I hope you're safe. I guess you don't want to talk to me, since you're not answering when I call. I'm trying to respect your space, but please get in touch with me so I know you're okay. I will come meet you so we can talk and work this out.

That's it. No "I'm sorry for being a total asshole last night," and no "things are messed up but I love you." Maybe she's as done as I am and too afraid to say it…like I am.

There are two pairs of eyes trained on me when I put my phone back on the table. "Lauren wants to know where I am," I say quietly. "She wants to meet me so we can 'talk and work this out,' whatever that means."

"You are going to have to talk to her at some point," my mom reminds me.

"Mom, I know. Believe me. I know. It's just not that easy."

"What is there to work out, though? I mean, do you think you guys can stay together?"

Now or never, Larsen. "Allison, look. There's someone else." Huh. That came out easier than I thought it would.

"Aw, no, Em—I told you, nothing happened between Lauren and Rachel!"

"No, I'm not talking about Lauren. I'm talking about me."

This leaves Allison in silence, a relatively rare phenomenon. I feel like a gigantic asshole telling this to my best friend who has dealt with a cheating girlfriend for years. I'm no better than Sidney right now, and I feel every ounce of judgment zipping through my brain.

"Oh," she finally says. I chance a look in her direction, and I can see the wheels turning. This isn't the Emery she knows and I'm going to hear about it. "Well. I wasn't expecting that."

My mom clears her throat. "It happens, Allison; sometimes people—"

"Oh, I know it happens." Ah, there it is: the expected bitterness and glimmer of anger. "My girlfriend cheats on me constantly. I just thought," Allison says, leveling her eyes with mine, "that you were different."

I half-laugh, half-cry and shrug. "You have every right to say that to me. I screwed up. I've done exactly what I swore I would never do again because I know the destruction it causes." The tears are really coming now, and I wipe at them furiously. My mom gets up to find tissues. "If I could have stopped it from happening, I would have. But when I tell you that I am completely in love with this woman, that I have *never* felt this way about anyone, I tell you that with every goddamn ounce of truth I have inside of me. I know what I've done is wrong. I know it's a huge break in trust and I know you're going to be mad at me for acting like such a fool. If I could hate myself for it, I would, but I love Burke more than I can stand, and I can't hate myself for that."

"Burke," Allison repeats, her expression changing slightly. "Oh."

I shake my head at her, frustrated by her lack of a complete thought. "What the hell does that mean?"

"Well, I didn't know who could affect you to the point where you would risk your relationship, but Burke..." She shrugs. "Yeah, I can see that."

"You can see that? So because it's Burke, it's okay?"

"No! It's still not okay. I was just worried that you'd done something stupid with some random girl from a club or some chick you met in New York or something."

My laugh sounds harsh and cold. "Thanks for having such faith in me, Allison. I appreciate that."

"Emery," my mom says, a warning.

"I didn't mean it like that," Allison says, and I know it's true. Because of her shit with Sidney, she and I will never see eye to eye on matters like this. "I didn't think you would, sorry Maryann, screw some random girl in order to end your relationship, or whatever. I guess I just wish you and Lauren could have, like, stopped before all of this happened."

"Me too," I agree. "But that's not how it happened and I have to deal with it now."

"It's gonna be messy," Allison muses. "But it's what you want, right? You don't want to be with Lauren anymore?"

"I can't." I push my hair out of my face and look at Allison so there's no chance for her to misread or mishear me. "Allison, I am completely in love with Burke. Staying with Lauren would be the worst thing I could do—for her, and for myself." Without looking at her, I can sense the smile on my mom's face. For once, a daughter who listens.

Allison studies me. "You're in love with Burke," she repeats.

"Yes. Totally."

She nods, taking in this information. "And does she know that?"

"That I'm not entirely sure about. I haven't exactly told her."

Allison and I stare at each other. I can tell she's watching me to make sure I'm not making an irrational decision based on flimsy feelings, and I know that nothing on my face would lead her to that thought. She nods slowly, seeming to accept my truth.

"So what's our plan of attack, girls?" my mom pipes up.

Allison and I exchange an amused look before we both turn our heads to my mom and her sudden enthusiasm for making a plan of attack.

"Well, wine, naturally," Allison says, as she gets up and moves into the kitchen in search of alcoholic reinforcements.

"Allison! It's too early for wine!"

"Oh, Maryann, live a little! We're at the beach! And it's four o'clock, definitely time for a drink or four."

* * *

An hour and a single glass of wine later, I'm sitting on the front porch of the beach house, enjoying the fading golden bands of the sun and a very gentle ocean breeze. My mother and Allison are inside, both on their second glass of wine, gossiping and working on dinner. Our planning session didn't get much further than agreeing that I need to go home tomorrow morning and prepare myself for a real conversation with Lauren—one that covers all possible corners, and creates a firm solution and ending. I've already contacted Caren and let her know I won't be in tomorrow, and then I had a weird moment of, 'oh my God, I'm my own boss now,' when I realized I don't need to report directly to anyone about my day off.

The other piece of our planning session, the far more sensitive portion, regards Burke. Just thinking about it makes my stomach turn in a thousand different directions. It's not a matter of, oh I'll only end things with Lauren if Burke still wants me. Not at all. It's more like…here is this woman that I am in love with, a woman that I am absolutely crazy about, and I've been lying to her, and what do I do now. I have no expectations. Okay, that's not entirely true. I expect that Burke will be angry (and I keep thinking back to those final moments in her hotel room in New York) and hurt and possibly want nothing to do with me. But no matter what comes of it, I owe her honesty, even if it's delayed and hurtful.

No point in prolonging the inevitable. I unlock my phone and open my contacts to Burke's name, then hit call. Maybe she won't answer. Maybe that'll be easier.

Oh, no, she answers, and just the sound of her voice flips my stomach again. "Hi," I respond, hoping to sound confident but knowing the mountain of conflicting feelings can be heard in my voice.

"Hi, Emery." Okay, she doesn't sound like she hates me. In fact, she sounds like the Burke I'm used to talking to. I can do this. "How are you?"

"Oh," I laugh a little, "I'm, you know, I'm okay. How are you?"

"I'm well."

Aaaaand a screeching halt, which never happened in any of our previous conversations. Wonderful. Any confidence I'd mustered is blown across the street and dissolves into the sea foam.

"I need to talk to you," I blurt out.

"I've gathered that much."

"I just, uh, this isn't really a conversation I wanted to have over the phone, but I'm in Rockaway right now, and I wanted to talk to you before I'm back in Portland, so, yeah." I pause; she's silent. Not helpful. "Okay. First of all, I want to apologize for my dig about Krista, and implying things that are really none of my business. I'm sorry for that. It was shitty of me."

"I understand."

I take a deep breath, realizing this conversation probably isn't going to go the way I'd hoped it would. "There's more. I haven't been completely honest with you. I mean, I didn't exactly lie, but I definitely didn't tell you the specifics of how involved I was with someone else. My feelings for you started to come out and I got so caught up in them that, I don't know, I didn't think about—"

"Don't qualify, Emery."

"What? What do you mean?"

"You weren't honest with me, so say that. Don't say that you didn't lie, because ultimately, you did."

A knife spears my heart. "You know."

"About you being very much involved with someone else? I know enough."

"How long?"

Her turn to sigh, and part of me is glad that it sounds slightly pained—tinged with anger at herself, not at me. "Long enough."

"That's pretty vague, Burke."

"So were you, Emery. And you had plenty of opportunities to be open and honest with me. You chose not to be."

My instinctual anger flares up, but I manage to temper it because I know I am at fault here. I screwed up. "Burke, I just—"

"I don't think I can have this conversation right now. I appreciate your call. I'll see you at work. Good night, Emery."

With that, Burke hangs up and I stare mutely at my phone.

* * *

"So, let me get this straight," Allison says, reaching past me for the pepper. "You didn't actually tell her how you feel about her?"

"I couldn't! It was like she wasn't interested in hearing anything about that."

"Well, if she's known about Lauren, then can you blame her?"

"No. Not really. But that conversation did not go how I envisioned it."

"Maybe she just needs some time, honey," my mom pipes up. "This is an awful lot to take in."

"I know. I know it is. But I wasn't expecting her to be so... cold." I shiver just thinking about the total lack of warmth in Burke's tone after those first couple of words. That's not the Burke that I got to know, not the Burke I fell for, but it's apparently part of her, and I know I love her because I'm not even mad at her for responding that way.

"I just don't get why she never flat-out asked you about Lauren," Allison muses aloud with her fork poised before her mouth, into which a perfectly grilled shrimp waits to be deposited. "I mean, that's weird. Don't you think?"

"I don't know how much she knows. Or who told her." That part is bugging me; I know it wasn't any of my people, so to speak. So who else could it be?

"That's not really your concern, honey. Being honest with Burke is what's most important," my mom gently reminds me.

"I know that, but attempt number one didn't go so well."

"But it opened the door."

I sit with that for a moment, weighing its truth and power. My mom is right: the door is open. I 'fessed up to something that should have been laid out on the table but wasn't. I also apologized for acting like a brat about Krista.

Oh.

Krista.

It hits me like a solid punch to my stomach. Krista. Burke's ex-girlfriend who gets jealous whenever Burke tries to move on. Krista knowing Burke's interest in me. Krista having met me outside of Whitmore; Krista's athleticism and group of friends, some of whom play soccer. With Lauren. Krista, soccer, Lauren, me. Of course Krista knows about me and Lauren.

And of course she would tell Burke.

"Em?" Allison asks, poking my arm with her fork. "You in there?"

"Yeah, I just, uh, realized something. It's not important." But there Krista sits in my gut, right on a pile of the words that I should have said to Burke from the very beginning.

"I think what you need to take from that conversation is that the door opened, and it didn't slam shut. Right?" My mom waits for my nod before she continues. "She didn't say she never wants to speak to you again. She said she couldn't talk right then. And that she appreciated your call. And that she would see you at work. Right?"

"Yes, Mom."

"Right. So, really, you just need to find your courage and walk through that door when she's ready to listen."

"She may not be ready to listen for a while," Allison points out ever so caringly.

"That's helpful, Allison."

"It's honest, Maryann!"

"It may be, but from what Emery's told us, Burke sounds like a fairly mature woman who values communication."

The two of them semi-glare at each other like petulant siblings, both angling for the right answer and the parents' approval. And then the glares disappear and they dissolve into laughter as each of them reach for their wineglasses.

I snort. I can't help myself. Yet another shining moment for the woman whose sole purpose in her career is to facilitate communication—*failing* in communication. I have a good chuckle to myself before looking up to find Allison and my mother staring at me in open amusement and/or concern. I wave them off.

"Well, the door is open, right? Now we'll see who's able to walk through it."

* * *

The next morning, I take a long walk on the beach, dodging puffs of fog. Allison is headed back to Portland in order to make sure Perk makes it through the day. My mom's goodbye hug was warm and solid, and her words were ever reassuring. I'm still surprised at, well, how *okay* she was with all of this. Surprised, and thankful.

I scrape my bare toes on the damp sand. Part of me wants to hibernate, away from everything that's causing all my internal chaos. But I know it's time to go home and face that music, to have different dances with different partners, and to see what happens when the songs are over. There's no guarantee anywhere, except for the fact that my relationship with Lauren is over. And I'm hoping she realizes, as I do, that it's been over for longer than either of us has realized, or been willing to admit. It's never an easy thing, realizing that you've fallen out of love with the person you thought you would spend the rest of your life with.

But it's also not an easy thing to realize how your heart is going to love again, in a fiery new way, in a way that you never imagined possible.

Even less easy is having paved a path of omissions (okay, fine, LIES) to that love and hoping it would all work itself out before the bridge collapsed and someone ended up almost drowning. And here I am, on the shore of the Pacific, hoping against all hope that the tools I carry and the love I own are enough to build a new path beyond that rickety bridge…that is, provided the door to the path still opens.

CHAPTER TWENTY-SIX

"Wait, slow down. What's missing?"

"Her clothing. Shoes. All the shit on her bedside table. Everything that's hers is gone."

"But you said downstairs looked normal, right? Go look again, Em."

I'm silent on the phone as I walk downstairs. The living room looks no different than it ever does: TV, blu-ray player, couches, Lauren's favorite chair…it's all here. Lauren's books are here, as are a couple framed pictures of us, one of her family.

"Yeah. Normal," I reply finally as I sink into the sofa. I rub my eyes, feeling a headache coming on.

"So, even if she left, she didn't completely leave."

"Isn't that worse, somehow? That means she'll have to come back. We'll actually have to, like, break up and talk and split items."

"Yes, genius. That's what will happen. That's how it's done. And this is what you want, right?"

I exhale loudly. I love Allison, I do, but when she is more rational than I am I want to scream and/or pull her short hair until she squeals. "Yes, friend. That's what I want. We'll have to figure out the house situation too. I just…" My voice trails off along with my brain.

"You just what?"

"I don't know," I admit. "I know this relationship has to end. I understand that."

"Em, it still sucks, and it's okay that it sucks. No one will expect you to be totally happy immediately."

"I know that. I guess I just didn't think Lauren would move out until she actually knew that I'd cheated."

The silence on the other end of the phone zings a rising panic in my gut. "Allison? Oh for fuck's sake, please tell me you didn't tell her."

"God, no. I didn't. But…I don't know…I mean…" She trails off, and my patience is about zapped.

"Whatever it is, say it. Now."

She sighs. I know the sound of that sigh. It's the: I'm going to say something and it might hurt you but dammit, I'm going to say it anyway. And so she does. "What if she cheated?"

And there it is. The Great Possibility.

"You're the one who said you were pretty sure she hasn't," I remind her.

"I know. And Em, I just can't picture Lauren cheating. I know she has her whole history of dating a lot of people and whatever, but she's loyal. She's a loyal friend and she was loyal to her ex, and she's been loyal to you." Allison pauses to take a breath in her rambling. Meanwhile, my heart rate has slowed and I'm feeling weirdly calm. "Of course I was shocked as shit when you admitted you cheated, but—"

"You never know, Allison. You just never know what's going to happen."

"I guess not," she says after a slow, quiet beat. "But let's not jump to conclusions, okay? You and Lauren did have a really nasty fight before you left."

"We did," and her words drag up the memory of that verbal throwdown. I close my eyes briefly. The front door opens. My eyes snap open and land directly on Lauren, who is doing everything in her power *not* to look in my direction.

"Gotta go," I say quickly, and hang up.

Lauren stands in the foyer, door shut behind her, keys swinging gently from her finger. She looks normal, like herself, in dark distressed jeans that hang from her hips, and a lightweight gray hoodie. Her blond hair is in a ponytail, a few pieces of hair wisp around her face. Other than her keys, she's empty-handed.

I perch in my spot on the sofa, waiting for her to move, to acknowledge me, anything. I feel like my ass has been super-glued to the sofa cushion and my limbs feel like lead. I don't know how long we stay like that, her posture missing its confidence, my body stuck solid and unmoving.

It isn't until she takes the chance and looks my way that I feel the hitch inside of me, the sign that my own dam is about to break. While her eyes aren't nearly as cold and unfeeling as they were the last time I looked into them, the warmth is gone. I can see sadness, which I know is reflected back at her from my own eyes, but other than that, she's emotionally blank.

I open my mouth, willing words to come out, but it's just air, and she sees it, hears the silence and takes that as her cue to turn and walk away. I hear the open and quiet shut of the basement door, and I sigh loudly in relief and impatience.

* * *

Getting out of bed on Monday morning requires some serious deep breathing techniques. As soon as I woke up, way before my alarm despite having spent most of the night alternating between crying and staring at the ceiling, the anxiety settled into my body. I know I could make some excuse and spend the day in my office at PLAC as opposed to setting a single toe inside Whitmore. Truth is, I need to pack up my desk and move into a different office, but the real truth is that I don't need to do that quite yet. Whitmore is still the current project I'm assigned to, promotion or not. And because I've been promoted, it's more important for me to be onsite with my colleagues than it is for me to be fussing about a new office.

It's not until I'm getting dressed that I realize I will most likely see Burke today. My little emotional hangover from the weirdness with Lauren kicks into overdrive again at the thought of Burke. With no resolution from our brief phone call, the prospect of seeing her is littered with confusion, anticipation, fear, and some excitement.

It's the excitement piece that helps me get dressed because like hell am I going to sit in misery when I know I'm going to see Burke. I decide I need to fully embrace my new, promoted role, and I forgo my more casual work attire in favor of a sleek black pencil skirt that hugs my curves and pair it with a tucked-in ice blue button-down shirt. I slide my feet into black heels, and grab a snug-fitting black blazer to top off the look. I leave my hair down and wavy and aim to leave it as it is until I see Burke.

* * *

Walking into Whitmore doesn't instantly calm me, not that I imagined it would. Fortunately, I have a clear plan and agenda for the day, neither of which allows me much downtime to sit and stew or to wander around looking for someone who may not want to see me.

Caren pushes a stack of papers in my direction. "Here's the latest data analysis report on communication between IT and central office. I have a couple graphs I emailed you as well, but I know you still like the hard copies."

"Thanks," I mumble. I open my laptop while absently shuffling through the stack of papers. "You ready for the meeting with HR today?"

"I am. Luke is too. You?"

"Sure."

Caren abruptly leans forward, drops her chin in her hands, and bats her eyelashes at me. "Wanna talk about whatever appears to be killing you from the inside?"

I exhale heavily and shake my head. "Can we just pretend I'm absolutely fine?"

"Well, *I* can do that. But you?" Out of the corner of my eye, I see Caren shake her head and stifle a laugh. "You're not exactly the best at that, you know."

"But she is great at a lot of other things," Luke announces as he breezes into the room. "Lovely to see you two New York debutantes back on the real coast. It was hell here without you."

"Really? Why?"

Luke rolls his eyes dramatically. "That was a joke. I barely even realized you were gone."

"How kind," Caren muses. "That's why you sent me thirty-some emails, right?"

"No, that was simply me keeping you in the loop. Hey, by the way, congrats, boss," he says to me, and winks. "Does this mean I have to stop making lewd jokes at your expense?"

"Please don't. Your jokes are often the only entertainment I have in a day's work." I've been absently filtering through my email, and as I click open one sent this morning from Krista Whitmore, my heart sinks. Luke and Caren's banter fades into the background as I skim through the brief note. Looks like I've earned myself some one-on-one time with the boss lady.

* * *

Precisely at eleven a.m., I knock on Krista's closed office door. I shift nervously, not knowing exactly what this conversation will entail. Her email was too brief to glean any information from it, and I've wracked my brain to come up with any valid reason for this little sit-down aside from my rather sudden promotion.

"Come in." Her voice is clear and strong through the solid oak door, and I brace myself for the impact of the woman who is intimidating in both her beauty and her refined professional demeanor.

She's focused on her computer screen, but waves me in, gesturing toward the seats in front of her desk. "Give me one second, I need to shoot off a reply to our Texas people. Their head of HR is always in my business and it makes me crazy. You'd think she was my boss or something. It's the weirdest thing."

This is perhaps the most Krista Whitmore has spoken to me since I've been here. I settle into a chair and wait for her to finish typing like a madwoman.

"Okay, there. That should shut her up for a day or two." She spins in her chair and levels her stare directly on me. Something like a smile settles on her lips, and I'm struck, again, by her seemingly flawless skin and perfectly symmetrical facial features. "So, how was New York?"

Caught off guard, I fumble for an appropriate answer. "Very busy. Productive, but busy."

"That's good. I haven't gotten much information from my employees about their trips so I thought I'd come to you instead." She cocks her head to the side, and I admire her lack of beating around the bush. She clearly wants information and she knows she can get it from me because, technically, I *have* to report back to her.

"What kind of information are you looking for?" I'm smart enough to play her game and not give up all my cards at once.

Again Krista tips her head slightly to the side, and her hair swings with the move. "Anything, really. Frank's only comment was, 'Good, boss.'" Krista throws her hands up in an exaggerated shrug. "All this work on communication seems to be making them quieter but I think I miss the fighting."

I laugh in spite of myself because she has a point. Even Luke reported back to me that while Caren and I were gone the HR group seemed to settle down. Krista's used to her employees butting heads with her, not being appropriately communicative and measuring their words for important conversations.

"Well, I can't speak for your employees, but I can assure you it was a very productive and informative week for everyone. There were a great array of topics to choose from and I know for a fact that Charlotte pulled a lot of information from one speaker in particular."

Krista nods slowly, and I can't help but feel as though she is assessing me beyond my professional role. Unfortunately for me, this woman is insanely hard to read. I keep talking. I give her details about a presentation I attended with Frank and Erin, and how excited they were afterward, how empowered and enlightened they felt by the information delivered to them. I mention Burke's excitement after meeting one of the head IT people from a well-known national company. Similarly, I highlight the one presentation that both Caren and I attended with all of the Whitmore employees that were present with us in New York, and also cover the "team strategy meeting," as Frank called it, that we had afterward.

My rambling seems to appease Krista, and I finish with reminding her that all four of her employees have been tasked with putting together a presentation covering their experiences and gains that they'll be sharing with the rest of the staff.

"Yes, that's right. We need to do more of that."

I nod. "It's a great way to balance personal growth with team growth."

"Speaking of personal growth, I hear you've been promoted. Congratulations."

"Thank you. It was unexpected, but I'm ready for the challenge."

"I imagine so," Krista says, almost to herself, and almost as though she didn't mean to say it out loud, because she looks away and changes the subject. "According to our original contract, Pointworth is required to be here at Whitmore for two more weeks. Do you sense that's enough time to wrap up?"

I shift gears right along with her. "I do, yes. Libby and I have discussed this already and I'll be making the final adjustments in the schedule for the next two weeks to ensure that all of our loose ends are wrapped up."

Something tiny shifts in Krista's expression, and if I knew her better, I'd say a smug look passes over her face. "All of the loose ends?"

Aha. There it is. I had a feeling we wouldn't get through this meeting without an oblique reference to Burke. I take a slow breath and answer in the most even tone I can muster: "All of them." I pause, unwilling to let her take the upper hand from me. "Of course, Caren, Luke, and I don't start our next project until mid-June, so we do have some flexibility if you feel as though we need more time here."

Her answer comes fast, though cool and definitive. "I don't think that will be necessary. It seems as though everything is coming to natural conclusions."

A quick knock raps on Krista's office door. "One moment!" she calls out, her eyes still focused on me. I smile at her, unwilling to let her see that she has effectively gotten under my skin.

"I hope I gave you the information you were looking for," I say, rising. "I'm sure you'll be impressed by the conference presentations later in the week. I'm going to be checking with each of the presenters to ensure they have everything they need."

"You certainly did. Thank you for coming in, Emery."

Knowing that someone is waiting outside of the door, I make sure I have a calm smile stapled to my face. Yes, someone is outside the door, and naturally, of-fucking-course, it's Burke. I hover in the doorway for a second. I watch carefully as flashes of emotions pass over her face while wondering what's flashing over my own. We're held there in our silence, having come face-to-face in this spot.

I hear Krista clear her throat behind me and I pull myself out of the moment. Stepping aside, I offer a quiet "excuse me" before slipping past Burke and making my way down the hall into the HR office for my next appointment. For once, I'm glad I have a ready distraction.

* * *

"So...it went well?" Caren asks.

I shrug and roll my neck a few times. It's been a long day. "I think she wanted more information than I gave her, but it's not my place to tell her anything about me and Burke."

"Kinda weird that Burke came in after you, though."

"Knowing what I know about Krista, that was entirely planned. She's a bit...conniving."

"And controlling," Caren adds. "Burke didn't say anything to you?"

"No, but it's not like she had a chance. I don't want to overthink it."

"Okay, good, because she totally left something here for you."

Caren points to the corner of the conference room where a large brown-paper wrapped package sits.

"What the hell is that?" I ask Caren.

"How the hell would I know? Burke came in while you were in your last meeting, and asked me to make sure you got it. That was the extent of our conversation. She seemed nervous, if you want to know the truth."

I make no moves toward the package, and it remains untouched for the next forty minutes that Caren and I spend in the conference room. I do such an excellent job of ignoring it that Caren has to remind me to get it as we're leaving. It's an odd size, but flat and rectangular, and light. I have absolutely no idea what this is, but I know I don't want to open it in front of anyone.

* * *

Lauren's car is in the driveway when I pull in that evening. I run my fingertips over the edge of Burke's mystery package before lugging myself and it into the house. I'm greeted at the front door by the mouth-watering scent of roasted chicken. I know instantly that Lauren has made dinner; she pulls out her grandmother's recipe for roast chicken about twice a year, knowing that it's irresistible to the both of us.

I find Lauren standing in the doorway with oven mitts on both hands. "I made dinner," she says, though we both know it's an unnecessary statement. "Mer won't be home until later."

I register that afterthought and realize we'll be eating together...alone.

"Everything will be ready in about ten minutes," she continues.

"Okay. Great. Um, I'll go change real quick."

In the quiet of what's now my bedroom, and no longer *ours*, I gently place the package on the bed, then change into comfortable clothes before perching on the edge of the bed and cautiously eye the package. A card addressed to me is taped to the front of it.

I gasp as the mystery beneath the plain brown paper is revealed. A painting. I recognize the form immediately. The colors explode off the canvas, leaving behind an abstract rendering of a woman's body. I love it instantly, and my second thought is how beautifully this painting would pair up against the paintings hanging in Burke's loft. Keeping that thought in mind, along with a small thread of hope, I pick up the card.

Emery,

While I was in New York, I managed to get in touch with Ariel's brother, Adam. As you can imagine, he's extremely protective over what remains of his sister's artwork, but I assured him that you would take excellent care of this print. I realize this "gift" may come as a surprise, but I hope it's not unwanted. I want you to have this because I know you'll appreciate it.

Burke

I flop back onto my pillows holding the card in my hand. The painting is an incredibly sweet and thoughtful gesture and I can't help but to notice that the sweetness and thoughtfulness is not echoed in Burke's words. There's a formality to them, a clear line drawn between us.

* * *

Downstairs, I can tell Lauren notices I'm not exactly okay, but she doesn't ask questions. Our conversation is sparse, but not unkind. I compliment the dinner she's prepared for us, and she thanks me. I ask her when she starts her new job, and she tells me next Monday. She adds that she's looking forward to it, so she can feel useful and motivated again. For some reason, that hits me in my chest; I want to take it personally, that I haven't made her feel useful, but I'm not her employer. I stuff that feeling down and try to stay present for the rest of dinner and the sprinkles of our conversation.

I tell Lauren I'm happy to clean up. She doesn't argue, instead grabs a beer and heads toward the living room. Once the kitchen's clean, I pour myself a glass of wine courage, and slowly walk into the living room. Lauren's sitting on the sofa, her long legs stretched out in front of her. She glances up at me as I walk into the room.

"We should talk," I blurt out unceremoniously.

"Yeah, we should."

I sit cross-legged on the sofa, facing her. "Things have been off. I know that happens in relationships…"

"It does," she agrees. "But I can't tell if you want things to go back…on."

I take a swig of liquid courage before responding. I don't want to hurt Lauren, but I also don't want to hurt myself for the sake of saving her feelings. "I don't think that I do."

Silence. I don't dare look at her, because I can feel the relief rising inside of me and yet I have no doubt that my words hurt her.

"Think or know," she finally says.

"I'm not happy, Lauren. It's an awful thing to say, and I am so sorry, but it's the truth. Something shifted between us, and instead of paying attention to it, I feel like we both avoided it until we couldn't anymore, and here we are."

She nods slowly. "I felt it too. And I was angry at you for a while. I thought you weren't supportive of me when I lost my job, and when I was looking for one I felt like shit all the time and you didn't seem to care."

"I did care, Lauren. Truly. But I think something broke between us before you lost your job."

"Because I was sleeping in the basement?"

"Well, yeah. We never talked about that."

"And I don't know if I can explain it." She meets my eyes and shrugs. "I know I should. But I can't."

"We could spend years trying to figure out the exact moment something shifted between us," I point out. "But that's not really what's important here, is it?"

Lauren smiles, but it's wry. "No. We've been avoiding this conversation for too long, Em. I don't want to fight anymore. I do love you."

My chest gets tight. *Be honest*, I remind myself. *You have to be honest.*

"I love you, Lauren. But...but I'm not in love with you anymore." A little weight lifts from my chest.

I see her jaw clench and tears come to her eyes. "Yeah. I kind of figured that."

"I'm sorry...I...I don't want to lie to you."

"It happens, right?"

I reach out and gently touch her arm. "You didn't do anything wrong, Lauren. This isn't happening because one of us screwed up."

"I know. I've fallen out of love with people before." She shakes her head. "I just thought you and I were going to make it for the long haul."

Tears sting my eyes. How do two people want the same thing, but can't manage to make it happen? How do two people fall out of love when they both believe they are each other's forever?

"I did too," I finally respond.

"But that's not going to happen, is it?"

I shake my head. "No. It's not."

She nods slowly. "I knew this was coming. I'm sorry it had to come after a couple months' worth of misunderstandings and fighting."

She has no idea how badly I wish we could have amicably ended our relationship before Burke re-entered my life. "Me too, Lauren. Me too."

"Why?"

"I'm sorry." I can't look at her. "I've never wanted to hurt you. And I didn't want to destroy what we have."

"But?"

"I fucked up, Lauren."

She's quiet. I know she's looking at me, but I focus on my wineglass. "You don't want to hear this," I whisper.

"I don't think I do. But I want you to tell me."

"There's someone else."

"I figured."

That stings, and gets me to look at her. She holds my stare for a moment, then looks away. "For how long?"

"A couple of months," I say, then rethink that. "Sort of. It's hard to explain."

"Try."

And so, even though it's the absolute last thing I want to do right then, I tell Lauren the abbreviated but true story of me and Burke, including the fact that we're currently not really speaking. She listens silently the entire time, not showing much emotion at all. When I finish, she goes into the kitchen and returns with two glasses of water, and hands one to me.

"Are you in love with her?"

"Maybe. I think so." The lump in my throat returns, and swallowing that water becomes even more difficult.

She sits with that for a moment, seeming to weigh her response instead of firing back out of emotion, which reminds me of the Lauren I fell in love with. It's a warm memory, one now laced with sadness. "That was really shitty of you," she finally says.

"I know. I'm sorry, Lauren." I don't go further; I can't make excuses. All I can do is own my behavior.

We sit quietly for some time. I'd never let myself think about this inevitable conversation in too much depth. It strikes me, too, that after this conversation, I will actually be single, and it may not even matter to Burke. Another wave of tears rushes into my eyes and I let them fall, certain Lauren won't ask what they're about.

"I've had a problem too."

"A problem?" I ask, wiping my eyes quickly. "What does that mean?"

Lauren shifts in her seat, showing discomfort. "Nothing happened. I just...I don't know, Em. I think about her all the time, and I get so mad at myself because I know I should be thinking about you, but I can't stop thinking about her."

I know what's coming now. It should ease my pain and guilt, but it doesn't, because I know Lauren. I know she didn't act on her thoughts, and I did. "Rachel?" I ask, making sure to keep my voice gentle and calm.

She nods and tears collect in her eyes. Her struggle is so similar to my own that I can't feel anger or betrayal; I feel something like compassion. Or maybe understanding.

"I didn't sleep with her. I haven't even kissed her. I know I want to, and I know she does too, but I haven't. I couldn't do that to you."

Cue up my guilt again. "I don't want to hold you back from the things that you want."

"Well that's a fucking weird thing to say."

"Yeah, I know. Sorry."

And so the conversation continues, the back and forth of two people unraveling a relationship they'd thought would last forever. There are more tears, some snaps of anger, slivers of understanding, and even some laughter. But more than anything, there is resolution, and when Lauren and I go to bed that night, she in the basement and me upstairs, we both know that there is no more "us."

CHAPTER TWENTY-SEVEN

The June sun warms my face the moment I step onto the back deck of the house. It feels like my whole body sighs in relief as I settle into the lounge chair and stretch out my legs. I ran six miles earlier, and I'm feeling it. My muscles are happily worn out. Some relaxation in the sun is exactly what I need.

"Tell me again what the plan is."

I peer over at Allison, who's attached to her phone. "Carly and Jen are meeting us at Hank's around six. We're going to have a couple drinks, then go somewhere else for dinner. Carly mentioned a new vegetarian place."

"Oh, good. Rhianna's a vegetarian."

"Uh, hello? Who the hell is Rhianna?"

"Just this girl I met the other week. She's new to town, really cool. You'll like her."

"No. No, no, no. I am not fifth wheeling tonight. Nope."

Allison lamely swats at me and misses because she's too focused on her phone. "It's not like that, shut up. We're just friends. Getting to know each other. You know."

"Yeah, I know how you 'get to know' people, Allison. This was supposed to be a friends night out! Not a double date with a fifth wheel."

"Seriously, shut up. You can't play this pity card forever, you know."

I roll my eyes, grateful she can't see my expression behind my sunglasses. Then again, she's still glued to her phone, presumably texting this new Rhianna person, so she wouldn't have noticed my gigantic eye roll anyway. "I am not playing a pity card. I just don't care to be surrounded by couples."

The truth is, I'm happy Allison has her sights set on someone new. Things never improved between her and Sidney, who may or may not be living with another woman now, and I begrudgingly understand how sometimes we need to meet someone else who sparks us in order to recognize what we need to let go of. It's not pretty; in fact, it gets pretty damn messy sometimes. But love isn't meant to be kept in neat, organized containers. It needs room to breathe, room to spread, room to live.

"I don't want to pry, but..."

I know what's coming, and I know I can't get out of it. "No. I haven't heard from her."

"Wow. Shit. I'm sorry, Em. I thought once you were done at Whitmore, she might contact you."

"Yeah, so did I." I sit up and take a long sip of cool water. "It's been over three weeks since we packed up and left Whitmore. I guess her silence is the answer I need."

"Why don't you call her?"

I don't respond because I don't have a good answer other than the fact that I'm scared. In the time since Lauren and I officially called it off, I've had a lot of silence in my head. I've gone through, numerous times, my entire relationship with Lauren, trying to pinpoint the moment when we started falling apart. I still haven't found it and I'm working on accepting that. The general silence of my life has brought me to several conclusions about my interactions with Burke; I haven't invalidated my feelings, but I can't help to feel like our feelings weren't the same, because if they were…wouldn't she have reached out by now?

"I mean, maybe she's been waiting for you to call her and say, 'Hey! I'm single now!'"

"Very funny."

"You know I have a point."

She does. I don't want Burke to slip away again, so I know I can't keep waiting for the elusive right moment.

"Ooh, this looks heavenly!" Meredith bursts onto the deck from the back door. "May I join you ladies? I'm feeling like we need margaritas too. Sound good?"

"God, yes. I'm in."

I nod at Meredith. "That sounds great, thanks. I'll wipe down the other lounge for you."

Meredith squeals in happiness (I'll never know what it is about her personality that makes her so…Meredith) and retreats back into the house. She and Lauren were out running errands, so I assume Lauren's home too. I don't expect her to join me and Allison on the deck, though. While we've been able to be peaceful and respectful, we haven't exactly been friendly toward each other. There's a lot of hurt that's circulated between the two of us, and while we haven't had any more significant sit-down conversations about it, the looks that pass between us have been enough to realize that we need time, and space, before we can think about being friends, if that's even something we both want.

As if her goal is to prove me wrong, when Meredith comes back onto the deck with a pitcher of margaritas, Lauren is with her, carrying four glasses. Allison glances over at me, and I do my best to remain unaffected. This is fine. We're all friends. No big deal.

Meredith pours each of us a glass, and as I'm about to take a sip, she stops me with a raised hand. "Wait! No! We need a cheers moment."

"Cheers!" Allison cries, then attempts to take a sip of her drink. Meredith stops her, this time by putting her arm between Allison's mouth and her glass.

"Calm yourself," Meredith says, gently swatting Allison's hand. "I'm talking about a real cheers."

"Right, okay. To great friends. Okay! Drink!" Allison takes a swig of her drink as the three of us stare at her in bemusement.

Meredith nudges Lauren, and Lauren ducks her head in response. "C'mon, Cabrian. This is your moment!"

I bite my tongue, dying to ask what's going on.

Lauren slowly raises her glass, then meets my eyes. "To new beginnings."

Struck silent, the four of us clink our glasses together, then take sips. Naturally, Allison breaks the ice, because that's who she is.

"What kind of beginnings are we talking about?"

Lauren hesitates again, and Meredith's elbow lands in her rib cage once more. "Jesus, Mer, seriously."

"Stop keeping them in suspense, you asshole."

"Fine. Okay. I got an offer from my job. And I took it. I'm, uh, moving."

I fake a smile. I knew this would happen eventually—Lauren and I can't continue to live together. It's ridiculous, anyway, with her living in the basement. We need to go our separate ways and sell the house. But it still hurts to think about not seeing her every day.

"Congratulations. Where are you moving to?" It's my best offer of a friendly response, and it seems to go over well.

"California."

Allison chokes on her margarita, and Meredith reaches over to smack her back. Thankfully, I wasn't drinking at the moment she dropped that bomb, or else I would have earned a back slap too.

"It's a lateral move," Lauren continues. She looks a little flustered, but also happy. "My company is expanding, and they want me to be at the new office to help train people and become established. I know it sounds crazy, but...I think it's a good idea."

"I think it's a great idea, Lauren. I'm happy for you." Lauren nods at me, and for a moment, I forget that Allison and Meredith are there. So many things silently pass between me and Lauren:

acceptance, forgiveness, hope, and loss. This time, though, there's a ring of understanding surrounding the emotions, and the look in Lauren's eyes tells me she feels it, too, and we've finally arrived at our absolute ending.

* * *

The quiet bustle of Perk provides the perfect background for my late morning meeting, I decide as I glance around the café. I've been glued to this chair and table for nearly two hours going over reports and data sent in by Luke and Caren. Our new project isn't going as swimmingly as Whitmore, and the employees are…quite different. We're two weeks in, and by this point we generally have a good grasp on what we're dealing with. Then again, this is the first time we're working with a school district. Apparently there's a mountain of chaos sitting beneath the people who run schools, and the three of us have just begun to chip away at it.

So far we've found that talking to the district employees outside of the central offices is the only way we can get anyone to actually talk. Because of this Allison has been enjoying an increase in sales and I have been running on the fumes of caffeine and little else.

I look up from my laptop in time to see Brittany Sanders, secretary of Human Resources in the Elderbridge School District, enter the café. She finds me quickly and storms over to my table. I barely have time to brace myself before she throws herself into the chair across from me and begins to unload.

Somewhere around twelve minutes into her diatribe, my mind begins to wander. I think about Lauren who has been settled in California for over a week. She texted me to let me know she'd arrived and then, well, that was it. I don't know when or if we'll speak again. Mer, who's moving into her own apartment this weekend, told me that Lauren and Rachel are long-distance dating. I can honestly say I'm happy for Lauren— that her career is taking off and she's moving forward with someone else. Sure, there's a little part of me that's bitter, just as with all break-ups and losses, but I'd rather focus on the non-bitter feelings.

Allison drops by my table and pointedly gives me the check, a prearranged agreement to give Brittany the impression that I have to leave because it's the only way to get her to stop talking.

"Wow, look at the time!" I exclaim. "I can't believe we've been talking for this long!"

Brittany sighs. "I have so much more to tell you, and—"

"I'm really looking forward to hearing it. Unfortunately, I have another meeting set up, so we'll have to hit pause for today." I smile brightly at her.

And just like that, Brittany Sanders is gone. I take a moment to steady myself in her absence, and wonder how anyone gets any work done when she's around.

My thoughts don't have time to move much further, because the seat across from me is filled again. I open my mouth to encourage Brittany to get moving but when I look up, I'm knocked speechless.

Now, in the seat across from me, is Burke.

We sit quietly and if I wasn't so dumbfounded I'd laugh because it feels like one of those scenes in a movie where every element of the busy background environment disappears, and the lovestruck duo is left alone and silent, drinking each other in.

"You look good."

"Thank you. Hello to you too."

There. A smile. Small, but I see it.

"Hello, Emery."

A pause. Wow, we're out of practice. Burke looks around Perk and I do the same, wondering where Allison is and how in the world she missed this moment.

"I was wondering when I'd run into you here."

Does that mean she's been looking for me?

"Well, I'm surprised it took this long."

Her eyes are focused on me again, and while I can't read her, I do think her features have gotten a little softer from when she first sat down. Okay, I tell myself. That's progress. Now don't blow it.

And then, I just start talking. It's as if my mouth takes control of my mind, and it decides, yep, we're gonna do this—we're gonna do ALL of this, and I find myself walking Burke, willingly or not, through the last month of my life. I reach back a little further, too, in order to fully explain the Lauren situation, and how that collided with the Burke situation. As I speak, Burke sits silently, but I can tell she's listening, and I can tell she doesn't hate me because her eyes are warm. I blab on and on, sparing few details, which I'm sure is my late attempt at showing Burke how open and honest I am.

Finally, my mouth stops, and I sit back in my chair. I feel exposed, but appropriately so. I'm ready, too, for whatever questions Burke may have for me even though I can't imagine that I left anything out of my verbal avalanche.

"So, here we are," I sputter, apparently uncomfortable with this silence as Burke takes in my words.

She's still looking at me, which is good, I think. "Here we are," she echoes, and I grit my teeth. She's not letting me off the hook.

I don't know if Burke and I even stand a chance anymore. And if we do, I have no idea what that chance will look like, or what it could become. But I do know I am not going to let her walk away from me until I know for sure if that chance exists.

And so, I keep talking. "One thing I've learned through all of this is…I have to listen to myself. If I'd done that, Lauren and I would have broken up way before you and I even ran into each other. I know that sounds so simple, but I was so caught up in not paying attention to myself that if I'd taken time to look at what was happening instead of avoiding it, well," I shrug, "this would be a different conversation right now."

"And you've learned?" Aha! She speaks!

"I've learned."

Burke watches me carefully, her body not moving except for the rise and fall of her chest. "I don't know if I can trust you," she says, her voice steady and calm.

I nod slowly. "I can't blame you for that."

Silence again. Months ago, I would have squirmed beneath that intent stare, wondering if she could see through my secrets and half-truths, wondering if that would be the moment she'd turn on her heel and leave me behind. But now there's nothing to be nervous about. She can take a chance on me, or she can decide not to. Either way, I'll still be here, my life will still be intact. I'll still be moving forward.

Burke smiles slowly, and I wonder if she's been reading my thoughts. "Well."

"Well," I echo, my own smile snaking onto my lips.

"There's one way to find out whether or not you can be trusted."

"That so?"

"Yep. I believe I owe you a celebratory dinner."

My heart bounces, taking over my confident I-don't-need-no-woman attitude. "I'm free tonight," I offer.

"Hmm, yeah, tonight doesn't work for me. I'm, you know, *involved*."

My bouncing heart skips a dangerous beat before I recognize that teasing grin on Burke's face. I lean forward and kick her gently beneath the table. She laughs and reaches across the table for my hand. Her skin melts over mine and my heart goes back to bouncing distractedly, remembering those brief moments of exploration and how I always wanted more.

"I need you to understand, Emery, that I take loyalty and honesty very seriously. I don't want to play guessing games. I want to know the truth, even if it hurts. If you'd been honest about your relationship with Lauren, we could have been just friends."

"Friends who were very attracted to each other," I interject.

"Were and *are* very attracted to each other," she corrects me. "But I'm serious about this. If you expect me to trust you, you have to be open with me."

I inhale slowly, not sure if I should admit what I was about to admit. "Okay. I'm being honest and open when I say that I want to date you. And I want to date just you." She watches me carefully, body language steeled against revealing too much. "I also want you to date just me."

She squeezes my hand. "See how easy that was?"

"Oh, yeah. Baring my soul is my favorite thing to do in the middle of the workday."

She laughs and holds onto my hand. "Thank you for being honest with me."

"And your moment of honesty is…" Because like hell am I letting her get away with leaving me wondering.

"I want that too. I want us to give this a real shot. But I'm also being honest when I tell you that I don't trust you right now. I want to trust you. I think I will trust you, in time. But I need you to be patient with me."

I stand up and cross the table, bend down and press my lips to hers. I feel her body release its tension and her hands find their way to my face. That kiss is bliss. That kiss is promise.

And that kiss is hope.

Bella Books, Inc.

Women. Books. Even Better Together.

P.O. Box 10543
Tallahassee, FL 32302

Phone: 800-729-4992
www.bellabooks.com

www.ingramcontent.com/pod-product-compliance
Lightning Source LLC
Chambersburg PA
CBHW061608100726
47898CB00002B/577